E. & M.A. RADFORD
MURDER JIGSAW

EDWIN ISAAC RADFORD (1891-1973) and MONA AUGUSTA RADFORD (1894-1990) were married in 1939. Edwin worked as a journalist, holding many editorial roles on Fleet Street in London, while Mona was a popular leading lady in musical-comedy and revues until her retirement from the stage.

The couple turned to crime fiction when they were both in their early fifties. Edwin described their collaborative formula as: "She kills them off, and I find out how she done it." Their primary series detective was Harry Manson who they introduced in 1944.

The Radfords spent their final years living in Worthing on the English South Coast. Dean Street Press have republished three of their classic mysteries: *Murder Jigsaw*, *Murder Isn't Cricket* and *Who Killed Dick Whittington?*

E. & M.A. RADFORD MYSTERIES
Available from Dean Street Press

Murder Jigsaw

Murder Isn't Cricket

Who Killed Dick Whittington?

E. & M.A. RADFORD

MURDER JIGSAW

With an introduction by Nigel Moss

DEAN STREET PRESS

INTRODUCTION

DOCTOR HARRY MANSON is a neglected figure, unjustly so, amongst Golden Age crime fiction detectives. The fictional creation of husband and wife authors Edwin and Mona Radford, who wrote as E. & M.A. Radford, Manson was their leading series detective featuring in 35 of 38 mystery novels published between 1944 and 1972. A Chief Detective-Inspector of Scotland Yard and Head of its Crime Research Laboratory, Manson was also a leading authority on medical jurisprudence. Arguably the Radfords' best work is to be found in their early Doctor Manson series novels which have remained out of print since first publication. Commendably, Dean Street Press has now made available three novels from that early period – *Murder Jigsaw* (1944), *Murder Isn't Cricket* (1946), and *Who Killed Dick Whittington?* (1947) – titles selected for their strong plots, clever detection and evocative settings. They are examples of Manson at his finest, portraying the appealing combination of powerful intellect and reasoning and creative scientific methods of investigation, while never losing awareness and sensitivity concerning the human predicaments encountered.

The Radfords sought to create in Doctor Manson a leading scientific police detective, and an investigator in the same mould as R. Austin Freeman's Dr John Thorndyke. Edwin Radford was a keen admirer of the popular Dr Thorndyke novels and short stories. T.J. Binyon in *Murder Will Out* (1989), a study of the detective in fiction, maintains that the Radfords were protesting against the idea that in Golden Age crime fiction science is always the preserve of the amateur detective, and they wanted to be different. In the preface to the first Manson novel *Inspector Manson's Success* (1944), they announced: "We have had the audacity – for which we make no apology – to present here the Almost Incredible: a detective story in which the scientific deduction by a police officer uncovers the crime and the criminal entirely without the aid, ladies and gentlemen, of any outside assistance!" The emphasis is on Manson as both policeman and scientist.

The first two Manson novels, *Inspector Manson's Success* and *Murder Jigsaw* (both 1944), contain introductory prefaces which acquaint the reader with Doctor Manson in some detail. He is a man of many talents and qualifications: aged in his early 50s and a Cambridge MA (both attributes shared by Edwin Radford at the time), Manson is a Doctor of Science, a Doctor of Laws and author of several standard works on medical jurisprudence (of which he is a Professor) and criminal pathology. He is slightly over 6 feet in height, although he does not look it owing to the stoop of his shoulders, habitual in a scholar and scientist. His physiology displays interesting features and characteristics: a long face, with a broad and abnormally high forehead; grey eyes wide set, though lying deep in their sockets, which "have a habit of just passing over a person on introduction; but when that person chances to turn in the direction of the Inspector, he is disconcerted to find that the eyes have returned to his face and are seemingly engaged on long and careful scrutiny. There is left the impression that one's face is being photographed on the Inspector's mind." Manson's hands are often the first thing a stranger will notice. "The long delicate fingers are exceedingly restless – twisting and turning on anything which lies handy to them. While he stands, chatting, they are liable to stray to a waistcoat pocket and emerge with a tiny magnifying glass, or a micrometer rule, to occupy their energy."

During his long career at Scotland Yard, Manson rises from Chief Detective-Inspector to the rank of Commander; always retaining his dual role of a senior police investigating officer as well as Head of the Forensic Research Laboratory. Manson is ably assisted by his Yard colleagues – Sergeant Merry, a science graduate and Deputy Lab Head; and by two CID officers, Superintendent Jones ('the Fat Man of the Yard') and Inspector Kenway. Jones is weighty and ponderous, given to grunts and short staccato sentences, and with a habit of lapsing into American 'tec slang in moments of stress; but a stolid, determined detective and reliable fact searcher. He often serves as a humorous foil to Manson and the Assistant Commissioner. By contrast, Kenway is volatile and imaginative. Together, Jones and Kenway make a powerful combination and an effective resource for the Doctor. In later books, Inspector Holroyd features as Manson's regular assistant. Holroyd is the lead detective in the non-series title *The Six Men* (1958), a novelisation of the earlier British detective film of the same name, directed by Michael Laws and released in 1951, and based on an original story idea by the Radfords. Their only other non-series detective, Superintendent Carmichael, appeared in just two novels: *Look in at Murder* (1956, with Manson) and *Married to Murder* (1959). None of the Radford books was ever published in the USA.

The first eight novels, all Manson series, were published by Andrew Melrose between 1944 to 1950. The early titles were slim volumes produced in accordance with authorised War Economy Standards. Many featured a distinctive motif on the front cover of the dust wrapper – a small white circle showing Manson's head superimposed against that of Sherlock Holmes (in black silhouette), with the title 'a Manson Mystery'. In these early novels, the Radfords made much of their practice of providing readers with all the facts and clues to give them a fair opportunity of solving the riddle of deduction. They interspersed the investigations with 'Challenges to the Reader', tropes closely associated with leading Golden Age crime authors John Dickson Carr and Ellery Queen. In *Murder Isn't Cricket* they claimed: "We have never, at any time, 'pulled anything out of the bag' at the last minute – a fact upon which three distinguished reviewers of books have most kindly commented and have commended." Favourable critical reviews of their early titles were received from Ralph Straus (*Sunday Times*) and George W. Bishop (*Daily Telegraph*), as well as novelist Elizabeth Bowen. The Radfords were held in sufficiently high regard by Sutherland Scott, writing in his *Blood in their Ink* (1953), a study of the modern mystery novel, to be afforded special mention alongside such distinguished Golden Age authors as Miles Burton, Richard Hull, Milward Kennedy and Vernon Loder.

After 1950 there was a gap of five years before the Radfords' next book. Mona's mother died in 1953; she had been living with them at the time. Starting in 1956, with a new publisher John Long (like Melrose, another Hutchinson company), the Radfords released two Manson titles in successive years. In 1958 they moved to the publisher Robert Hale, a prominent supplier to the public libraries. They began with two non-series titles *The Six Men* (1958) and *Married to Murder* (1959), before returning to Manson with *Death of a Frightened Editor* (1959). Thereafter, Manson was to feature in all but one of their remaining 25 crime novels, all published by Hale. Curiously, a revised and abridged version of the third Manson series novel *Crime Pays No Dividends* (1945) was later released under the new title *Death of a Peculiar Rabbit* (1969).

During the late 1950s and early 1960s the Radfords continued to write well-conceived and cleverly plotted murder mysteries that remain worth seeking out today. Notable examples are the atmospheric *Death on the Broads* (1957) set on the Norfolk Broads, and *Death of a Frightened Editor* (1959) involving the poisoning of an odious London newspaper gossip columnist aboard the London-to-Brighton Pullman Express (a familiar train journey for Edwin Radford, who had worked in Fleet Street while living in Brighton). *Death and the Professor* (1961), the only non-Manson series book released after 1959, is an unusual exception. It features Marcus Stubbs, Professor of Logic and the Dilettantes' Club, a small private dining circle in Soho which meets regularly to discuss informally unsolved cases. Conveniently, but improbably, the Assistant Commissioner of Scotland Yard is among its members. The book comprises a series of stories, often involving locked room murders or other 'impossible' crimes, solved by the logic and reasoning of Professor Stubbs following discussions around the dining table. There are similarities with Roger Sheringham's Crimes Circle in Anthony Berkeley's *The Poisoned Chocolates Case* (1937). The idea of a private dining club as a forum for mystery solving was later revived by the American author Isaac Asimov in *Tales of the Black Widowers* (1974).

Edwin Isaac Radford (1891-1973) and Mona Augusta Radford (1894-1990) were married in Aldershot in 1939. Born in West Bromwich, Edwin had spent his working life entirely in journalism, latterly in London's Fleet Street where he held various editorial roles, culminating as Arts Editor-in-Chief and Columnist for the *Daily Mirror* in 1937. Mona was the daughter of Irish poet and actor James Clarence Mangan and his actress wife Lily Johnson. Under the name 'Mona Magnet' she had performed on stage since childhood, touring with her mother, and later was for many years a popular leading lady in musical-comedy and revues until her retirement from the stage. She also authored numerous short plays and sketches for the stage, in addition to writing verse, particularly for children.

An article in *Books & Bookmen* magazine in 1959 recounts how Edwin and Mona, already in their early 50s, became detective fiction writers by accident. During one of Edwin's periodic attacks of lumbago, Mona trudged through snow and slush from their village home to a library for Dr Thorndyke detective stories by R. Austin Freeman, of which he was an avid reader. Unfortunately, Edwin had already read the three books with which she returned! Incensed at his grumbles, Mona retaliated with "Well for heaven's sake, why don't you write one instead of always reading them?" – and placed a writing pad and pencil on his bed. Within a month, Edwin had written six lengthy short stories, and with Mona's help in revising the MS, submitted them to a leading publisher. The recommendation came back that each of the stories had the potential to make an excellent full-length novel. The first short story was duly turned into a novel, which was promptly accepted for publication. Subsequently, their practice was to work together on writing novels – first in longhand, then typed and read through by each of them, and revised as necessary. The completed books were read through again by both, side by side, and final revisions made. The plot was usually developed by Mona and added to by Edwin during the writing. According to Edwin, the formula was: "She kills them off, and I find out how she done it."

As husband-and-wife novelists, the Radfords were in the company of other Golden Age crime writing couples – G.D.H. (Douglas) and Margaret Cole in the UK, and Gwen Bristow and husband Bruce Manning as well as Richard and Frances Lockridge in the USA. Their crime novels proved popular on the Continent and were published in translation in many European languages. However, the US market eluded them. Aside from crime fiction, the Radfords collaborated on authoring a wide range of other works, most notably *Crowther's Encyclopaedia of Phrases and Origins*, *Encyclopaedia of Superstitions* (a standard work on folklore), and a *Dictionary of Allusions*. Edwin was a Fellow of the Royal Society of Arts, and a member of both the Authors' Club and the Savage Club.

The Radfords proved to be an enduring writing team, working into their 80s. Both were also enthusiastic amateur artists in oils and water colours. They travelled extensively, and invariably spent the winter months writing in the warmer climes of Southern Europe. An article by Edwin in John Creasey's *Mystery Bedside Book* (1960) recounts his involvement in the late 1920s with an English society periodical for the winter set on the French Riviera, where he had socialised with such famous writers as Baroness Orczy, William Le Queux and E. Phillips Oppenheim. He recollects Oppenheim dictating up to three novels at once! The Radfords spent their final years living in Worthing on the English South Coast.

Murder Jigsaw

MURDER JIGSAW, the second Doctor Manson series book, was published in late 1944, the same year as the first, *Inspector Manson's Success*, which had been well received. Both titles were published by Andrew Melrose and designated as Crime Book Society selections. The Crime Book Society was operated by the Hutchinson publishing group and modelled on the prestigious Collins Crime Club. In the preface to *Murder Jigsaw*, which introduces Doctor Manson to the reader, we learn that on the rare occasions when Manson takes a holiday from Scotland Yard, he likes to indulge his only hobby – fly fishing. Moreover, as a purist he fishes only dry fly – a small throwaway detail, but one which later has a unique bearing on the case.

The setting for *Murder Jigsaw* is a small Cornish fishing hotel, The Tremarden Arms, and its adjacent waters in which guests fish for salmon and trout. It is July, and the hotel is full. A peppery old Colonel (ex-Indian Army) is found drowned in a salmon pool in the hotel grounds. He was dressed for fishing and his rod was on the bank nearby. The local Police concluded it was an unfortunate accident: the Colonel had fallen down the steep slope, hitting his head on a boulder close to the water edge and falling unconscious into the pool, where he had drowned. Unfortunately for the perpetrator, Doctor Manson had arrived at the hotel for a short fishing holiday on the day of the Colonel's demise. Curiosity led Manson to the scene, where two peculiar circumstances convinced him that this was no accident, but rather a skilfully contrived murder. There were fellow fishermen out on the river banks near to where the Colonel was found dead, two of whom had publicly uttered threats against him. Furthermore, several other hotel guests had strong financial motives for removing him.

In keeping with the book's title, the analytical mind of Doctor Manson gradually unravels, piece by piece, a perfect jigsaw of murder. The Radfords play fair by presenting all relevant facts and evidence, so readers can follow the Doctor's thought processes and deductions as the investigation unfolds; and a 'Challenge to the Reader' to solve the murder mystery appears towards the end. The Doctor's knowledge of fly fishing helps to pin down the identity of the murderer. Edwin Radford was himself a keen angler, especially for salmon and trout. Science too plays its part. Manson's analysis of the mud and weed discovered in the Colonel's throat and stomach results in a key finding relating to the killing – a pure Dr Thorndyke moment! Manson's careful sifting of the evidence and clever deductions display a great detective's mind at work. The denouement is suspenseful and dramatic, with Manson's trademark clarity of exposition leaving no stone unturned and providing a satisfying resolution. *Murder Jigsaw* is a well-constructed, soundly plotted murder mystery, with clever investigative methods and ratiocination, in the attractive, atmospheric setting of a small fishing hotel in the height of summer. The characters are skilfully drawn, but it is the commanding and reassuring figure of Doctor Manson who takes centre stage throughout and imbues the story with his authority and formidable logic.

The first edition of 1944 was in a dust wrapper which evocatively portrays the old wood-beamed fascia of The Tremarden Arms hotel, with a passing couple carrying fishing tackle. The book attracted encouraging reviews upon publication. The novelist and critic Elizabeth Bowen commented: "*Murder Jigsaw* is a return to the type of detective story of which we have not had enough lately". J.R. Spencer in the *Liverpool Evening Express* wrote: "If these Radfords can keep writing thrillers of this class, they are going to take their rightful place very near the top". *Queen* added: "The authors lay all their cards on the table, and this reader found Doctor Manson's methods of working quite absorbing".

Murder Jigsaw is one of a sub-genre of British Golden Age mysteries which incorporate a fly fishing background. In *The Five Red Herrings* (1931), Dorothy L. Sayers shows her famous amateur detective Lord Peter Wimsey demonstrating fly fishing talents in the rivers of Galloway. Sayers also wrote a favourable review for the *Sunday Times* of Nigel Orde-Powlett's *The Cast of Death* (1932), commending its special appeal to trout fishers and vouching for the accuracy of its technical fishing details. Cyril Hare's *Death Is No Sportsman* (1938) is arguably the finest British detective title with a fishing background. It centres on the river bank murder of the owner of a trout stream syndicate, and fly fishing intricacies play into the story. Jack Vahey (John Haslette Vahey), better known under his Vernon Loder pseudonym, wrote *Death by the Gaff* (1932) featuring murder at a North Wales hotel catering for anglers. In 1940, British author Harriet Rutland released *Bleeding Hooks* about murder at a

Welsh fishing lodge hosting a group of fly fishing enthusiasts. *Bleeding Hooks* was deservedly rescued from obscurity and re-published by Dean Street Press in 2015. Later detective novels to feature fishing, worthy of mention, are Macdonald Hastings' *Cork on the Water* (1951) set on a Scottish salmon river and featuring insurance investigator Montague Cork; Josephine Tey's *The Singing Sands* (1952) in which Tey's Inspector Alan Grant describes fishing as "something between a sport and a religion"; Ngaio Marsh's *Scales of Justice* (1955) concerning the murder of a Colonel found dead by a stream in an English village setting, with a large trout next to his body; and Colin Willock's adventure-thriller *Death at the Strike* (1957) where, on the first night of a short fishing trip to the West Country, the protagonist sleuth Nathaniel Goss hooks, not the record breaking carp hoped for, but what appears to be a drowning man. (Willock was a noted authority on angling).

Nigel Moss

TO OUR PARENTS

INTRODUCTION
Doctor Manson

TO THOSE WHO may not yet know Chief-Inspector Manson, some introduction may seem to be necessary. Let us then make the presentation:

Harry Manson, Chief Detective-Inspector, and head of the Scotland Yard Crime Research Laboratory, is the Medical Juris-prudist of the national Police Force. Aged in the early—the very early—fifties, he is a Master of Arts of Cambridge University; a Doctor of Science, also of Cambridge; and a Doctor of Laws. He is the author of a number of standard works on Medical Juris-prudence, and other branches of the Pathological side of crim-inal investigation. These, then, are the officer's qualifications.

As for the man himself, he is six feet one inch in height; but he does not look it. The stoop of the shoulders, habitual in a scholar, is even more than usually evident in Manson, a cir-cumstance due undoubtedly to the many years spent peering through the eyepiece of a microscope—a natural bent for his bent, if we may crack a joke! On occasions of moment, however, the stoop vanishes, the man straightens to his full stature—and then his colleagues at the Yard know that something is "corking up" for the individual to whose trail their noses are pointing.

The inspector's face is rather on the long side, but is broad in the forehead, which is the only part of any face that matters! The grey eyes are wide-set, though lying deep in their sockets. They have a habit of just passing over a person on introduction; but when that person, after the greeting, chances to turn in the di-rection of the inspector, he is disconcerted to find that the eyes have returned to his face and are seemingly engaged on long and careful scrutiny. There is left the impression that one's face is being photographed on the inspector's mind.

During most of his appearances in public Doctor Manson's expression is that described by card players as "poker-face." But, now and again, wrinkles mark the broad brow in deep furrows, and curious crinkles surround the corners of the eyes. And when they see this his colleagues silently fade away like the Arabs. The Doctor, they will tell you, is in a spot.

Manson's hands are, possibly, the first thing that a stranger meeting him notices. The long, delicate fingers are exceedingly restless—twisting and turning on anything which lies handy to them. While he stands, chatting, they are liable to stray to a waistcoat pocket and emerge with a tiny, yet powerful, magnifying glass, or a two-inch micrometer rule, to occupy their energy.

Most of the days of the year the scientist is working—if not on an investigation, then in compiling microscope slide exhibits which may, at some future time, be useful for the purpose of identifying some object of investigation. But occasionally he will take a few days away from the Laboratory at the top of Scotland Yard, and then he indulges in his only hobby—fishing. With a seven-foot trout rod, a 4x cast, and an assortment of flies, and with a swiftly-running stream in front of him, he finds the acme of relaxation. One last point: he is as much a purist at fishing as he is at investigation; he fishes only dry fly!

CHAPTER I
The Colonel Alive

AT TEN MINUTES to six on a July evening the lounge of the Tremarden Arms showed no indication of the tragedy that was soon to envelop its guests in an evil cloud of mystery and suspicion.

A babel of bustle and sound came from it. Men sprawled in armchairs, tired feet, a'weary from much walking, resting in slippers as they gathered in groups discussing the day's "business."

With the ticking of every minute the door from the hotel yard swung open to admit other figures to the company; strange figures, perspiring in water-proof trousers reaching up to the armpits, and with water-proof coats; and, at the other end, nail-studded, sodden brogues. They called for "George!" He pulled off brogues and tugged waders from nether limbs as he had done at this hour of the day for more than twenty years. The thirsty newcomers, freed from the trammels, joined the babel in the lounge.

Winding a way between this restless kaleidoscope, waitresses came and went, tray-loads of glasses, sparkling with the colours of the rainbow, raised perilously above the heads of the crowd. The conversational babel deteriorated for a moment into a single phrase, "Good health," only to break out again with renewed enthusiasm a minute later. Cocktail time was in full swing in the Tremarden Arms.

If you know the Tremarden Arms (and if you don't, then you should do) you will be under no necessity of eavesdropping on the chatter. For the people who stay at the Arms come under three classes only; they are either fishermen, or commercial travellers, or they are London folk, bound for the Cornish coast, breaking their journey for a night.

And since, at six o'clock, the commercial travellers are busily engaged copying out the orders decoyed from the Tremarden tradespeople—for the post goes out at seven o'clock—and the night sojourners are washing the dirt of the long trek from the metropolis in the hotel bathrooms before dinner, that leaves only the fishermen to fill the lounge. Therefore, the talk is FISH.

From April until the end of September the lounge of the Tremarden Arms echoes to "fish," as the anglers gather round the circular table beneath the great palm tree, which reaches up into the glass canopy, twenty feet above. "Walter" ministers at the table. As though by sleight of hand a plate or a dish appears in Walter's hands at the sight of an entering fisherman. One by one, the trout are taken, almost reverently, from the creel, and laid in speckled lines on the plate to occupy a show-place among the score of other collections on the table. In long, shallow dishes in the centre, salmon glisten like silver in pride of place above the plates. For the display of the fruits of a fly and a cunning hand has been a ritual of the Tremarden Arms for a generation, and each angler adds his devotions, whether he returns with a brace of trout or a score of brace. And the fight is fought over again as the fishermen recognise an old campaigner from the pools, now laid low.

This, then, was the scene in the Tremarden Arms on the evening of 21st July, just before dinner gave the first inkling (although it was not until next day that it was known to be an inkling) of tragedy.

The day had been an ideal one for the Prince of Sports. A warm sun had been tempered by a zephyr wind, which gave the water just enough ripple to cover the angler, and disguise the artificial fly from the less plentiful natural insect! Some hundred brace of trout lay on the table; light-speckled from the swift and clear-running waters of the Inney; others, sandy-hued, from the reddish-stained, shallow Lyner; and the dark-backed and larger fish which had lost in game fight in the slower and deeper waters of the Tamar.

A little group of men stood beside the table, apart from the throng of drinkers. "A nice day's sport, Major," commented the tallest of the group.

Major Smithers nodded. His practised eye surveyed the catch. "And mostly Linney fish, Sir Edward," he said. "I'm glad to see the old stream is picking up again. We've had a pretty thin time in there this last year or two. Eh, Padre?" The major smiled across at the grey-suited figure of a clergyman.

"Indeed, yes," was the reply. "I could not catch them myself." A chuckle greeted the reply, for the padre's prowess with trout was almost a legend. Where others, who prided themselves as experts, came back with half-a-dozen brace of trout, the padre would table a creel of a couple of dozen brace. The local tackle shops coined a fortune from flies which were sold as "The Reverend Williams pattern." He had once, years ago, in a turn of elfish humour, condoled with a despondent journalist, who had only a brace of anaemic trout for his day's labour. The padre brought in a laden creel.

"How the devil do you catch them, Padre?" the disgruntled journalist had asked.

"Well, I tie my own flies," was the guarded reply.

The journalist subsequently regaled a company with the padre's "secret." A day later, the padre missed half-a-dozen of his flies; within a week the fly-drawers of the local retailers were filled with the "Reverend William's pattern" in Pheasant Tails, Red Spinners, March Browns, and the other varieties of fly bait. That they were not any different, but generally not so good, as any other flies did not matter! What the padre did *not* tell the journalist was that he had been whipping the waters of the Tremarden Arms for thirty years, and knew them as well as he knew his prayer-book. But to return to the group.

"Well, if *you* couldn't catch 'em on the Williams fly they must have been scarce." Sir Edward Maurice accompanied the compliment with a dig at the old story. "What d'ye think was the reason?"

The padre frowned. "I think Franky had too much timber cut back," he said. "You've got to have cover for trout, especially in the Linney's crystal water."

Major Smithers nodded.

"You don't think it was the bad angling we had?" Sir Edward frowned as he made the suggestion. "Remember the bunch of doggers we endured. And they nearly all fished the Inney. Said there was room to cast there." Sir Edward snorted. "I saw one fellow ploughing through the water with enough wake to put down every trout for a mile ahead."

"No," the padre replied. "I think it was cutting back the timber. And Franky is doing it down at Three Bridges this year."

"The devil he is," ejaculated Sir Edward. "Where is he?" He turned his head and, catching the eye of Frank Baker, beckoned him across.

The proprietor of the Tremarden Arms was one of those men who fitted into hotel keeping as a glove fits the hand. Tall, slim and aesthetic looking in countenance, he had run the Arms for just over twenty years. He also ran Tremarden; for not only was he the principal farmer in the district, the chief milk producer, but he was also Mayor, Chairman of the Chamber of Commerce, Chairman of the Conservative Club, and a magistrate.

He was a bundle of nerves, but managed successfully to live on his nerves, and that kept them from breaking point. No frequenter of the hotel had ever seen from him a display of impatience, much less annoyance. "Franky," as he was called by these anglers who came year after year to the Arms for the fishing, was as popular a figure as a host as he was a good friend.

The group of men who now waited for him were his oldest customers. They had not missed spending July and August at the hotel since the days when Franky was in short trousers, and Old Man Baker was building up the hotel on a mile of water, adding a furlong here and there as it prospered.

"Even' Major, Even' Sir Edward, Even' Reverend," Franky hailed the company. "Had a good day?"

"Evening, Franky. What's this I hear about Three Bridges? Padre says you're cutting the timber back there."

"Only in a few places, Sir Edward."

"But, dammit, Franky, look what happened to the Inney when you cut the banks back."

Franky spread his hands apologetically. "I know, Sir Edward. But then, you and the major, and the Reverend here, are experts. We're getting a lot of amateurs at the game now. Half of them haven't learned to cast horizontally, they can't use a backhand, and haven't heard of a Spey. I've got to give them a reasonable chance of catching fish. And I can make open water more easily at Three Bridges than I can anywhere else. I'm keeping the other streams for the experienced people like yourselves."

"Well, I suppose if you must, you must, Franky. But I should have thought there was enough open water at Three Bridges, in the fields alongside the quarry and beyond." He dismissed the subject. "Who's caught all the fish to-day? Doesn't seem much from the Tamar. The colonel had another bad day?"

A smile passed round the company. Mention of Colonel Donoughmore and his fishing generally raised a grin.

Franky glanced at the table. His eyes picked out the dark-backed lower Tamar trout. "Fred Emmett brought three brace of these in," he said, "and I think the major grassed the others. The colonel hasn't come in yet."

"Bit late for him, isn't it? I thought he generally gave up about four o'clock."

"He does," Major Smithers said. "He—" His voice ceased as his eyes caught sight of an article leaning against the hall-stand, amid a welter of bagged rods. "Isn't that the colonel's landing net?" he asked.

The four stared at the six foot long pole at the top of which was fastened a square-ended net.

"That's the colonel's all right," agreed Sir Edward. "Nobody else would use a ruddy butterfly net—pardon, Padre—to save getting his waders wet." He walked over to the stand. "That's funny," he said. "It's wet."

"I'm pretty sure he hasn't been in," said Franky. "His rod isn't there." He turned to the porter. "Seen the colonel, Walter?"

"Noa, Mister Frank. He hasn't a ben."

"Ruddy good job if he never comes back," said a voice; and Fred Emmett joined the company. "Why all this loving anxiety for the old devil?"

"He doesn't seem to have returned, and that's unusual for him. Did you see anything of him down there, Fred?"

"Saw him this morning, edging into my beat. Said he'd been chasing a big 'un and hadn't noticed that he'd passed the mark. I told him if he didn't get back into his own kennel I'd chuck him in the ruddy river."

"What's all this about throwing people in the river? It is my duty to warn you that anything you may say will be taken down and may be used in evidence."

"Doctor!"

The exclamation came in a chorus as the little group swung round on the interrupter. He stood in the doorway, a six-foot figure in tweeds, a raincoat over one arm. The smile on his face lit up his wide-spaced, deep-set eyes and the crinkled, pleasant contour of the broad forehead.

For a moment the Doctor stood thus. Then, dropping the raincoat on a basket chair, he stepped to the side of the group with outstretched hands.

"I'm glad you are here, all of you," he said. "I rather thought you might be."

He shook hands warmly with the four men; grips that were returned as warmly, for Doctor Manson, though an infrequent visitor to the Arms, was a popular guest when he did pay a visit, not only because of his skill as a fisherman—an achievement which was usually the first consideration of good fellowship in the house—but because his charm as a conversationalist was allied to a scholarly mind, and any argument in which he took part never failed to entertain as well as instruct his company.

His Doctorship had little to do with medicine, though it was in many respects allied to it. His degree was in Science; the alliance with medicine lay in the fact that he was the scientist attached to the Criminal Investigation Department of Scotland Yard; its investigator into pathological mysteries, and its expert in medical jurisprudence.

It was two years ago that the Chief Commissioner of Scotland Yard had called him into the Yard's Service and given him *carte blanche* to equip a Laboratory in an attempt to stay the growing list of unsolved crimes. Since that date there had been no single case the solution to which had not been reached by the Yard. This, then, was the man who, having been welcomed, now called for a long, cool, drink, which the host himself brought.

"But what the deuce are you doing here, Doctor?" from the major. "Don't tell us the Squire's daughter has been foully murdered, and you're after the villain."

A roar of laughter greeted the major's histrionic pose and declamation.

Manson laughed. "No, nothing so important," he said. "I've just got a few days' leave, and thought I'd like to spend them on the water. Sorry to come without warning, Franky, but I didn't know until this morning. If you haven't a bed I'll sleep in the hayloft."

A smile crinkled the face of Baker. "Sure, us always has a room for yew, Doctor." The words came in the soft sing-song of the Cornishman.

"But you still haven't told me what this throwing in the river business is about," said Manson.

"The sleuth on the track already!" Sir Edward chuckled. "Fact is, Doctor, we've got an unpleasant gent here named Donoughmore—Colonel Donoughmore—don't think you've met him. He's usually back from fishing about five o'clock, but hasn't turned up to-day. Funnily enough, his landing net is in its usual place, and it's wet. Emmett, here, said the blighter had been poaching on his beat this morning, and threatened to chuck him in the water if he didn't get out and keep out. What d'ye make of that?"

Franky laughed. "Yieu'd best 'fess, Emmett," he said. "Doctor will get you in the end."

The company chuckled at Emmett's embarrassment. "He's probably been in with an empty creel, and gone off to avoid the banter. Anyhow, I'm not interested, and the gong has gone."

"I expect he'll be in for dinner," said the major. "He's a pretty good trencherman, isn't he, Franky?"

Franky grimaced. "He is," he agreed.

But dinner came and went, and still the colonel made no appearance. Franky sought the lounge's advice on his missing guest.

"May have run into a good evening rise and wants to show what he can do."

"More likely gone after another kind of fish." The sneer came from Bill Braddock.

"Oh," from several voices. "Who is she, Braddock?"

"Didn't know he went in for that kind of fish. Spill her name."

Braddock shook his head. "I'm saying nothing," he said. "But what I hope is that he's fallen in the Tamar and drowned his damned self."

"Well, I think I'll run down to the river and have a look round," said Franky. "He may have fallen down and hurt himself, and there's nobody down there he could call to for help."

He returned an hour later without the colonel. "No sign of him down there," he said. "I walked down to the flats at the bottom of our water."

"It's what I said. He's engaged elsewhere," Braddock said. "And he don't want any flies for that fish."

There was a guffaw of laughter. "Well, he'll have to make an honest woman of her now it's out. The padre here will see to that, won't you, Reverend? There's seventeen-and-six in the kitty for you."

The padre smiled deprecatingly.

"You'll fix the lounge out as a chapel, eh, Franky?" The major joined in the joke.

"And give 'em the bridal suite as a wedding present," added Sir Edward. "That ought to induce the colonel to wed—free board and lodging."

"Ef so be you make it a funeral, I wud give 'ee a coffin free." The voice came from the back of the company. If the softness of the Cornish accent belied the words, the look on the face of the speaker removed the impression. He eyed the company. "You be outlanders and friends of his'n. Tell him to kep hisself to hisself." Turning on his heel, he put his glass on the table, and walked out.

Manson eyed his retreating figure, and then looked inquiringly at Franky.

"Willie Trepol, our carpenter and undertaker." Franky answered the question in the Doctor's glance. "He's a queer chap, and religious, but his bark is worse 'n his bite. There was a mort of trouble atwixt him and the colonel last year."

"Well, I'm off to bed, Colonel or no Colonel." The major finished his drink and gathered his papers. "Want to be out early in the morning. Anybody fishing the top beat in the Inney, Franky? I'd like to have another try for Old Glory."

"I'll keep the beat for you, Major."

"Bet you five to one you don't grass him." Sir Edward spoke hopefully. "Old Glory" was an institution!

The major grimaced. "I've been trying for him for five years," he said. "I'll take it, Sir Edward. Lend me a fly, Reverend."

A chorus of protests rose, followed by a howl of laughter as the padre handed over a Red Spinner. "I've used that on him for ten years, Major," he said.

Still laughing at the joke, the company dispersed to the bedrooms. It was eleven o'clock.

CHAPTER II
The colonel Dead

Doctor Manson came downstairs at seven o'clock next morning, walked through the deserted lounge and into the dining-room.

"Just coffee and rolls, John," he said.

John brought them with his news. "Did 'ee hear about Colonel, sir?" he asked.

"No. What's he been up to now, John? Out on the tiles all night?"

"He be proper dead, he be."

"Dead!" Manson looked up, startled.

"Ay. Dead as Cornish Laamb. He were found in river the mornin'. Master Frank, he's there now. Master Budd, he be farmer, told him on telephone, and Master Frank fetched Sergeant."

Manson pushed his chair back from the table. "I think I'll get up there too, John. Corpses are rather in my line, you know. Where was he found?"

"In Tamar, Doctor. You goes down to farm, turns right and goes a mile alon' river bank just afore big pool."

"I know the way. Do you mean by the Gulley?"

"That be right. Master Budd see'd 'un goin' thru Gulley."

Manson whistled softly. "If he's got into the round pool they'll have a job to get him out," he thought, as he got his car out of the garage.

It was a perfect July morning, and Manson whistled more cheerfully than the occasion warranted as he drove in the direction of the river Tamar. The narrow Cornish lanes, in which there is never room for two cars to pass except where banks are broken by wide gateways into fields, were at their best, he soliloquised, at this time of the day and year. The sun, just getting into its first warm rays, glistened on silvery, dew-spangled cobwebs, thrown as though by fairy hands across the lanes, or festooned in delicate tracery along the hedgerows. Ahead, and on either side, a blue haze shimmered over the trees of the valley, at the foot of which ran the river, sluggishly moving between the rapids, then racing into the deep salmon pools, where its turbulence spent itself in the cool depths.

Behind, the town perched on the hill stared down as it had done for eight hundred years. Its crowning point, the Castle, dominating approaches from every side for twenty miles around. It must have been a formidable object in the Norman Days that saw its rise, soliloquised Manson.

Wild roses towered over the low hedge-rows, fox-gloves spread a purplish carpet in the fields beyond. Manson sniffed in the morning perfume as he drove. He waved a greeting to the postmaster at the little roadside office, which lay in the shadow of the big barn that Cornish Baptists had changed into a Bethel, turned a forgotten right-hand hairpin bend on two wheels, and stopped in front of a five-barred gate, enclosing a farm-yard from which a solitary cow gazed reflectively as she chewed the cud.

Opening the gate, Manson drove through and parked the car beside two others in the shade of a store-barn. Closing the gate behind him he struck right, climbed a fence and entered a field. The river lay below him, and in the distance he saw a small group of men gathered on the bank half-a-mile or so away.

He approached by way of a winding track between two fields of oats, to find himself standing on a rocky bank, with a deep pool thirty feet beneath. The pool was almost circular in shape, some 160 feet in diameter. At the top end, a wall of granite rock imprisoned it, except for a narrow, funnel-like, opening through which the water raced like a mill-stream. This was "The Gulley," known to all fishermen as the place where a salmon could invariably be taken on a "Devon Spinner" when the fish were running. At the bottom end of the pool, the water flowed sluggishly forward, and so on to the four-feet-deep shallow flats where trout abounded for the wily angler. Manson knew every inch of the water; he had fished it off and on for several years.

A labourer greeted him with excited explanation. "He be down there, zur," he said. "We found where he fell in. He comed down the rapids and water tuk'n thru t' gulley. Sergeant and Constable be tryin' to get 'un to bank."

Manson moved towards the bank.

"If you go down, be careful: Et's dangerous."

"I'll watch out," was the reply, as Manson began to clamber down the steep slopes to the water edge.

Sergeant Jones looked round as he heard the scrambling approach. He greeted the Chief Inspector with a grin. The two had met before, both as fishermen and also when the sergeant had visited Scotland Yard!

"Heard you were down, Doctor, and expected you'd be about afore long. But there's no need for 'ee to be troubled. We found where he slipped in, a mile back."

Manson smiled a reply and looked out across the pond. Fifty feet out the dead man was floating, just below the surface of the water. "Dashed queer he's floating like that, isn't it, Sergeant?" he asked.

"We reckon it's his wading clothes keepin'n up," he said. "They'll be water-proof and there'll be air inside." He scratched his head. "I don't know how we'll be gettin'n out," he said. "The current goes circular-like, and we have been countin' on it sweeping him to the bank. But he just goes round and round in middle of the pool."

"You can't get a boat in the pool, of course?"

The sergeant pointed to the Gulley. "We couldn't get a boat through there, Doctor, as you well know. And, anyways, the only boat is ten miles away."

"Swimming any good?"

"I wouldn't let any man risk his life theer fur a corpse."

Manson nodded. "I think you're right," he agreed. "But I don't think he'll float much longer. If you don't soon get him out you'll lose him for good. If he once touches bottom, the granites will hold him."

He paused in thought for a few moments, then bent forward and whispered in the sergeant's ear. The officer recoiled. "Aw jiminy," he gasped, "for a ghoulish thing you be thinkin' of.

Howsever, if you think we should do it, all right. Franky is the best of us, if he'll do't."

Manson climbed the bank and beckoned to his host. The two walked a few yards apart from the waiting group before the Scotland Yard Chief Inspector broached his suggestion. Baker looked at the scientist dumbfounded. "I'd never have the nerve to do it, Doctor," he said, slowly. "I'd never be able to go to the river again."

"But you *must* try it, Franky," Manson insisted. "I'd do it myself if I could, but you know damned well I'd be no good at the job." He eyed the hesitating hotelier for a moment, and then took him by the arm. "After all, Franky," he said, "he's your guest, and he's been your guest for years. He's entitled to a decent burial."

Manson's eyes twinkled a little as he saw a changing expression in Baker's face. The Cornishman will break the law for a little smuggling; he will kill; and he isn't above a little poaching; but Cornish hospitality is something not to be betrayed or broken. And, as Manson knew, so it happened. "If-so-be you look at it that way, Doctor, I'll do my best," Franky said.

"I thought you'd see it that way, Franky," said Manson. "But I think you'll have to hurry."

"I've got some things in the car, Doctor. Always keep them there. I'll be back in ten minutes." He turned on his heel and strode rapidly away in the direction of the farm.

He was back in less than the ten minutes, a bag over his shoulder and a long canvas case under his arm. From it he produced a twelve-foot salmon spinning-rod. Fitting the joints together he slipped in a reel, and threaded the line through the eyelets.

The group of men had watched these proceedings in puzzled silence. Suddenly their meaning penetrated into the mind of one of them. "Jiminy! He's going to fish for him," he shouted.

Franky fitted a salmon spinner to the line. He eyed the eye of the barbed triangle of hooks with concern. "I doubt it will grip him, Doctor."

Manson nodded.

With a figure-of-eight knot, Franky added an additional cast to the line, attaching to it a large spoon spinner with three sets of triangle hooks. Thus equipped, he scrambled down the bank. The colonel still moved sluggishly along with the circling current.

There followed thirty minutes: thirty minutes that hung beneath the azure sky, each minute seeming an hour to the watching men, in a setting so bizarre as was never imagined, even by Poe. Trout rose to the morning hatch of fly; a salmon leaped six feet above the centre of the pool, to fall back with a mighty splash, the suddenness of which sent the hearts of the crowd into their mouths.

Perched precariously with his left foot on the crumbling earth edging the water, and the other resting a pace forward on a jutting rock, Franky sent his line spinning towards the body of the colonel.

Forty, fifty, feet the line flew out from a free-running reel. The host of the Tremarden Arms was as expert a salmon-spinning fisherman as he was an hotelier; the spinners slipped into the water at the end of the cast with hardly a splash, were reeled in subtly, only to go whirring through the air again.

Once, the hooks made contact with the colonel, but failed to drive home. The body rolled over, and Franky was violently sick before he could reel in the sinking baits. He put down the rod. "I'll have to wait till he comes round again," he said. "There's too much lag on the line to get a strike."

The next cast was the last. The line stretched athwart the body, the hooks a good three yards beyond. For a matter of three seconds Franky stood motionless, letting the baits sink into the water. Then, slowly, he reeled in, until he felt touch. With the line just tautening he struck hard, rod horizontal to the water, with a swift left-handed snatch.

"He's held, zur." A voice came from the top of the bank. "You ben got him below the shoulder."

Franky began slowly to wind in, the stout rod bending in an arch as the weight took effect.

"Take it gently, Franky."

The angler nodded at Manson's unconsciously whispered warning. Slowly, the colonel's body came towards the bank, the rod lifting as he gained weigh, until at last it touched shore, and the sergeant and constable, kneeling down, held it against the bank.

"Us'll never get him up the bank here," the sergeant said.

Manson nodded. "If Franky can bring him down to the bottom of the pool we'll be in the flats, and he can be lifted straight out. You men get a gate and carry it down to the shallows," he called up to the group on the bank.

So Colonel Donoughmore came to grass, as does a salmon in the steep-banked Tamar, which had fought for life to a finish—towed at the end, motionless, to a convenient landing-place. And when he was lifted out Franky took the salmon-rod, snapped it across a knee, and hurled the pieces into the river. He had 'played' salmon with that rod for nearly twenty years.

Doctor Tremayne came to the waiting body, panting and angry. "I wish to heaven you'd leave hunting corpses until I've finished my morning patients, Sergeant," he protested.

The sergeant giggled. "The patients may have something to thank us for, Doctor," he said. "We may have saved their lives."

The Doctor glared. "Where's the body?" he demanded.

He eyed the still figure clad from head to foot in khaki-coloured wading outfit. "Fisherman, eh?" he said. "Fell in, I suppose? Not surprised. Most dangerous water in Cornwall, this blasted Tamar. Shoals and pools, and blasted great boulders you fall over. Well, get the things off him."

Stripped of his outfit the colonel was almost bone-dry underneath. The Doctor ran his hands over him. "Well, he's dead right enough, beyond a doubt," he said. "And he's been dead a long time. Rigour is well developed. What do you want me to do about him?"

"Would he have ben drownded?" asked the sergeant.

"Now how the devil d' ye expect me to give you an answer to that, man, by just looking at him?" snarled the Doctor. "You found him in the water. You pulled him out. I should say he was drowned right enough. But I cannot make any such pronouncement as you well know, Sergeant, until I have opened him up and looked at the inside of him."

"Just so," agreed Manson. "And he's had a nasty blow on the forehead. It probably knocked him unconscious, though the actual cause of death may have been drowning." He stooped over the body, and, taking a magnifying glass from a waistcoat pocket, peered closely at the bruised tissues. Then, returning the glass to his pocket, he ran a hand over the dead man's skull; his long, tapering fingers exploring the area of the wound. He felt the bone give under their pressure. "Yes, skull fractured," he announced.

Doctor Tremayne stared at him. "Would you be a surgeon, sir?" he asked.

Manson smiled. "No, Doctor," he said. "No."

"Then ye ought to have been; you've been given the very hands for the job."

"But not the brains nor the desire for it, Doctor," Manson retorted. His hands moved over and along the corpse. "There's a rib broken too, and the hands and arms are bruised."

"That 'ud be the rocks in the water," the sergeant opined.

"Mebbe," Manson said. "Well, I don't see that you can do any more, Sergeant. You'd better get him away to the mortuary and leave him to the Doctor. Then we might have a look at the place where he fell in."

CHAPTER III
BITS AND PIECINGS

IT WAS A THOUGHTFUL chief inspector who led the procession of three back to the river after the colonel's body had been started on its journey to the town. His brow was puckered; any of the officers at the Yard would have read the symptoms, but Franky and the sergeant put his abstraction down to the grimness of the scene just ended.

"There's a short cut, Doctor, to where he went in across the field," suggested Franky.

Manson shook his head. "I'd rather follow the river, if the sergeant isn't in any hurry," he said.

The sergeant nodded. He made it plain by his attitude that his job was finished. The colonel wasn't a young man, he was at pains to point out, and the Tamar was, as Doctor Tremayne had said, a dangerous place for anyone who wasn't pretty active. Still, it was a pity all round. "It do give the water a bad name, when a fisherman is drowned," he explained.

"Still, if it had, betimes, to be, I'd rather it was the colonel than anybody." He coughed apologetically. "Mebbe I shouldn't have said that, if he was a friend of yours, zur."

"No," Manson smiled. "Never met him. I gather he wasn't popular round here. What was the trouble?"

The sergeant hesitated. "To be shure," he said, "there have been tales of goings-on with wimmen-folk, and he gived 'isself airs with the men, and that doesn't do from an outlander. I've the idea, Doctor, that Master Frank wouldn't have took'd it bad if he hadn't comed to the Arms again." He glanced at the hotelier, but Franky made no sign.

The two men walked in silence until the river bank was reached. Turning by the Gulley, they headed up-stream along a track worn by the feet of fishermen.

Salmon were leaping in a pool, and the three halted to watch the bow of their bodies. "Fresh run," commented Franky. "Getting rid of the sea-lice. This is the best pool for fish in the river and hardest to catch 'em in. There's none but one place which yiew can spin it, and it do run too fast for anybody but an expert to cover with a fly."

"The Rostrum Pool, isn't it?"

"Yes, Doctor. They called it that after Pass'n—the Reverend Williams, you know. That bit of jutting rock is the only place you can stand to spin from, and they said that the Reverend, when he was there, looked like he was in his pulpit. If he can spin a sermon same as he can spin a Devon, he's sure a good pass'n."

The inspector pointed a few yards ahead. "That's the place Doctor," he said.

A constable stepped from behind the trees. "Ah, there you are, Bennett. There been any visitors?"

"No, Sergeant." He eyed Manson.

"This is a scientist gen'nlman from Scotland Yard, comed to have a look over."

Manson acknowledged the constable's salute, and standing on the verge of the clearing, let his eyes wander over the foot-wide track worn hard by feet. Between it and the edge of the bank was four feet of grass, growing in uneven tufts. The land had, in the spring, been ploughed up with the field. Sowing had left the edging for anglers to traverse, and the grass had grown over and between the furrows. It was, in effect, a plateau some six yards square and clear of the bramble bushes which grew thickly along the path at either end of the clearing.

Manson surveyed it carefully for a few moments, taking in the rod, fishing reel and bag lying on the grass.

"Where did he go in?" he asked at length.

"Here, sir." The sergeant led the way to the bank, Manson noted with a frown the clear, steep slope to the water, twelve or fifteen feet below, scored with scratches and torn-out tufts of grass.

"I misdoubt he catched his foot in a rut, sir, and comed over headlong. Straight into the water he'd go."

"So I see." The reply came mechanically; Manson was staring thoughtfully at the slope. His eyes puckered into creases. Manson's eyes always puckered that way when he was puzzled. He returned to the path and walked upstream, the sergeant following him. He walked slowly, eyeing keenly the bushes which dotted thickly the shelving sides of the bank down to the river. At last he spoke to his companion.

"You'll notice, Sergeant, that the bushes and brambles, though they are not continuous along the bank in a line, overlap at various depths down the slopes."

"That is true enough, zur," the other agreed.

"And that, mostly, in order that we can inspect the water, we have to crane our heads either over or between the bushes, thus. . . ." Manson stretched up and looked over a blackberry bush.

"Now, if I slipped over the edge here, I do not think I would come to much harm. What do you think?"

"No, zur. The bushes would catch you for certain."

"Quite. Now, if the colonel had fallen in anywhere along here he wouldn't have gone into the river?"

"That be true. But he didn't. He fell somewhere else."

"The river bank is the same all the way up and down, isn't it, Sergeant?"

"Yes, zur. 'Ceptin' where Colonel fell in."

Manson eyed the sergeant speculatively. He seemed to be about to speak, but changed his mind. Instead, he retraced his footsteps to the plateau, and continuing down-stream, subjected that side of the spot to a similar examination. Not until he had exhausted all that the bank seemed to have to tell him, did he turn his attention to the actual place of the colonel's fall. There, he peered intently at the scored scratches, examined the grass of the tufts torn out by the colonel as he tried to break his fall, only to find the grass pull up by the roots as he grasped it.

Finally, taking a magnifying glass from a waistcoat pocket, Manson passed a critical gaze over the surface of the granite boulder that edged the river and towered two or three feet over the waterside.

"It's all very singular," he said half aloud as, back at the top of the bank again, he looked down at the scene of the tragedy.

"What is singular, Doctor?"

"Everything, Franky," was the reply.

He turned to the sergeant. "I cannot, of course, give you any instructions, Sergeant," he said. "But I *can* tell you that, were I professionally in your shoes, I should leave this place undisturbed, and exactly as it is now, until it could be examined by an expert investigator. Perhaps you could take it on yourself to see to that, purely as a precaution, until you have had a chance to talk to your Inspector."

The sergeant hesitated. The scientist's examination seemed to him to be directed to making a mountain out of a molehill. There, on the bank, were the plain marks of the angler's fall. They had taken the body out of the water. It was as clear a case of accident as ever he, the sergeant, had seen. But there, these Scotland Yard men always saw suspicious circumstances in everything. The sergeant supposed that was natural. It was what they were paid for.

Still, Dr. Manson *was* a Scotland Yard Chief-Inspector and a famous one at that. And if there *should* be anything wrong, he, the sergeant, would be on the carpet if a clue was lost when he had been given a warning by a Scotland Yard Chief. Perhaps, he declared, it wouldn't do any harm to humour the Doctor. So—

"All right, zur," he said. "I can arrange that. I'll leave Constable Bennett here, and if you are finished I'll be gett'n back and telling the inspector."

Manson nodded. "I think you'll find it a wise move," he said, and started on the return to the farm. Franky, following, stopped suddenly. "Shall we take the colonel's rod, Doctor?" he asked.

"The rod?" echoed Manson. "Oh, I'd forgotten that, Franky."

He retraced his steps and looked down at the rod. A split cane, seven-foot, dry-fly, it lay alongside the path, and parallel to it. Some eight feet of line trailed idly along, and beyond its length, ending in a fine-gut cast. Manson put it as lx to 4x strength. Near the rod was the colonel's fishing bag, and creel, the latter holding half-a-dozen light-coloured trout.

Lifting the line, Manson let it run through his fingers, noticing the tapered end. He grunted with satisfaction. Whatever else he might be, he reflected, the colonel was a purist in fishing. A tapered line should go with a dry-fly. His fingers ran down the gut to the fly and there—!

Manson stared at it unbelievably. It was a Sedge and wingless, known as a Hackle Sedge. The hackles ran backwards from the hook, streamlined, and almost flat to the shank—a fly that, no matter how lightly it came to rest on the water, would go below the surface within a fraction of a second. Manson stared at it. His gaze moved upwards again above the cast to the tapering of the line; and back once more to the fly. Then, still gazing, he spoke: "Franky, what kind of fisherman was the colonel? I mean in habit?" Manson asked the question casually, over his shoulder.

Franky laughed. "Much the same as you, Doctor; too much of an artist to fill a creel. Everything had to be correct—line to cast, cast to hook, and so on. Hemingway was his Bible."

"He wouldn't fish wet fly, I suppose?"

"Not judging by what he called other people who fished wet fly."

Manson dropped the line and opened the colonel's bag. He lifted out a spare reel, and after examining the tapered end of the line wound on it, placed it on the grass. Next, he laid out the contents and went carefully through them. He examined the cast-box and the spare casts in envelopes, and the envelopes of "points." Finally, he opened the colonel's fly-case. Kneeling in the grass he emptied the contents of each compartment into his hand, in turn. Only the most cursory of glances were given to each, but it seemed enough for the scientist. There were Red Spinners, Greenwells Glory, Pheasant Tails, Gnats, Red and Black Palmers, March Browns and Olives.

Each sat jauntily in his hand, wings set and spread daintily—perfect wings—at the correct angle.

Placing the fly-case with the other contents, Manson next spread his handkerchief on the grass and up-ended the colonel's fishing-bag over it. Finally, he turned the bag inside out.

What he sought was obviously not there, for he rose to his feet and, starting from the path, went step by step over the grass down to the water's edge, and back again.

Sergeant Jones, looking on in bewilderment, broke the silence. "Can I help, zur?" he asked. "Would it be important?"

Manson glared at him. "Important! Of course it's important. Should I be crawling about on my hands and knees in this grass if it wasn't—"

He stopped, and an apologetic smile lightened his face. "I'm sorry, Sergeant," he said. "I got carried away. Instinct of the investigator, I suppose.

"But what I'm looking for is the most important part in your case, and it ought to be found. In fact, it must be found. If you like, I'll help you to search for it. But search must be made by somebody. Every inch of the bank, the paths, and if you can tuck up your trousers, get along the water near the bank and see if it's fallen into the stream. I'll go over to the farm and telephone the mortuary. It may be in the colonel's waterproof jacket pockets, and I may have missed it when I looked into them—but I don't think I did. But get busy as soon as you like."

"What are we looking for?"

The sergeant and Franky asked the question simultaneously.

It was a reasonable question to ask.

Manson told them—

The party scattered. Franky and the sergeant began their searching of the path and banks. Constable Bennett, discarding socks and boots, and with trousers rolled up, waded along the river edge, peering through the transparent water.

It was upwards of half-an-hour when Manson returned from his telephoning. He was greeted by the company with head shakes.

"We've searched nearly every inch for a quarter-of-a-mile square, Doctor, and there's no trace of any such thing," said Franky; "and I don't think it ever existed—not on the colonel," he added.

"It wasn't in his pockets," said Manson. He sighed. "That settles it." He turned to the sergeant.

"Sergeant," he said; "Colonel Donoughmore did not fall in the river. He was thrown, or pushed in."

"Murdered!" The exclamation came from the sergeant in a gasp.

"And, Sergeant, take care of that rod, and don't handle it," added Manson.

He strode off with Franky, leaving the sergeant with open mouth, staring after him.

"Well, oi'l be jiggered," said Constable Bennett, who was a man of Devon.

CHAPTER IV
GOOD FISHING

BACK AT THE Tremarden Arms Doctor Manson decided to put the colonel's death out of his thoughts. It was for a few days' fishing that he had come to Tremarden, and he intended to have them. He had done his obvious duty in pointing out to Sergeant Jones certain conclusions which had occurred to his analytical mind, and that, he argued, ended his concern with the matter. How the colonel came to be killed, and he had no doubt from the facts deduced that he had been killed, was a job for the Cornwall detective force.

He would ask Franky to give him a fishing beat furthest in the opposite direction to the Tamar, this afternoon—the upper Lyner would be best—and beguiling trout from that rushing mountain stream would take all his agility of mind. It was in this state of mind that Manson went in to lunch.

There are few people in the Tremarden Arms to lunch during the fishing season. The fishermen are more likely to be found eating sandwiches on the river bank; sandwiches which the cook had risen in the early hours of the morning to prepare. To-day, Manson found himself the only occupant of the luncheon-room.

John, the waiter, hovered silently over the scientist until he brought in the coffee. Then, as he poured the liquid into Manson's cup, he whispered in his ear. "Superintendent Burns and another gentleman would like to see you for a few minutes when you've finished lunch, Doctor," he said.

Manson swore under his breath.

"Where are they?" he asked.

"In the coffee-room, and Master Frank says you'll not be disturbed." Manson pushed back his cup and, rising, walked to the coffee-room. Superintendent Burns was an old acquaintance. The two had met on several occasions, when the superintendent had sought the aid of the Yard in London; and advice from Manson had enabled him, on one occasion, to solve a problem that had puzzled the Cornish police for weeks. It had, in fact, resulted in Burns being given his promotion from Inspector. In return, Burns had introduced the Doctor to the Cornish fishing streams, and to the Tremarden Arms. He now came forward with a smile to greet the scientist. The two shook hands cordially.

"Sorry to have broken in on your lunch, Doctor," he apologised, "but our Chief Constable, Sir William Polglaze, wanted to have a word with you. I don't think you've met." He made the introduction.

"Know all about you, of course, Chief Inspector," said Sir William. "Been a follower of your methods for a long time." He chuckled. "Between you and me you've made me the most unpopular man in the Force here, since I made our bobbies study your *Scientific Rules in Criminal Investigation*. I've even bought them a microscope; the superintendent here says he's going blind peering through it."

"Cigarette, Doctor?" Superintendent Burns proffered his case to his two companions, and there was silence for a few moments as the three men lit up. It was broken by Manson.

"And now. Sir William, to what do I owe the pleasure of this unexpected visit?"

The Chief Constable polished a monocle nervously. He screwed it into an eye. "This river business," he said, "Sergeant Jones has reported what happened on the bank, and what you said to him. I gather you think it was no accident?"

Manson held up his hand. "There is no question of thinking, Sir William," he said, quietly. "I know it was no accident."

"You mean that he was murdered?"

"I did not use that word, Sir William." Manson was quietly emphatic. "I have not enough data to say that the colonel was murdered. Let us say that I think there is urgent need for a very thorough inquiry."

The Chief Constable coughed deprecatingly. "Y'know, Doctor, we're peaceful people down here. We don't usually go about killing people. It doesn't do the place much good—"

"It didn't do Colonel Donoughmore any good, either, Sir William."

"Er . . . no. But it seemed a clear open case to our people, you know. What makes you think that it is not an accident?" Manson made no immediate response. He rose to his feet and walked nervously across to the window. A stranger would have taken his tall figure, with the stoop of the shoulders, for that of a scholar. A glance at the thin, aquiline face, with its broad and high forehead and deep-set eyes, would have strengthened his opinion. For a few minutes the eyes of the scientist stared through the window at the busy market-place of the old Norman town. It was market-day. Stalls lined the centre of the square, selling their cheap wares to the farmers' boys and girls who flocked into the centre from twenty miles around, for their one day a week among the busy throng of life. The Sunday-best suit—that had done duty as such for many years—betrayed the farmers, and showed its age by its cut. The Cornish son of the soil is a frugal and careful soul; he buys rarely, but he buys well.

The striped canvas hoods over the stalls fluttered idly in the breeze that blew up the hills on which the market-place was perched. Around the stalls wandered, aimlessly, from stall to stall, a circle of people; it seemed a continuous and unending circle of meandering sight-seers. Cars whizzed along that side of the square which is the main road from London to the Cornish coast, some twenty miles away; cars covered white with dust of the journey, picked up in the mad rush from the Metropolis; cars with luggage grids laden with trunks, cases and packages. And, over all, the ruin of the castle looked down as it had looked down on shoppers and travellers to the sea year after year for centuries.

Doctor Manson drank in the sight, slowly. Then, he turned round and resumed his seat—and answered the Chief Constable's question. "There are several good reasons," he said.

"Such as?" the superintendent queried.

Doctor Manson countered with a question of his own. "Have you, Superintendent, visited the scene?" he asked.

Burns nodded. "I have, Doctor."

"Did you notice anything that might have been called unusual?"

"I . . . er. . . ." The superintendent screwed his face into the contortion of thinking introspectively. He eyed the Chief Inspector suspiciously. It occurred to his mind that he might have missed something which Doctor Manson had seen and regarded as important. The Doctor, he noted, seemed very sure of his ground. He couldn't have seen anything that I haven't seen, he argued; so the superintendent thought hard and fast, hence the facial contortions. There is not, as a rule, much police business in the town that requires concentrated thought. He made up his mind at last. "No, I don't think I noticed anything particularly unusual, Doctor," he said.

Manson let his eyes dwell on the man's face. His look reflected disappointed concern. The superintendent saw it, and wriggled slightly. It was nearly a minute before the Doctor turned his eyes away, switched them over to the Chief Constable, and explained his views.

"Well, Sir William, I did. I noticed one very marked coincidence." He pressed the tips of his fingers together. "Now, I must say here, that I have a very profound suspicion of coincidence. Coincidence is a combination of circumstances coming together. Any one of the circumstances taken by itself is a perfectly normal happening; it is only when they come together in a combination that the happenings develop into what we call coincidence. As a rule, there is a substantial and altogether natural explanation of coincidence, when it is examined properly. To be quite candid, I do not believe in coincidence as a general rule. I view it with suspicion when it is connected with police matters. I view it with *very* serious suspicion when I come across it in connection with unnatural death. So that, when I came across coincidence of more than usual marking, I began to take a more than usual interest in the circumstances."

"What was the coincidence?" The challenge came from the superintendent.

"When I had examined the body of the colonel after it had been taken from the water, Frank Baker, your Sergeant and myself walked up the river bank to the spot where I was told the colonel had fallen in. Now, I know the water. So do you, Superintendent. And I dare say that you, too, Sir William, know it?"

The Chief Constable assented.

"I noted without any reason, except a developed habit of observation, as we walked, that it was pretty well impossible to get any clear, unobstructed, view of the water from the top of the bank. From the scene of the fall I walked upstream, and there the same peculiarity struck me. Bushes covered the waterfront. I do not mean that there was a continuous line of bushes; but where there were gaps between them along the top of the bank, these gaps would be filled in at intervals down the slope. By that chance arrangement, there was no part of the slope, from the shallows up to the Meeting Pool, where there was any clear drop to the water's edge. It was covered completely by a breastwork of bush. All except one spot, a couple of yards in width."

The scientist paused.

"Now, do you see what I am getting at?" he asked.

"Had Colonel Donoughmore fallen, or fainted, at any point along the two-mile stretch of water on which he was supposed to be fishing . . ."

"He *was* fishing there, Doctor," the superintendent interrupted.

"I'll come to that, later, Superintendent," retorted Manson. "As I was saying, had the colonel fallen anywhere along that bank he could not possibly have crashed into the water except at one spot—and that was the spot at which he DID go into the water according to all the signs. It is the only couple of yards where the descent straight to the water edge is not obstructed by bushes, or trees, which would have stopped a falling body, and held it. That occurred to me as an exceedingly unfortunate coincidence for the colonel.

"As I have said I do not believe in these kind of coincidences in the case of violent death. I suspect them. The effect of this observation on my part was to set me looking for signs that would take the 'co' out of coincidence. Yes, Superintendent?"

Superintendent Burns had started to interrupt, but had stopped. Invited, he now made his point. "At the water's edge, upstream from there, Doctor, a large blackberry bush juts out into the river over quite a deep hole. Most fishermen come out of the stream there, climb the bank, and go back to the water on the other side of the bush—at the spot where the colonel fell in."

"I saw the bush," Manson acknowledged, dryly. "Which brings me to my second point. Colonel Donoughmore was a dry-fly man, and a purist at that. Why should he come out of the water to round a bush which took him a few yards DOWN-STREAM? Does a dry-fly man fish downstream, putting every fish 'down' as he goes? You are a fisherman, Superintendent. Would you do that? Ask yourself the question. That is what I did." He eyed the superintendent's start of surprise with a smile. "And if the colonel was fishing upstream," he continued, "why should he go to the water there at all, *when he couldn't go any further upstream because of the blackberry bush?*"

Manson paused, invitingly, but there was no response from his audience.

"Thirdly"—he marked the point off on his fingers—"Why was the colonel going down to the water at all? His fishing-bag was on the bank. So were his creel and his rod. Oh, by the way, you are a fisherman, superintendent, and as good a one as the colonel. Tell me, how do you rest your rod when you are not, for some reason, using it?"

The superintendent looked puzzled. "Why, Doctor . . . er . . . put it up against a tree or a bush, I suppose."

"Of course. So do I. So would Sir William. And so, I imagine, would Colonel Donoughmore. He was a good angler, whatever else he might have been. But where was the colonel's rod when his body was found, Superintendent? Tell me that?"

"Lying in the gra. . ." The superintendent stopped suddenly.

"Quite," said Manson. "Lying in the grass, and alongside a path where anybody might have come along and trodden on it. Now, Superintendent, I will repeat my question: Why should he have been going down to the water at all? He wouldn't be going down to fish, would he? He hadn't got his rod with him.

"There were other points at the spot which struck me as suspicious, but these I will pass by because I was able to give them only cursory examination. But I suggest, Superintendent, that you pay close attention to the marks on the colonel's face and to the displaced tufts of grass on the banks, and, further, the marks of the fall. I suggested to your Sergeant that they should be left undisturbed. I suggest, also, that the head injury should have your very careful attention, in conjunction with the Police Surgeon. It may surprise you.

"Lastly, although the colonel went out to fish in the morning with his landing-net and never returned, his landing-net was in the umbrella-stand of the lounge of the Tremarden Arms at six o'clock in the evening—*and it was wet.*"

Manson paused to let the emphasis of this fact sink into his hearers' minds. "Now, any one of these circumstances, taken separately, might be just a coincidence," he went on; "but not all of them put together."

"It's a perfect jigsaw of coincidence. And the pieces, to my mind, fall together in a pattern. It may be that the post-mortem will turn up other pieces. They may, of course, alter the pattern as a whole, but I feel that we must start putting together the pieces we have."

The three men smoked in a silence that lasted some minutes. It was broken by the Chief Constable. "Well, Superintendent, what do you think of it, now?" he asked.

"Put like the Doctor has done, it does seem a bit queer-like, Sir William," was the answer. "I suppose we'll have to make some inquiries." The addition came regretfully.

"The point is, Burns, do you do the job, or do we call in Scotland Yard?"

Manson thought that the superintendent seemed to grow a little more cheerful at the mention of the Yard. "That would be for you," he reminded him. "But I would point out that we haven't had a deal of experience of murder round here. It looks like we've got a ready-made case for Dr. Manson. I've always heard that corpses were the Doctor's hobby, same like gardening is my hobby."

The Chief Constable guffawed. "What you mean, Burns, is that you don't want to go raking among people you've known half your life, eh?" He looked across at Manson. "What do you say, Doctor?" he asked. "Would you take over?"

"That, Sir William, is for the Assistant Commissioner to say. You'll have to ask for the Yard's help, and they'll depute a senior officer to come down. You can, if you like, mention that I'm here, and can give any help that may be required."

* * * * *

"Telephone call for you, Doctor." It was an hour later. Manson walked to the box and took up the receiver.

"That you, Harry?"

Manson groaned.

"What's this corpse you've nosed out? Thought you'd gone for a few days' fishing." The Assistant Commissioner of Scotland Yard was inclined to facetiousness.

"So I had." Manson explained briefly the details of the colonel's death, and the conclusions at which he had arrived.

The A.C. chuckled. "Well, Harry, they particularly want you to go on with it. You started the hare—it looked a perfectly good accident. I should think, now you'd better catch it. You've asked for it. Any help you want you can have."

"All right, A.C. Send Sergeant Merry down."

"And the Box of Tricks?"

"And the Box, A.C.," Manson agreed.

"They'll be down there to-morrow—and, Harry—"

"Yes."

"Good fishin'."

The phone went dead to the sound of a chuckle.

CHAPTER V
JIGSAW PATTERN

DOCTOR MANSON had told the Chief Constable that the post-mortem examinations on Colonel Donoughmore might alter the pattern of his hypothesis; it was accordingly to the post-mortem that he turned his attention as a first step in the investigation of the colonel's death.

From his brief examination of the body on the river bank, and his subsequent discoveries at the scene of the fall, he had been guided into a certain line of thought. The direction of his mind had produced the points which he had suggested to the Cornish police as being such as to call for investigation. He had not, however, mentioned his more tentative suspicions.

Like all scientists of any standing, Manson was a cautious man. He evolved an idea from certain suspicions, which, to his analytical reasoning, seemed sub-normal; but he used that idea only as working datum until the suppositions were converted into hard fact. Until he had proved them hard facts, indeed, no hint of theory passed his lips.

In the case of Colonel Donoughmore he realised that active investigation could not usefully be proceeded with until the cause of death had definitely been ascertained, and until the body had been exhaustively searched for any indications likely to help in explaining how the colonel came to be in the water. Nor did Manson think that the police surgeon, Dr. Tremayne, was likely to be a competent authority for such an examination without a hand to guide him; he had little or no criminal or pathological experience of what to look for, especially as he could not possibly read his (the Chief-Inspector's) mind. But Manson had not been impressed with his examination on the river bank. He decided to attend the post-mortem personally, and satisfy himself first-hand on the points which he had mentally pigeon-holed.

With that object in view, the Doctor, on the morning after the discovery of the body, left the Tremarden Arms for the mortuary. He turned through the great iron-studded door of the hotel, with its huge, wrought-iron knocker, and into the Market Place. The Tremarden Arms is almost as old as Tremarden itself, with, inside, narrow, winding corridors which go, oddly, up two worn steps here, and down three equally worn steps there. Finding one's bedroom is a switchback adventure to the newcomer in the Arms. There is a story, still told, of new guests who were presented on their arrival with a packet of coloured cardboard chips, which they dropped one by one, as they walked from their room to the hotel lounge and dining-hall, in order that they might be able to find their winding way to bed later on!

The oak-studded hotel door is the oldest part of the Arms. It had once been the door of the Friary, the ruins of which still stand.

Those were the days when the hunted man, once he had raised the massive knocker and dropped it, had secured sanctuary; when the hungry wayfarer, achieving the same, could not be refused food and lodging. Times have changed, but even now the wayfarer still raises and drops the ages-old knocker to secure food and lodging; the Tremarden Arms disdains a bell at the front door.

Traversing the Market Place, Manson turned right, at the end, and began walking down the steep, sloping street to the town's gate. In whichever direction, north, south, east or west, one walked from the Market Place of Tremarden, one found oneself going downhill. The Normans, who built the town, knew how to build for security. They first laid the roads; and they built the towns on the road. But the towns straddled the highway at their highest peak. That is how Tremarden was built, on a plateau, cut out from the hillside. The plateau was the living square of the fortress. Two hundred yards down from it, the wall of the fortress encircled the hill-side; above it rising to a pinnacle, the castle poised, the eyes in the window slits commanding a view of twenty miles of the countryside around. The road path was broken twice—at the north gate which gave entrance to Tremarden; and at the south gate which gave exit.

The south gate has vanished; but the north gate still stands, its centuries-old stone now crumbling here and there; its cells for malefactors now open to the public gaze. The Keeper of the Gate will show you his relics if you ask him—the cell in which lay imprisoned for a year Fox the Dissenter, who would rail against the established authority of the Bishops; the whipping cell, the dark cells where no light penetrated.

It was through this gate that Manson proceeded on his way to the mortuary. It lay outside the town, on the long white road, so that the ugly side of life was by-passed for the people of Tremarden.

Manson opened the door and stepped in the room, clammy with the touch of death.

Doctor Tremayne, informed by telephone of the intention of Doctor Manson to assist him in the post-mortem, was inclined to resent this as an intrusion on his domain, and a reflection on his ability as a surgeon. When, on their meeting in the mortuary, he found that the Doctor was the man of the river bank, he showed himself even more resentful.

"I thought, sir, you told me that you were not a medical man," he said.

"Neither am I, Doctor," was the reply. "But I am a Professor of Medical Jurisprudence, an authority on pathological examinations, and I am in charge of the investigations into this man's death." He passed over his card.

Dr. Tremayne's eyebrows rose on reading the name. "So you are THE Manson, are you?" he replied. "That is quite a different matter. I shall be very glad to have you with me, and to watch you practice the methods of which I have read so often in print. I base my examination in these cases on your medical jurisprudence, you know. But we don't get much opportunity for that kind of thing down here, Dr. Manson. We are a peaceable crowd really, you know."

Manson smiled an acknowledgement of the compliment. "And may not have much this time, Doctor," he warned. "So far, it is only a case of unusual circumstances which, I think, ought to be straightened out."

"Well, I've had the body prepared. Shall we start?"

Colonel Donoughmore, stripped of his clothes, was revealed as a well-preserved man of some sixty years of age, of good physique, and development associated with military drill and discipline. There was an inclination to obesity in the stomach, the obvious result of abandoned exercise in later life. The two men stared at the body with professional interest.

"Shows all the obvious signs of drowning, don't you think, Chief Inspector?" commented Dr. Tremayne. "Skin is pallid enough, *cutis anserina* (goose-flesh, if you like), a little froth in the mouth . . . let's have a look at the eyes . . . yes, pupils considerably dilated. Very satisfactory, I should say. Is there anything you want to see before we open up?"

"Nothing that I know of, except the head injury, Doctor. But I think I will run over it, nevertheless. Good rule in medical jurisprudence not to miss an opportunity of examination. Wish I could make every police officer realise that before it is too late."

Manson was examining closely the skin of the dead man as he spoke, spending some moments over small discoloured patches here and there.

"Hypostasis, would you say, Doctor?" he asked.

Doctor Tremayne bent over the markings. "Possibly," he agreed. "One or two, perhaps, are bruises caused doubtless by knocking against the stones when he went through the Gulley."

"And these?" Manson was now peering at slight discolourations on the upper arms. Half a dozen in number, and spaced over the muscles, they were only just visible even against the pallidness of the skin.

"Slight bruising, eh, Chief Inspector?" Dr. Tremayne stared closely at the faint markings. "Possibly occasioned on his attempts to swim. Bound to use his arms, you know, and in his wading outfit constriction of the flesh against the clothing would be pretty tight."

"Quite so, Doctor," replied Manson; but he produced a powerful magnifying glass from a pocket, and made a further examination. Next, with a pair of micro-calipers he measured the sizes of the separate bruises, carefully entering the figures into his note-book. A rough drawing was added, showing the position of the marks.

Catching the doctor's smile at this meticulous care, Manson answered it. "Sorry to be keeping you, Doctor," he said. "It may seem a waste of time, but you never know. I have a very suspicious mind, and I don't like bruises on dead bodies. If I don't note them now, against the future, I would never note them at all. Once we've put the body underground, it's gone. Now what about that head wound?"

In contrast to the other injuries on the body, the bruise stood out in ugly conspicuity. It was a reddish purple, deepening into blue along its three-quarters of an inch centre of violence. A livid ring encircled it. Dr. Tremayne probed the surroundings with his rubber-gloved fingers. "Depressed fracture of the frontal bone ... I should say that there is a rupture of the meningeal artery."

Manson nodded. "I think so, too, Doctor. You will have noticed the blood in the tissues? I remarked it on the river bank. But we'll be better able to read it, probably, from the inside. How long before death would you say it was inflicted?"

The doctor considered the point. "Knocked his head on a boulder as he went down the bank, the sergeant tells me," he said. "Possible, of course. I should say that that is the answer."

Manson looked up sharply. He seemed about to speak. But he changed his mind. When he *did* speak it was only to say: "I would rather like a section for microscopic examination later, if necessary."

It was in the actual post-mortem examination, however, that Manson evinced the keener interest. It was obvious that drowning had played a part in the death of the colonel. The lungs were voluminous, spongy, pale in colour and with air vesicles distended. On the trachea being slit, fine froth was revealed lining the tubes. There was a quantity of water in the stomach.

"That seems to settle the question, Chief-Inspector," said Dr. Tremayne. "There is nothing here not compatible with death by drowning, so far as I can see."

"No?" The scientist's voice was more of a query than an agreement. "Do you not think, perhaps, that there is either too much or too little water in the body?"

Dr. Tremayne considered the question. "I see what you are driving at, Doctor," he said. "In an ordinary case of drowning I agree that the lungs would be bellowed, so to speak, and that the stomach would contain considerably more water than is apparent here. But we have to remember that the deceased had fractured his skull with a heavy blow on a boulder as he entered the water. The shock of the immersion, coming on top of the head injury, would materially hasten the death; he could not have lived more than half-a-minute or so. Consequently, the water drawn up into the lungs would be correspondingly less than in the case of a person drowned in the ordinary way."

"I appreciate that, Dr. Tremayne, but I would like to feel more satisfied on the point," the scientist replied. "I shall, I think, take a sample of the water both from the lungs and the stomach, for examination."

From a parcel which he had brought with him, Manson took two laboratory exhibit bottles. He filled them with liquid extracted from the lungs and from the stomach of the dead man. Sealing them, he labelled each bottle, and completed the operation by writing his own signature on the label, and obtaining also the confirming signature of the surgeon. The liquid seemed to excite his attention after the sealing, for he held the bottles up to the light, and directed his gaze to a number of floating, tiny objects, green-coloured. Dr. Tremayne noticed the inspection and joined him.

"Bits of weed, are they not, Chief Inspector?" he asked. "Common enough in cases of drowning, as you will know. There are generally fragments of detached weed in water, and they are naturally drawn through the mouth while the power of breathing still exists and into the lungs and stomach while the power of swallowing obtains."

"Quite so, Doctor."

"I noticed a few pieces in the throat."

"You did?" Manson looked nonplussed. He returned to the body and, throwing the beam of a dentist's pencil torch into the throat, picked out with a pair of the doctor's tweezers a number of fragments still adhering to the sides of the mouth and throat. These were slipped into envelopes and labelled. Then, taking a third bottle, Manson placed inside a section of the tissue from the bruise on the colonel's head, afterwards sealing the bottle with an identifying label, which Dr. Tremayne, at his request, signed.

That ended the examination with the exception that, as Dr. Tremayne completed the after-examination details to the body, the Chief Inspector browsed round the colonel. Firstly, he paid special attention to the fingers of the dead man. Placing a piece of clean white paper under each hand he scraped from beneath the fingernails a quantity of matter. The collection he tapped into a seed envelope and this, again, was labelled.

Finally, he again examined the forehead wound, noting the varied colours of the bruising. It was while thus engaged that he noticed a discolouration on the chin. It had not before been apparent, but seemed to have developed since the post-mortem began. The skin was unbroken, and the mark appeared to be a bruise of less intensity than that of the forehead. Manson entered a description of the mark in his note-book, and then occupied himself with packing his bottles back into the parcel. "That, I think, is all the colonel can tell us Doctor," he said.

"I think so, Chief Inspector," was the reply. "I do not anticipate any difficulty in my report. Shall I send it to you direct or to the Chief Constable?"

"Oh, I think the Chief Constable, Doctor, if you don't mind."

"Very well. Nothing more you want, is there? What about the inquest?"

"I'll see the Chief Constable about that, Doctor. We shall have to wait, of course, for relatives of the man to get down here. The only thing I want to see now are the clothes he was wearing. I'll get the mortuary attendant to wrap them up and send them to me at the hotel."

The two men shook hands and parted.

Walking slowly and thoughtfully Doctor Manson reached the door of the Tremarden Arms at the same moment that a car drew up in front of the entrance. From it emerged a squat, and somewhat mournful-looking figure. A fishing creel followed, propelled by the hands of the driver; and a bundle of fishing rods, emerging suddenly from the same source, missed by a fraction poking into an eye of the Chief Inspector. He stopped dead and eyed the procession in dazed astonishment.

Detective-Sergeant James Merry, B.Sc., deputy scientist at Scotland Yard, had arrived on the job!!

"And what the devil do you suppose you have here, Jim?" asked Manson.

"Morning, Doctor . . . just a couple of rods, you know."

"Rods! I can see they are rods. Do you suppose I'm blind? What's the idea?"

"Well, I mean to say, Harry . . . All work and no play makes Jack a dull boy, as the saying goes. Combining a little pleasure with business, as it were, helps the grey matter to work better."

"My lad, you look like having enough fishing before we are through with this. But it's a man we'll be fishing for, not trout."

"How do you know it's a man, Harry? You're theorising." Merry wagged an admonishing finger at the scientist.

Manson eyed it. "*Touché* to you, Jim," he admitted. "I DON'T know that it is a man. Come along inside. You've brought the Box of Tricks, I suppose?"

Sergeant Merry pointed to the interior of the car. "And a few extras with it as well," he said.

"Good man."

The couple entered the hotel and walked up to the Chief-Inspector's room. "So it's phoney, is it?" Merry asked, as he washed away the dust of the journey from London.

"Very phoney, Jim; and, except for us, it would have gone into records as a very unfortunate accident. Now listen carefully. . . ."

For half-an-hour the scientist outlined the facts to his assistant. The two men had worked together since Manson had founded the Laboratory at the Yard. Indeed, they had worked together before that, for they had been room-mates and students together at the University. They followed the same train of thought, and each possessed the same aptitude for dismissing theory until proved facts pointed to one. The combination had proved a brilliant success in solving crime since it had first worked in the case of Joseph Petty.

"And what is the local police reaction, Harry?" asked Merry, at the end of the recital.

"They are hoping to establish that the thing was a pure accident, Jim. And I am prepared to find that the doctor's report on the post-mortem will strengthen the opinion."

"As bad as that, is he?"

Manson nodded. "He would not see anything unless it got up and hit him on the nose," he said.

* * * * *

Doctor Manson's prognostication was quickly justified. It was shortly after lunch that the Chief Constable and Superintendent Burns were ushered into the private sitting-room which Franky had arranged for Manson and Merry. The latter having been introduced, the Chief Constable announced the reason for his visit. "The superintendent here, has received Dr. Tremayne's report on the post-mortem, Doctor," he announced. He handed the document over. Manson read it aloud:

"I have this day carried out a post-mortem examination on the body of Colonel John Donoughmore. I find that the said Colonel Donoughmore met his death primarily by drowning, after having fallen in the River Tamar."

There followed a description of the injury to the head, and the notification that the usual full symptoms of asphyxiation by drowning were not present in the body. Reasons were given:

"I attribute this to the fact that the head injury was sustained by the colonel striking his head on some object a few seconds before immersion, rendering him unconscious, and thereby causing death more quickly in the water than would be the case had he fallen conscious into the water. I find no symptoms of foul play and attribute the decease to an accident.

"*(Signed)* Egbert Tremayne, M.D., F.R.C.S."

Manson handed the report back to the Chief Constable. "It is exactly what I expected to read, Sir William," he said.

"Then you agree with Dr. Tremayne?" The face of Superintendent Burns brightened.

"I do not. I disagree most emphatically. The death was *not* an accident," was the scientist's reply.

There was a pained silence. Superintendent Burns shifted uncomfortably on his feet. It was a full minute before the Chief

Constable broke the strain. "But, Doctor, do you not think you are a little . . . er . . . unreasonable?" he asked. "You yourself said that the post-mortem might alter the pattern of your hypothesis . . ."

"It *has* altered it, Sir William; it is no longer a hypothesis," was the reply. "It has become a definite fact."

The Chief Constable passed a hand over a puzzled brow. "But Dr. Tremayne insists that the affair was accidental, Doctor; and he gives what I should say is chapter and verse . . ."

"Dr. Tremayne's report is a complete travesty of the facts," interrupted Manson. "I said that his report was only what I expected to read, because I had seen the line, or lack of line, upon which Dr. Tremayne was working throughout the post-mortem."

"Um. Doctor Tremayne, Chief-Inspector, is our leading medical man. He is a qualified and excellent surgeon, who has worked with the police for many years." The Chief Constable had become distinctly antagonistic and showed it. "He carried out a pathological examination and this is his considered report of his findings. I feel that in view of these circumstances I cannot see the need for any further investigations and I am proposing to drop the case."

"That, I am afraid, you cannot do, Sir William." Manson's voice was grimly insistent.

"Why not, Chief Inspector?"

"Because, sir, I could not allow it and should not allow it," was the stern reply. "On certain opinions which I laid before you at your own request, you called in the aid of Scotland Yard. The Assistant Commissioner authorised me to take charge of the case. I am a competent police officer. I hold the opinion that the death of this man was not due to accidental means. I hold that opinion very strongly. It is my duty as a police officer to acquaint my chief of that fact, to explain to him why I hold that opinion, and to do all in my power to see that a proper investigation is made in the interests of Justice. That I propose to do."

He paused for any comment that either or both the two men might have to make. None was forthcoming, and he continued: "It is my intention to return to London immediately, hand a copy of Dr. Tremayne's report to the Commissioner of Police, and at the same time give him my personal report on the post-mortem as I saw it. The subsequent decision will be for him to make, doubtless after he has discussed the case with you."

Doctor Manson turned to his table. It was a plain dismissal and the Chief Constable and the superintendent accepted it. Half-an-hour later Manson was being driven to the station, on his way to London.

CHAPTER VI
MURDER IS OUT

"So THAT, A.C., is the position as I see it. I am convinced in my own mind that this man was killed. Every fact points that way. I feel that I should not have done my duty had I not have acquainted you fully with the circumstances as I view them. If you decide that the Chief Constable is justified in accepting the post-mortem report and calling off the investigations, that, of course, is the end of the matter."

For three quarters of an hour Dr. Manson had presented what he considered to be an unbiased chronicle of the case of Colonel Donoughmore from the moment that he had examined the body on the river bank to the last interview with the Chief Constable, in which that official had declared his intention of dropping further investigation. He had outlined his inspection on the bank, and the conclusions he had drawn from it. Very quietly he had sketched out the possibilities of foul play which had occurred to his quick mind from the jigsaw pieces which represented the broken pattern of the colonel's death. Finally, he had described the condition of the body as he had seen it during the post-mortem.

Before he had commenced the interview with the Assistant Commissioner, Doctor Manson had asked for the Home Office pathological expert to be present. "Not that I have any doubts as to my conclusions," he had explained, "but because I think you would be helped to arrive at a decision if those conclusions were confirmed or otherwise by an independent person who is also an authority on such matters."

The Assistant Commissioner had welcomed the suggestion; and it was to this expert that he first turned when Doctor Manson relaxed into the depths of his chair at the termination of his recital.

"What do you say about the position, Mr. Abigail?" he asked.

Mr. Abigail ("Stiffy" to his friends, for a reason obvious from his calling!) was a meek little man with a bulging forehead and protruding eyes. A pair of pince-nez spectacles usually sat on the extreme end of his nasal organ, but were now lying on the table in front of him. He had been pathological expert at the Home Office for nearly twenty years; and had been inclined at first to resent the appointment of Doctor Manson to the position of Scientific Investigator at Scotland Yard, and to the providing of the Laboratory at the Metropolitan Police headquarters. The antagonism, however, quickly vanished when he made the acquaintance of Manson, and the two had since worked together on numerous occasions, to the benefit of both. He had listened to the scientist's postulations and assumptions with keen interest, and had made copious notes during the dissertation.

"I think, Mr. Assistant Commissioner, that I must agree with Doctor Manson," he now said.

"Reasons?" snapped the Assistant Commissioner.

"Several," retorted Mr. Abigail. He arranged his spectacles at their usually precarious angle, and shuffled his notes into something like order. He cleared his throat. "Firstly," he began, "the wound on the head. The local sawbones, I see"—he peered at Dr. Tremayne's report—"says that the injury was sustained by the deceased striking his head on an obstacle on the river bank a few seconds before he entered the water. Doctor Manson says that the object was a granite boulder. Now Doctor Manson describes the bruise as a reddish-purple in colour, deepening to blue along the centre of violence, the whole being encircled in a livid ring. The skin was not broken.

"Now, Mr. Assistant Commissioner, in a bruise without a broken skin, blood has to escape under a certain amount of resistance. The force that overcomes this resistance is supplied by (i) the beating of the heart; and (ii) the elastic force of the arteries. At the moment of death the first of these factors disappears. The second factor sinks very rapidly and is probably lost in half an hour. It follows, therefore, from these facts that the amount of blood effused in a bruise can determine, within certain limits, how long before death the bruise was inflicted.

"Very well, sir. Now the utmost limit of time that an unconscious man can live when plunged completely underneath water is one and a half minutes. Doctor Manson is quite definite that in the bruise there was considerable infiltration of blood into the tissues, and, furthermore, that the blood had coagulated. Had the bruise been caused by the head of the deceased striking a boulder as, or immediately before, he entered the water, and had the man lived the full span of a minute and a half afterwards, there could not have been any such infiltration. A little there might have been, though even this is doubtful, but not to such an extent as to have been evident at a post-mortem examination.

"That is point one. Point two is the colour of the bruise. The changes which take place in the colour of a bruise enables an opinion to be given as to the time, before death, that a bruise was inflicted. Now a bruise shows itself at once as a red discoloration. In course of time changes in colour occur, due to the absorption of blood pigment. After death the blood, of course, ceases to flow. The red discoloration of the bruise soon changes to a purplish tint. Then the purple begins to turn bluish, firstly at the actual seat of the violence. The succeeding discolorations are green, lemon and yellow.

"But at least half an hour must elapse before the red discoloration of a bruise changes to purple. It may be longer—it probably will be—but half an hour is the minimum time. A further period must pass before the centre of the violence shows signs of blueness. It would, therefore, Mr. Assistant Commissioner, be impossible for a wound, inflicted a minute and a half before death, to show at a post-mortem, made a few hours after death, a purplish colour with the centre already turning blue. The fact that the outside ring, the extremity of the violence, was still red, suggests to me that the bruise was inflicted not seconds before death, but between half and three quarters of an hour. I think that is one thing worrying Doctor Manson."

He glanced at the scientist and received a confirming nod.

"This," the expert went on, "combined with the fact that the tissues were infiltrated with coagulated blood makes the time lag a certainty.

"Then there is the bruise on the chin, which showed up during the post-mortem. It is pretty well known that a bruise on the point, made, for instance, by a blow such as a boxer might deliver on an opponent, does not show any discoloration for from fourteen to eighteen hours after its delivery. I can imagine nothing which could cause such a bruise at that spot of the body except a blow from the fist. The skin, it is to be noted, was unbroken."

Again Manson nodded agreement with the expert's reasoning.

"So far as I am concerned, then, there remains only the water in the lungs and the stomach. Doctor Manson gave, I should have thought, a pretty plain hint to Doctor Tremayne when he asked whether that medico did not think that there was either too much or too little water in the body. Taking the limit of life for an unconscious body in the water, unable to help itself, as a minute and a half—the outside limit, mind you—it is impossible that there could be sufficient water inhaled to volumise the lungs, and half-fill the stomach. If a man died within the limit, and was unconscious, there was too much water in the body. If he died from drowning, then there was too little water. The lungs should have been ballooned, and the stomach distended.

"The crux of the matter, as I see it, is this: What happened between the time the bruise was inflicted and the time the man went under the water? The two were not caused at one and the same time. That is certain. There is a hiatus, and I agree with Doctor Manson that it invites serious inquiry. I have on many occasions tried to impress on the Home Office that the men who conduct these post-mortems should be not merely sawbones, but pathologists. This case is an excellent example of the need for some standard of knowledge on the part of police surgeons."

Mr. Abigail dropped his spectacles from the end of his nose and lay back in his seat.

It was some moments before the Assistant Commissioner spoke. He sat, leaning forward, left elbow on his desk and the hand cupping his chin. His right hand drummed a pencil on the blotting pad in front of him.

"I am in a difficult position," he said at last. "But I think that I must accept the opinion of both of you. That means that there is something to investigate. Without committing myself to admitting that Colonel Donoughmore was killed, I shall inform the Chief Constable of Cornwall that there are very unsatisfactory aspects of the inquiry, which we feel cannot be allowed to pass without investigation; and that Doctor Manson is authorised by the Commissioner to proceed with those investigations, originally asked for by the Cornish police. Many thanks for the assistance you have given, Mr. Abigail."

"A privilege, I assure you, Mr. Assistant Commissioner," was the reply, as the Home Office Expert left the room.

"Well, Harry, that's that. You're going to be a trifle unpopular in Cornwall. Was the local doctor really as bad as you said?"

When they were alone together, the Assistant Commissioner and Manson were Harry and Edward, or "A.C." together. The two were firm friends and members of the same club, and formality was dropped between them.

"He was even worse, A.C.," was the scientist's retort. "His examination on the river bank was no examination at all. He would not have taken the temperature of the body, had I not asked for it to be done, although I, then, had no authority to make the request. The sergeant naturally knew nothing of how vital the time and temperature may be."

"And the post-mortem?" the Assistant Commissioner asked.

"Farcical. The sergeant and constable had told him what they thought had happened and he accepted it. He went to the post-mortem to look for all the things of which he had been told, and of course, he found them. But he didn't find anything else, because he wasn't looking for anything else."

"That's a queer thing about the fishing line and the fly, isn't it, Harry?"

"Most peculiar, to my mind. It was the second thing to excite my suspicions. I'm keeping the thing quiet for the time being. It will give me more time for inquiries."

"And then there is the landing net."

"True. If everything was above board someone would surely have come along to admit having seen the net lying on the bank, and to have brought it back to the hotel. It's a perfectly natural thing to do, take a found net to the headquarters of the water."

"Anybody in mind, Harry?"

Manson shook his head. "I haven't looked round yet, you know," he answered. "The colonel seems to have been a pretty nasty type of man. Nobody I have spoken to has a good word to say for him."

"Well, good luck, Harry. I expect you'll find things a little uncomfortable with the police down there now. If you want any help from here we can spare you a couple of men."

"Thanks, Edward. I think I shall be able to square Burns, anyhow. He owes me something, you know."

CHAPTER VII
JIGSAW BASE

DURING THE ABSENCE of his chief in London, Sergeant Merry was occupying his time in laying a foundation for future inquiries. Having read and re-read the notes made during his talk with Manson, and having studied the *mise-en-scène* of the tragedy, he decided that the start of any investigations must be with the people who had access, or could have had access, to the colonel during his last hours of life. The obvious possibilities were those who had that day fished the River Tamar. The sergeant accordingly sought their identities.

Franky was disturbed, to say the least, at the sergeant's questions. He had known his guests for almost as many years as he could remember; and could conceive none of them in the role of a killer of a fellow guest, however obnoxious that guest might be. It was unfortunate, and he said as much to the sergeant, that there should have been so cordial a dislike between the colonel and the rest of the hotel crowd, because fishermen, as a rule, are a cordial company, and angling seemed to bring about a comradeship and camaraderie more than any other sport he knew of.

Merry appreciated the repugnance of the hotelier at discussing his guests in such circumstances, and hastened to apply healing balm to the wound.

"I am not suggesting that any of them are concerned, Franky," he explained. "I can't see any fisherman going round killing even Colonels when there are trout waiting to be killed. But we cannot ignore their presence near the scene of death. In point of fact, the quickest way to dismiss all of them from the business is to get their alibis as quickly as possible."

Franky acknowledged the point. He fetched his fishing diary and weight book, and opened them at the day of the tragedy. "As you know full well, Sergeant, there are five beats on the Tamar," he said. "All of them were allotted for that day. Now, Mr. Emmett had the bottom beat—that is the one from the lowest extent of my water up the shallows and to as far as can be fished of the Round Pool. You cannot fish all the pool; you have to walk past it and start again at the top end, and take in the Gulley. The next beat starts a hundred yards from the Gulley, going upstream, takes in the Rostrum Pool and the Meeting Pool, where another stream joins the Tamar, and ends at the Gorge. That is the beat the colonel was fishing."

"And in which he went into the water, eh?"

"And in which he went into the water," the hotelier agreed. "Then there is another break because the Gorge is unfishable owing to its depth, and the fact that the banks rise so sheer that one cannot walk along the water edge. Also, it is too thickly lined with trees for casting. So the next beat starts beyond the Gorge and runs up wide shallows until it enters the Avenue. That's the stretch you yourself have often fished. There it runs pretty deep wading again—up above the waist—for a good distance. Mrs. Devereux had that beat. It ends near the Pylons. From there, the fourth beat goes in timbered and open country up to the Farm. The major was fishing that one; and Sir Edward had the deep water beyond, up to the end of my stretch."

Sergeant Merry visualised the river. "So that, one side of the colonel—the lower side—Emmett was fishing; and on the other side—above—Mrs. Devereux, with the major next to her again?"

"That's it, Sergeant."

"Now, about the landing net, Franky. Is it certain that the colonel took it with him that morning?"

"Absolutely certain." Franky grimaced. "I handed it to him after he had got into the bus that took him down to the water. It was strapped to his rod."

"And you've no idea how it came to be in the umbrella stand in the hotel lounge?"

Franky shook his head. "I've asked all the staff. Nobody saw it brought in, though there was hardly a moment when one of them wasn't in the lounge."

"Urn. Well, somebody brought it in, anyhow." Merry looked across at the landing net carefully hung on the wall of the room. "We shall have to see what it's like for fingerprints," he said.

"Now while you are here, Franky, we might as well draw a map of the river. It will give the Doctor a bird's-eye view of the scene, as it were." He drew a sheet of official paper towards him. "Let's see, now. Hadn't you used to give a plan of the water to newcomers as a guide to their beat?"

Franky nodded. He rummaged in his pockets, and produced a folded sketch map of the hotel's waters. "That's it, Sergeant," he said.

"Good! Then we'll draw it out, large-scale, and mark in all the beats and pools and the spot where, as the newspapers say, 'the foul crime was committed'."

The plan completed and checked up, Merry pasted it on a large sheet of cardboard and laid it on the Doctor's desk for reference.

"And now, Franky—" Merry reached for his hat—"and now, supposing you wanted to hear a bit of gossip about this township and its people, where would you go, and to whom?"

Franky let a broad smile break over his face. "Well, now, you are an outlander, as they call strangers round this part, and you're a presentable kind of man with a pair of trousers on. They do say that a couple of young ladies, waitresses at the tea-shop round the corner of the Market Place, by the old church, have a bit of time to spare about 10.30 o'clock, before a few of the business men drop in for a cup of coffee; and they do say that the young ladies talk rather a lot. And then there's old Tom Tregarron, him that sits in the ticket office of the old ruins; he seems to know a lot about the people round here. How he gets to know, sitting there in a one-roomed eyrie, I don't rightly know, but he does. I shouldn't be surprised but what you'd hear quite a lot of things, if so be you went in there."

Merry put on his hat. . . .

And went!

* * * * *

The Ivy Tearooms were an innovation in Tremarden; they were also the most modern "contraption" in the eyes of the older portion of the populace. In fact, they were so modern, set amidst the ruins of the past, as to appear even to the visitor somewhat incongruous. Visitors coming on the tearooms suddenly, as they emerged from the older parts of the town, were apt at first to shy away like a startled horse.

To reach the Ivy, those who fancied its contents walked across the east side of the Market Place and down a cobbled back street, until the ancient church, with its flint-built walls, came into vision. There, on the left, stood open a vividly green door. Futurist curtaining looked out from the panes, set over window boxes of gay geraniums. The geraniums nodded their plumes at ivy-covered ruins across the way, which were all that remained of what had been the wall of the old fortress town. Hence the "Ivy" name in the Tearooms.

The young ladies of the Ivy were also gay to the point of incongruity. "Outlanders" they were in the sight of the townspeople. There was nothing much in that, because old William Porter, who was nearing seventy-five, and had lived in Tremarden for forty years, was still an "outlander." However, even he looked askance at the hair à la Garbo or Grable, and the Ivy girls' abbreviated, bright blue silk skirts that did not even pretend to hide the sheer silk of the beautifully filled hose beneath. The bloodied, lacquered finger-nails, designed to allure, seemed to confirm the opinion of the good women of Tremarden that them girls at The Ivy were hussies. The opposite sex, however, did not share the opinion; and the Ivy Tearooms did a good business in coffee and cakes, teas, luncheons and discreet little dinners.

Merry first tried the coffee and cakes, and as the Synthetic Glamour placed them before him, he endeavoured to display the interest he really felt in the ministering angel. He felt pretty sure that there was no need for originality here. He opened the attack frontally, so to speak. "It's a lovely day," he said.

"Yes," drawled the languid one. "Pity to be inside a day like this. Of course, it will rain to-morrow—that being our closing day."

Merry was away!

"You don't belong to Tremarden, surely?" he ventured. "You sound more like a Londoner."

"Oh. 'Ow could you tell? Are you from London?" was the reply.

"Yes. Down on a few days' business."

"Lucky you!" The damsel sighed. "I've got to stop here till the winter. My place in town was closed down, and as I wanted a change, and a gentleman friend of mine knew this place, I came down. But I don't like it. Too much fresh air to suit me. Give me London and quiet."

Merry jumped to it. "But you must do a good business here; and you must meet lots of nice people."

She looked around, and seeing no more "coffees" crossed one foot over the other and, one arm leaning on the back of a chair, settled down for a chat.

"Oh, yes, we get some very nice gentlemen come in here. Mostly them as come down for a holiday, though what they can see in this place beats me."

"Fish," Merry explained. "They mostly come to catch trout and salmon. All right in the daytime, but the place must be pretty dull in the dark period. No theatre, cinema twice a week, and no other amusement."

"That's all *you* know." A broad wink accompanied the remark.

"What!" Merry looked startled. "Why, this is the goody-goodiest place I've ever been in. Can't even speak to anything in petticoats."

"That's what *you* think. Hypocrites these people are. Place is full of them. But you've got to know 'em, see? All go-to-meeting on top, but, boy, when you've got underneath! Could I tell you something about other men's wives! And other wives' husbands!"

"No!" Merry moved his chair nearer.

"It's mostly the visitors, of course. I expect they're your fishermen, 'cos they've been coming every year. It's a good job the men round here don't know what their wives are doing when they expect 'em to be at a sewing-bee, or something. And the girls! We have one here who's got a fine old sugar-daddy; just like on the pictures, believe me."

"You don't say," protested Merry, after the whispered story. "Well, I'd never have thought it. Now how about the girl with the sugar-daddy? Who is she?"

"I think she works in a hotel here. But they had that table in the corner several nights a week, she and him did. And somebody else had it with him the other nights. But I've done very well out of their suppers. Now he's gone."

"Gone? What, left?"

"No. He's dead."

"Dead?"

"Yes. Damned nuisance if you ask me. Can't think how the silly old codger fell in the river. You must have heard about him. Whole place is talking about him. Old Colonel, he was."

"I've only just come, you know."

"Oh well, it's a funny business. . . ."

It was an hour before Merry left.

* * * * *

"So, as far as I can see, Harry, the colonel seems to have been a gay Lothario; and things don't look too good for one or two people in these parts."

The sergeant's wanderings had taken him well over the lunch hour. On his return to the hotel he had found Doctor Manson back from his London trip and swallowing a cup of after-luncheon coffee. To him he sketched an outline of his morning's verbal angling in the Tremarden gossip waters.

"Is it fact or just spiteful gossip, do you think, Jim?" The scientist's voice carried a doubting note. "You know, or perhaps you do not, the vicious scandal-mongering in these small towns. They'll probably be saying to-morrow that you have designs on the tea-shop girls, especially as you seem to have spent the greater part of the morning there."

"Oh, I think it's true enough, Harry," was the reply. "I set one or two booby traps for the girl, but the story hung together. Anyway, it seems to be pretty well talked of behind the scenes. As to old Tom, he says, quite definitely, that the carpenter's daughter met the colonel in the castle ruins after dark on several occasions. Used to wait in the shade of the old gateway to the tower. Says he used to watch 'em. You know the type."

"Still, Jim, I don't see that meeting the carpenter's daughter in the dark is any reason why she should murder the colonel. She seems to have had no objection to the meetings."

"No. But, you see, someone else had."

The sergeant waited in tantalising invitation for Manson's inevitable question. It came, sharply insistent: "Who?"

"Mrs. Devereux."

"What!"

"Mrs. Devereux, Harry. According to Tom she was walking along the path from the lower part of the town, and was near the entrance to the ruins when she must have spotted the colonel and the girl. Tom says she suddenly stopped, slipped behind a tree, and stood watching them. Tom had just locked up the office, after counting the takings, and was about to start for home when he saw what he described as 'queer goings-on.' He propped his door open—it was fairly dark, you know—sat back in the room and waited. He says he didn't know who Mrs. Devereux was, not then; and didn't know who she was watching until the colonel walked past his door. The Trepol girl followed about a minute afterwards, and when she reached a spot opposite the tree out jumped Mrs. Devereux. The couple of women had a 'hell of a go-ing-to-it,' in Tom's language. He couldn't hear what they were saying, mind you, but it was a row all right. Then the girl flew out of the gate, and Mrs. Devereux followed more slowly."

"I see. And how did Old Tom know that it was Mrs. Devereux?"

"He didn't, until a couple of days later, when he passed the hotel as Mrs. Devereux came out. He saw her, and recognised the scarf she was wearing as that worn by the woman in the ruins. It's a yellow scarf with dogs scattered all over it. He had noticed it as the woman of the ruins passed close to his peephole after she had parted from the girl."

"That seems pretty conclusive, Jim."

"There is something in it, Harry, I think, because the Tea-room couple say that the Trepol girl said she was friends with the colonel, and that her father had threatened he'd give her a hiding if she saw him again. She said she didn't care, and would see the colonel whenever she wanted to."

"It doesn't seem very sensible to me, Jim, if you are suggesting that Mrs. Devereux killed the colonel. If she wanted the colonel, it doesn't make sense that she should go shooting him into the river."

"May not have been intended, Harry. And you've got to allow that she was on the water on the beat next to him. You've seen the map I sketched out?"

"Yes, thanks. Well, we'll have to look into it, of course. I think we should have a talk, after dinner, with all the fishing folk. You had better arrange that before the meal, and tell Superintendent Burns. Meanwhile, perhaps we had better do a bit of investigating here."

On such occasions as Doctor Manson had to leave his laboratory at Scotland Yard to conduct personal inquiries at some distance from the Metropolis, there went with him a portmanteau which was, in effect, a most effective mobile laboratory. It lacked few of the essentials of a fitted "lab"; in other words it was a laboratory in miniature, in the early days of the scientist's appearances as the Yard's Medical Jurisprudist, the opening of this portmanteau at the scene of investigations had given rise to much hilarity among police officers. Manson had borne the amusement in good part, sometimes joining in it. He was a great believer in the efficiency of its contents as a means of investigation, and as a means of proving, or disproving, certain lines along which the police proposed, or were already, working.

After one or two spectacular results, hilarity against the portmanteau declined; in its place, a marked respect for the uncanny disclosures due to its contents sprang up. One prominent police officer, commenting on its workings among his colleagues, referred on one occasion to the portmanteau as "a box of tricks." The name was greeted with approval, and it stuck. Doctor Manson and his Box of Tricks became inseparable, and indivisible, in the minds of Scotland Yard's investigators.

It was the Box of Tricks—which Merry had brought down from London—that Manson now set on the table and opened. From it he took a small, but powerful, double-eye-piece microscope, prepared slides, two pairs of small tweezers and a capillary tube.

Taking an envelope from a drawer he tipped out on to a piece of clean Litmus paper the fragments of weed which he had picked from the mouth of Colonel Donoughmore. First, he made a cursory examination of the weed through his magnifying glass. He next separated a fragment with the tweezers and placed it on a slide, which he fixed to the stage of the microscope. After a few moments of staring through the eyepiece, he removed the slide.

Then, using a long pair of tweezers, he picked out one of the floating fragments from the bottle of liquid which had come from the dead man's lungs. Transferring it to a second slide, he again submitted the exhibit to microscopic scrutiny. The result seemed to satisfy him, for he pushed back the microscope, first removing the slide and exhibit to safety.

"A member of the *Monocotyledonous* natural order of *Hydrocharideae*, Jim," he said. "*Elodea*, and undoubtedly *Elodea Canadensis*, called by the unscholarly, water-thyme."

"Kind of thing you would expect to find in the inside of a man drowned in a river, Harry," was the sergeant's comment.

"Yes, I think we might go as far as to say that the body of a drowned man usually contains, in the watery contents, specimens identical to the medium in which the body was found. But . . ." He paused and considered the specimens, his brow furrowed.

"But what, Harry?"

"But I should not have thought that we would have come across this stuff in the Tamar. It is a native of North America, and has been a curse over this side of the Atlantic since it was brought across. Ireland had it first, when it was introduced into County Down. It found its unfortunate way into England in 1841, since when it has been a curse to ponds, ditches and streams. But I should have put the Tamar as unlikely to harbour it, because of the fast flow. Still, there it is. I'd like to have a look at the stomach water, Jim."

Merry, taking the capillary tube, lifted a spot from the bottle and set it in a prepared slide, sealing it with a mica cover. Manson, examining the exhibit through the microscope, made a note on his pad. "You had better seal off the other slides, Jim, and label them. They have told us all they can for the moment," he said.

The colonel's clothes now came up for examination. As the scientist untied the bundle and laid the unwrapped waders and suit on the table, now bared of its ornamental cloth, the sergeant took from the Box of Tricks a contraption that looked more or less like a doll's-house vacuum cleaner. That, in effect, was exactly what it was, except that it served a more useful purpose. It was, in fact, a Soderman dust extractor, but fitted with a small motor for use with a battery. The motor had been Manson's own improvement on the original Soderman. The difference between a Soderman and any other dust extractor is that paper filters and bag can be fitted inside to take the extracted material, and can be removed and sealed for examination later, while another bag and filter can be fitted for immediate operation.

While the sergeant was fitting the Soderman and testing it, Doctor Manson proceeded to pore over the colonel's waders. They had been dried and a number of stained patches stood out from the surroundings. To these the Doctor paid special attention, marking each with a piece of chalk as portions over which the Soderman should be run. He next directed his search to projecting portions such as buckles, straps and pocket-flaps. Twice he called his magnifying glass into service, and each time he picked off a strand of something with his tweezers, transferring it, in each case, to a seed envelope which he sealed and labelled before placing it on one side. Finally, from a button of one of the breast pockets he unwrapped a small tuft of some material, which went into a third envelope.

Merry then began work with the Soderman, passing the suction nozzle over the patches marked by Manson. "Not that I expect we will get much satisfaction," Manson said. "I'm afraid the water will have washed away most of the traces. But we may as well try . . . Have a good run over the greenish patch, Jim. It looks the most promising."

Three of the patches were "Hoovered" before operations were suspended. Each operation saw the paper bags and filters changed, and the used bag sealed, labelled, and initialled by each of the two men. The scientist was a stickler for accuracy in examination; he held that there could be no mistake, if correct identification were made of material for examination, instead of the simpler, but less reliable, human recollection.

As the last of the envelopes was put away the dinner gong sounded.

"That will do for now, Jim," said Manson. "We'll refresh the inner man ready for the interviews afterwards."

CHAPTER VIII
SHAKING THE PIECES

IN THE YEAR 1921 the impish mind of Sir James Barrie evolved the first act of a play; and no play, before or since, has so exasperated the playgoer. For, either because he wouldn't or because he couldn't, Barrie never wrote another act to *Shall We Join the Ladies?* Perhaps you know the little piece? A party of ladies and gentlemen are the guests at a dinner party, perfectly happy and contented. But the host has evil intentions. A brother of his was murdered some time previously; the company at this dinner party were also present in the vicinity when the brother died. And the host lets them know that HE knows all about that, and hopes to be able to name, before the party ends, which of them killed his brother. You can imagine, therefore, the atmosphere at the dinner table. *Shall We Join the Ladies?* however, never gets through the dinner party, and there is no ending to it!

It was an environment similar to this that enclosed the diners in the Tremarden Arms, on this July night, in a circle of constraint. One of the company had lately been killed. The tall, scholarly man sitting with a lugubrious companion at a table apart was the man whom, the company knew, hoped to name the murderer sometime after the dinner.

Barrie would have seen his play come nearly to life. The sidelong glances cast at each other, the nickerings, made the usually jolly meal in the Arms an ordeal uncomfortable not only for those who knew they were to answer questions which, for all they could say, might throw suspicions upon each other, but also for those of their fellow guests who could be in no even dim light of suspicion, but who, nevertheless, felt the duress in the air, and found themselves involuntarily speaking in whispers.

Nor did the conclusion of the meal bring any relief or lessening of the strain. On the contrary; for while the diners took coffee in the lounge, Manson and Merry were absent, and the company waited the summonses to the ordeal.

The evening had not been less uncomfortable for Manson; all the company, with the exception of one or two, were, if not actual friends, very good acquaintances of his, with whom he had dined and wined and, what is more, fished. To an angler that is a bond of fellowship. The task of questioning them was not one to which he looked forward with any anticipations of pleasure.

Superintendent Burns was waiting when the Doctor arrived in his sitting-room. It says much for the two men that no word was said of the disagreement over the proposed dropping of the investigations. Instead, Manson greeted him with a friendly smile. "Before we start, Superintendent, I want to run over one or two exhibits," he announced. From the Box of Tricks he extracted, again, the microscope, and the envelopes in which had been placed away the strands taken from the colonel's wading outfit. The first of these was fitted under the microscope, and an examination made of it.

Manson, having looked his fill, made way for Merry. The sergeant, scrutinising, made the first remark: "Looks like a strand from a tweed, Doctor," he said.

Manson agreed. "I think so, too," he said. "And as it is a trifle on, shall we say, the tight weave, I should put it as Donegal tweed. It's a little less fluffy than Harris. Let's see how the others compare."

A double scrutiny of the remaining threads, and the tiny ball of fluff, seemed to leave no doubt in the minds of the two scientists. They agreed, unhesitatingly, that the threads or strands had been pulled from a tweed garment.

The Super had by now developed an interest in the proceedings. "Then, if there was foul play, Doctor, it looks as though the person responsible was wearing a tweed suit at the time," he suggested.

"We cannot go quite so far as that, Superintendent," Manson answered, with a twinkling eye. "It might not, you see, have been pulled out during any conflict, or even during that day. But should we find anyone who had been in the company of the colonel during the afternoon of the tragedy, and had been wearing a suit of Donegal tweed, we should, I think, be justified in looking at him with a certain amount of suspicion."

He replaced the exhibits in the Box of Tricks as he spoke. Then: "Now I think we can start our friendly little chats." He grimaced. "Shall we have Mr. Emmett first?"

The man who obeyed the summons, and sat gingerly in the armchair provided for him, was a magnificent specimen of the human animal. Some six feet in height, Fred Emmett had the bronzed face and easy carriage of the out-of-doors man. His clothes, sitting easily upon his broad figure, served to emphasise the impression. He was, in matter of fact, a country gentleman, as much at home with a gun as with a fishing-rod; and equally efficient and enthusiastic with a horse beneath him and the hounds in full cry to a "Gone Away." He had known Manson as a fisherman with whom he had spent many enjoyable days, long before the Doctor's profession was public property; and it was to the Doctor that he now turned. Manson smiled, reassuringly.

"This is a bad business, Emmett," he said. "You know, now, of course, that there are certain circumstances connected with the colonel which lead us to believe that his death might not be the accident it appeared to be."

Emmett nodded gravely. "I'm sorry to hear that, Doctor. I didn't like the man, but I've fished with him, and . . . well . . . I'll do anything I can to help hang the person who did it. It wasn't a fellow angler, I'm sure of that."

"I'm quite sure you will help all you can, Emmett. That's why we've asked you here. What we are trying to do is to trace the colonel's movements in order to narrow down the time of his death. Now, we know he left the hotel at 10 o'clock and reached the farmhouse yard at 10.15. At twenty past ten, the farmer met him carrying his rod, waders and brogues in the direction of the river. That is as far as we have progressed. Including the colonel, there were five people on the Tamar that day. You were one of them, and we gather from Franky that you were fishing the beat next below the colonel. That is correct, is it not?"

"Quite right, Doctor."

"What time did you reach the river?"

"About 9.30. I left the hotel at nine—immediately after breakfast, and cycled down."

"Where did you leave the cycle?"

"Not in the farmyard. When I am on that beat, I take a short cut through the fields and wheel the cycle along a path between the big field of oats and the ditch."

"So you were fishing half an hour before the colonel arrived?" asked Superintendent Burns.

"If you say he didn't arrive till 10.20, that would be about right. I did not see the colonel arrive."

"You began at the bottom of the beat, I suppose?" Manson put in. A nod from Emmett. "However, I did not work up-river," he said. "The water was pretty well coloured. Old Giles's cows had been having their morning paddle, I suppose. Anyway, there wasn't a fish rising, so I thought I would leave the water to clear itself, and fish higher up."

"I've had the same experience," Manson commiserated. "Giles's cows are a damned nuisance in the early mornings on that beat. It's the best time of the day for the shallows. How far up did you go?"

"Just above the Flats, on the first salmon water."

"How long would you have been there?"

"I should say a good half-hour. I was wading pretty deep, as you will realise, and there were a few big ones rising. They were coming short, though, and I decided to put up a Red Spinner—I had been using a Greenwell. That is how I put it at half an hour; I reckon to give a fly half an hour's trial before changing."

"You had seen nothing of the colonel up to now?"

"No. I wouldn't be likely to, you know, unless I came up on the bank."

"When did you first see him?"

"When I reached the top of my beat."

"Bit of trouble, was there not?"

Emmett grimaced. "There was, rather," he agreed. "You know that beat finishes about 200 yards below the Gulley? Well, that is the best bit of fishing on the beat. The water is just losing its rush through the Gulley, and there is generally a good fish hanging about in the tail. If you can fish fast water—and I can—you can be sure of two or three brace of two-pounders. You can't fish the Round Pool, as you know. I had come out below the pool and walked up the bank—quietly, so as not to disturb the fishing. There is a mass of bushes just there. As I came round them, there was the colonel fishing about fifty yards from me—in the water he was. That means he was 150 yards down in my best water. I asked him what the hell he thought he was doing. He said he'd been chasing a big one, and hadn't noticed that he was in my water. I told him he was a ruddy liar, and if he didn't get back to his own kennel I'd throw him in the river."

"I was pretty mad," Emmett continued. "It wasn't the first time he had been poaching on another beat, as the others can tell you. Damn it all, there was a board on the bank with the beat number painted on it."

"Any argument about it?"

"No, Doctor. He just turned round and walked upstream."

"You didn't hit him?"

"Hit him!" Emmett looked staggered. "Good God, Doctor, he was an old man. Shouldn't think of it."

"I did not suppose you would, Fred," replied Manson in a soothing voice. "Only I had to ask the question. There is the matter of a bruise, you see. When did you see him again?"

"I never did see him again."

Superintendent Burns looked up. "Never?" he asked. "That was funny, wasn't it? The river bank is pretty open from there on, and you can see a pretty way upstream. Then, the river itself isn't timbered, and I should have thought that any one wading would have seen a wader on the next beat. I reckon you can see half-a-mile up the stream."

"That is so, Superintendent," agreed Emmett. "But the fact remains that I cannot recall seeing the colonel again. Mind you, I wasn't looking for him. And I dare say he was keeping away from me. Most likely he was at the top of his beat, and I went down to the Shallows again later."

"But you came up to the Gulley again, I take it?"

"Yes."

"Did you see any of the others?" asked Manson.

"No, I don't think so, Doctor."

"I suppose the colonel did not leave the landing net at your feet when he walked away?"

"No."

"And you did not find it at any time and do him the service of bringing it back to the hotel?"

"No, Doctor."

"And you did not, I take it, throw him into the river?" The smile which accompanied Manson's pointed question drew an answering one from Emmett. "No, Doctor, I didn't," he said. "But, all the same, I wish I had not made that remark in the hotel that night."

"Well, I think that is all, Emmett, old chap." The Doctor stood up. "Thank you for coming. Oh! By the way, what suit were you wearing that day?"

"Suit?" echoed Emmett. "Why, my old tweeds, Doctor. Always do for fishing."

"Of course! I ought to have remembered that. Donegals, aren't they?"

"They are."

"Right. See you in the lounge later. Would you mind asking Sir Edward to come up?"

"So he was in Donegal tweeds, Doctor! That seems to be getting us somewhere." Superintendent Burns entered the fact in his notebook. "That's the kind of information I like to get hold of. You find Donegal tweed round the buttons of a dead man, and now we've a man who quarrelled with him and he was wearing the same tweed."

"A similar tweed, Superintendent . . . a similar tweed, you know," Manson replied. "There are, I believe, hundreds of Donegal tweed suits made in the course of a year. . . . Ah! . . . come in, Sir Edward. We're sorry to disturb your nightly game of Bridge, but needs must . . ."

The baronet sat down ruefully. "Dammit, Doctor, the colonel has spoiled *everybody's* Bridge. Dashed if he isn't more nuisance dead than he was alive." He paused. "Perhaps, though, I should not have said that," he apologised. "Well now, how can I be of any help to you?"

"I'm afraid that you cannot help overmuch, Sir Edward, but we must be sure that no point is missed. Franky says you were fishing the top beat, so you would hardly have much contact with the colonel. I suppose you drove round by the road to the water?"

Sir Edward cast a rueful look at the three men. "That, Doctor, is just what I did not do," he said quietly. "I've put myself right in this business, up to the neck. The previous day I had fished the beat the colonel was now on and I dropped, somewhere along the bank, my leather cigarette case. It has a sentimental value, so I thought I would walk along the bank and keep a lookout for it on the way to my water. I guessed I would be bound to come across the colonel. I wasn't keen on that, but if I found the case it would be worth it. So I drove up to the farm as usual, left the car there, and struck across the field to the river."

"Did you find the case?"

"Yes, I found it."

"What about the colonel?"

"I never saw him."

"You walked along his beat? I suppose you must have done to reach your own beat?"

"As you say, I walked all along his beat. Never saw a sign of him."

"What time would that be, Sir Edward?" It was Superintendent Burns who asked the question.

"As near as I can say, about 11.15 o'clock. I was a little late in starting out that day."

There was a moment's silence. Superintendent Burns caught the eyes of Doctor Manson in a questioning glance. The scientist nodded slightly. The superintendent resumed his questioning.

"Now we know, Sir Edward, that the colonel reached the water about 10.30 o'clock. Mr. Emmett left the bottom of his water about a quarter of an hour later, which makes the time a quarter to eleven. Then he fished for half an hour, finally walking up past the Round Pool to find the colonel fishing in his (Emmett's) beat. That would be, by the process of simple addition, at 11.15. He says that the colonel, after their few words over the poaching, walked up into his own water. Yet, you reach that water at precisely the same time, as far as you can say, but saw nothing of the colonel."

"Dammit, Superintendent, that's a queer business." Sir Edward's surprise had a convincing note of naturalness about it. "But I can assure you I did not catch a glimpse of the colonel, and I certainly walked along his beat."

"Sir Edward,"—Manson took up the questioning—"I take it that from the Gorge you would pass through the wood and strike the road which runs parallel, a field's distance away, with the beats of Mrs. Devereux and the major, further up?"

The baronet agreed.

"Did you see Mrs. Devereux or the major?"

"Never saw a soul, Doctor. I thought I saw the tip of a rod waving on the major's beat, but if he was in the water, you know, I would hardly be likely to see him. There's a four-foot bank along most of that stretch."

"That's true. Where did you find your cigarette case?"

"Where I thought it might be—at the hollow tree almost in front of the Meeting Pool. I remembered having had a cigarette there at tea-time."

"How about your return walk?"

"I left about half past four, walked to the gorge wood, and then struck diagonally across the fields to the farmyard, picked up my car and drove home."

"See anybody then?"

"Nobody I could recognise. I saw the figure of a man on, I thought, Mrs. Devereux's stretch, but who he was I couldn't say. Probably one of the farmer's men. I didn't notice a rod."

"I suppose you didn't see the colonel's landing net en route, at all?"

"No—and I certainly didn't bring it to the hotel, Doctor. I wouldn't have been seen dead with the abortion."

"What suit would you have been wearing that day, Sir Edward?" The superintendent waited anxiously for the answer.

"Suit? What the deuce does that matter, Superintendent?" He wrinkled his brows in memory. "My tweeds, I think."

"They would be Donegals, I suppose?" Manson's question came jestingly, since Sir Edward was a fervent Irishman.

"They are," was the reply.

Superintendent Burns's jaw dropped, and Doctor Manson chuckled.

Sir Edward was succeeded by Major Smithers. He listened to the formal inquiry precis; and replied in the crisp, workman-like, method and tone which he had been wont to use on the barrack square.

"I can't help at all, Doctor," he announced. "I drove along the upper road, parked my car in the gateway of the field I usually park in, and went straight to the water, and fished all day. Did I see anybody? Well, I caught a glimpse of Sir Edward walking along the road. I was whipping the bit just past the pylons and came in to the bank to put on a new fly. Just saw Sir Edward's head. Time? I should say about 11.15. Then, about two o'clock, I saw Mrs. Devereux—at least, I suppose it was Mrs. Devereux. She had a rod and was standing at the Avenue, the other side of the pylons."

"You did not see the colonel, I suppose?"

"Couldn't, Doctor. I never went near that side of the gorge."

"It may seem a funny question, Major, but what suit were you wearing that day?"

"Suit? Always wear fishing tweeds, Doctor, and was wearing them that day."

"Harris?"

"What! In July? No! Donegals."

Manson looked across at the superintendent and grinned wickedly. It was a grin that developed into a wide smile at the entrance of Mr. Braddock. For he was wearing a suit of Donegal tweeds as he stalked in. The superintendent scratched his head.

"Now, Mr. Braddock," said Manson, "you are not a fisherman, are you?"

"Never fished in my life, sir. Never wanted to."

"And, so far as we know, you were not near the water when the colonel met his death? But you will remember that on the night of the tragedy you said that you hoped he had fallen in the Tamar and 'drowned his damned self.' Well, apparently he DID fall in, and drown himself. We do not suppose, for one moment, that the two things are related, but we think it only fair to you to give you an opportunity to convince those who heard you make the statement that you know nothing about his death. How do you feel about that?"

"Well, that's very good of you, gentlemen, I'm sure. I was not near the colonel on that day. I have no interest in fish, except as a course at dinner; but I am sure glad that the colonel did fall in and drown himself, so why hide it?"

"We won't discuss that, Mr. Braddock. Our task, at the moment, is to find the motive for murder, which is what we believe happened to the colonel. For instance, Mr. Emmett quarrelled with the colonel over poaching on his beat; but fishermen do not push one another in the water because one of them has taken a fish that the other might have caught. Now you were suggesting, were you not, that the colonel had other interests here besides fishing? You have probably heard the phrase 'Cherchez la femme' as an elementary step in detection. What can you tell us about the colonel and a lady?"

"Nothing—except that he was pestering a woman here and there if you want exact details, one of them was the daughter of the carpenter, and acts as an extra chambermaid in this hotel. And it was the same with another chambermaid. And I've heard things about a woman somewhere near the hotel. Apart from that the colonel was as nasty a card-player as ever I've struck, and I've seen a few bad losers in my time. In fact, he was a man much better dead than alive."

"Where were you on the afternoon of that day, Mr. Braddock?" asked the superintendent.

"I walked over to Callington through the woods."

"Many thanks, Mr. Braddock."

"And to you, gentlemen." And Mr. Braddock left the room.

"Now Superintendent, we come to the last one—the lady," said Manson, as Braddock closed the door behind him. "You have a go at her, and I will hold a watching brief until such time as I see a point I may want to make. We have to remember that she was on the beat next to the colonel, the same as Emmett was on the other side."

The three men rose to their feet as Mrs. Devereux swept in and took an armchair. She settled herself comfortably, one silken-sheathed leg crossed over the other, displaying a length of hose which caused Merry to edge a little forward. Then, having lit a cigarette and nestled down into the cushions, she spoke. "I do not know why you gentlemen want me, or what you expect me to say," she began. "But perhaps I should tell you that I am shortly to marry Sir John Shepstone, and he is furious at the idea of my being connected with this business . . ."

"We are not connecting you with this business, Mrs. Devereux," Manson broke in. "We are only asking you, as a citizen, to help the Law if it is within your power to do so. You see, you had been allotted the beat next to Colonel Donoughmore, and we are seeking information as to the times you might have seen the colonel during the day, in order that we can lessen down the inquiries from the time that he was last seen. Quite simple, really."

"As you put it, sir, it IS quite simple—for me. I cannot help you at all in the inquiry, I am afraid. I did not see the colonel, nor did I see Major Smithers or Sir Edward, or anybody else there. I did not see them for the simple reason that I wasn't there to see them I wasn't fishing."

"What!" The ejaculation came from the superintendent.

"I thought I spoke quite plainly. I said that I was not fishing there at all that day."

"But the Ma. . . ."

Manson broke in hurriedly before the superintendent could complete the sentence. "We understood from Mr. Baker that you were on the beat between the colonel and Major Smithers, Mrs. Devereux?" he said.

"I was allotted that beat the previous night, Doctor Manson, but when the morning came I did not feel inclined for fishing in the circumstances, so I decided to spend the day elsewhere. Therefore I was not at the water, and did not see the colonel at all."

"Um . . . er . . ." The superintendent recovered from the shock. "Then it doesn't seem that you can be of very great help to us, Madam."

"I cannot help you at all."

She rose to go, but Doctor Manson pursued the subject. "I was wondering, Mrs. Devereux," he said, "whether, from the tone of your voice, the fact that the colonel was fishing the next beat to you had anything to do with your disinclination to fish that day?"

If the question was presumptious, the smile and air of assumed deference which accompanied it, changed the answer which the woman had started indignantly to make. "That, sir, has nothing to do with you . . ." she started, but stopped. "It might have made the fishing less desirable," she said, mollified by Manson's manner. "He was not a nice man."

"No? Now, we understood that he was something of a lady's man."

"Indeed!" was the retort. "I did not like the colonel. I hated the sight of him. I never *DID* like him, and I don't know a woman who did." The words poured from the woman in a torrent which swept the men before her into momentary silence.

Manson's eyes narrowed, and the puckers appeared on his brow. "I understood that you met the colonel only when you came to the Tremarden Arms, Mrs. Devereux," he said. "Do we understand that you had known him previously?"

The startled look which appeared in her eyes, only to vanish in an instant, and the stammering reply, served to intrigue the scientist, for he watched her closely from behind his half-closed lids.

"I . . . I . . . I . . . Of *COURSE* I did not know him previously," Mrs. Devereux protested. "What I meant to say was that I never did like the colonel from the first day I met him here. You do not know much about my sex, Doctor Manson, if you cannot appreciate the fact that a woman can, and does, sum up a man within a few minutes of meeting him. Surely it was noticed that the women in this hotel avoided the company of the colonel. His attentions towards us were objectionable."

"Had he been annoying you, Mrs. Devereux?" asked the superintendent.

Doctor Manson was writing on a slip of paper. He passed the note over to Merry who, after a moment's hesitation, left the room. He sat back in time to hear Mrs. Devereux's answer.

"He was always pestering me—inside the hotel and outside it. I think his death is an advantage to the feminine guests in this hotel, and the women in this town. If he was killed—as people are saying he was—I hope you never find the person who did it."

"I am afraid you are pretty well correct in your estimation of the late Colonel, if what we hear is true, Mrs. Devereux," said Manson. "By the way . . ." he spoke affably and charmingly . . . "you are the only angler in the hotel whom I have not met at some time or other. Most of them have fished the waters with me for years. Is this your first visit to Cornish waters?"

"It is, Doctor—the very first."

"And what do you think of the fishing?"

"Well, really, you know, I haven't had enough of it, so far, to be able to say. And this business has rather spoiled things."

"True! It is a pity that your first impressions should be so unfortunate. What kind of fisherman are you, Mrs. Devereux? I mean, have you any fads about it?"

"If you mean do I fish wet fly or dry fly, Doctor, I assure you I am no purist. I fish to catch trout—and I don't care whether I do it on a dry or a wet fly, or on a spinner, so long as I catch them. It is fish I go out for, not foolish fancies. I have generally caught more brace than anyone else in the party, and that is what I like."

"Yes, there is something in that," agreed Manson; and the men in the lounge below, could they have heard the smooth expression of the scientist, would have written him down a blasphemous heretic!

"Well, Mrs. Devereux, it has been very pleasant to meet you, although I wish it had been under more pleasant circumstances. Perhaps, when this is all over, you will, if you are still here, allow me to show you the secrets of the waters. Oh, by the way, the superintendent had better have your complete alibi, if you don't mind me using that nasty word. We must have things in order, you know. Where did you spend the day on which you should really have been fishing?"

"I went over to Tavistock."

"By train?"

"Yes."

"You lunched, of course, at the hotel?"

"No. At the Devonshire Tea Rooms. They'll remember me I am sure, if you want to check me up. I dropped and broke, very carelessly, a cup and saucer at tea, and left my scarf there at lunchtime—altogether a most unfortunate day."

"Accidents will happen, Mrs. Devereux. Good-night, and many thanks."

Manson opened the door and bowed her out. Before he could close the door Merry slipped in. He bowed in mock acknowledgment.

"Thanks for the reception, Doctor," he said. As he sat down he grinned broadly at his chief and at the superintendent.

"Well?" demanded Manson.

"The lady's fishing costume, according to the chambermaid, is a tweed shooting suit."

The superintendent jumped. "You aren't going to say that she wore Done . . . ?"

"She did an' all, Super."

Manson, at the sight of the Cornishman's face, for once in his life lost all decorum. He threw himself back in the chair and roared. "I told you, Superintendent," he gasped between his laughter, "that you could not take the tweed strands for granted. Now, where are you?"

"Five people—and every damn one of them in a suit of Donegal tweed!"

"Not quite so bad as that, Super."

"How—not so bad, Doctor?"

"Only three of them on the river, you know."

"That helps a lot, doesn't it?"

"It *does*—by the one reliable method of detection—elimination. Elimination, my dear Superintendent, is the only really conclusive way to solution. When you have eliminated all the suspects to one—then he is your man, and there is no door through which he can get out. He may appear to be perfectly innocent; if you have eliminated everybody down to him, he's guilty. But that's enough for to-night. We will call it a day. To-morrow morning, Superintendent, I want to go along the river, and perhaps you will come along with me. If you can get a tin bowl and a quantity of plaster of Paris, I would be glad. I may want a few casts of any footmarks we may find."

CHAPTER IX
THE PATTERN FORMS

"WHAT I WANT to do, Superintendent, is to see if the three of us, with your Constable Lee, can reconstruct the scene which occurred here when the colonel went into the water. There are two things which I noted on the day of the tragedy, when we found the body, and I think they will pay for a little investigation to-day."

The four men—Merry was, of course, in the company—were standing at the top of the bank down which Colonel Donoughmore had crashed. Constable Lee had rolled back the tarpaulin, with which the marks of the tragedy had been protected from the weather, and from casual observers. They now showed plainly on the grassy slopes, irregular scratches in parallel lines, broken once or twice, but recurring again until they finished some two feet from the water's edge. Here and there tufts of grass, pulled up by the roots, lay scattered down the slope.

Doctor Manson went down on hands and knees and peered through his magnifying glass at the scars, taking elaborate care not to disturb them in any way. He followed them to the water-side, comparing each mark with that above it; and it was fully five minutes before he motioned the superintendent to make his examination.

Burns made an equally close investigation, emulating the scientist's thoroughness. At the end he stood up and dusted his knees.

"Well," asked Manson. "What do you make of them?"

"Heel marks, Doctor, I should say."

"Agreed, Superintendent. But rather queer heel marks, don't you think? I would like a cast of each set, if your constable will hand over the plaster of paris."

Tipping a quantity of the powder into the bowl, the scientist added water from the river and stirred the mixture until it had the consistency of a stiff, creamy liquid. Taking a few pinches from the remaining powder, he sprinkled them in the first set of marks, satisfying himself that the powder covered the base. Then, with the utmost care, he poured a couple of spoonfuls of the liquid into the indentures, making sure that it lay evenly and level in them. Satisfied of this, he filled up the already hardening mould level with the surface. Leaving the plaster to harden, he repeated the operation with the next two sets of marks. Finally, when the plaster had set, the moulds were lifted and turned upside down. A brief inspection, again through his glass, satisfied Doctor Manson that the casts were accurate copies. He marked each one with the position of the indentures on the bank, and the superintendent added his confirming signature. When all the marks had thus been dealt with, they were packed into the Box of Tricks, which had accompanied the Doctor to the river bank.

The superintendent had followed the operation with keen interest. "I had always heard that you were remarkably painstaking and meticulous in your examinations, Doctor," he said, "but do you always go to such lengths as this in the case of marks of a fall?"

"Not always, Superintendent. Frequently, when I think it necessary, but not always. It happens to be necessary in this case, because I want to show you something later, which will, I am afraid, ruin the original marks. Now that we have a permanent record of them that will not matter."

"Something that I ought to have seen and have missed, Doctor?"

"It may be. I am not sure. You can tell me afterwards." Manson smiled. "I am not sure that you are not holding something out on me." Flattery was a card which the scientist had frequently found to be a trump when dealing with the provincial police. That it worked on this occasion was apparent from the smiling countenance of the Cornishman. But he said nothing. Behind his back, Merry caught his chief's eye—and shook with laughter.

"Now you said, Superintendent, that the marks were obviously heel marks. I remarked that they were curious heel marks in the circumstances. I still think them curious." He eyed the puzzled gaze of the officer, which flickered over the marks for the third time, and then returned to meet the scientist's eyes. "No?" Manson queried. "Well, let's try another line."

Sergeant Merry interrupted the duologue. "If the constable will stand at the bottom of the bank to catch me, Doctor, you can push me down the bank." He winked.

Manson nodded, slowly. He realised Merry's insinuation, and knew that his assistant had confirmed his own suspicions. "That will certainly help, Merry," he said. He turned to the superintendent. "Now, Burns, what do you surmise happened here to send the colonel down into the water?"

"We cannot be sure, of course, Doctor, but I should say he was probably stepping back from where he put down his rod, and that he either fell backwards down the slope, or caught his heel on a projecting clump of grass—there are several about, as you can see—and was thrown backwards down the slope. He caught his head on something, he was knocked unconscious, and went into the water. That is assuming that his death was an accident. If he was pushed into the water, then I should say that he was pushed over backwards by a sudden and violent blow."

"You think that a sharp push would produce these effects?"

The superintendent considered the point again. "It would, I think, give an approximate result," he decided.

"Very well. Now, you stand back where you can see, and Merry will walk backwards towards the slope. I'll give him a hard push. No—don't worry"—as the superintendent protested. "Don't worry about Merry. He's used to demonstrations, and he won't hurt himself if the constable will wait at the water's edge in case he reaches the water."

Merry, his hands clasped behind his head to protect it, stepped to the edge of the slope. A sharp "unexpected" push from the scientist sent him unresistingly over the edge. He slithered down the bank after going flat, and then his body, trying to recover as the colonel would undoubtedly have done, rolled over and over until it reached the boulder, where the constable, acting as a buffer, stayed his course.

"Show me the heel marks made by Merry, Superintendent," demanded Manson.

The superintendent looked down the bank. There were two short scratches only at the top of the bank, where Merry had instinctively tried to recover his balance as he fell. The Cornishman looked from them to the scientist.

"I see," he said, slowly.

"Of course! That is what intrigued me on the day of the tragedy, Superintendent. *It would be absolutely impossible for a man to fall full-length down a slope such as this, and remain at full length dragging his heels*. The man, alive or dead, would begin to roll almost as soon as his body struck the ground. I know of only one method by which a man going down a bank could make heel drags such as these."

"You mean that the colonel was dragged down?" The superintendent looked up, startled.

Manson shook his head. "I am not going to admit anything, Superintendent. I never admit anything until I am quite sure of the fact. I will give you my opinion when I have made a more careful examination of the moulds of the heel marks. You had better examine them again, also, and see if you can make anything of them, in view of the demonstration you have just seen. They may have a story to tell. I don't know yet."

"There is another point I would like to urge, Doctor."

"Yes, Merry?"

"To make heel marks the colonel, in any case, would have had to go down the bank on his back. The marks pass the boulder on the right side, so how could the colonel, lying on his back, have hit his forehead on the boulder on his right temple? It's the side away from the boulder."

"The point is well taken, Merry. I had not mentioned it because I never, for a moment, believed that the head injury was caused by the boulder." He moved forward. "I think we have seen all we can see here," he added. "But I want to have a look at the water up and below. I don't think we shall need the constable again, Superintendent, unless you want to keep him here. But he might take the Box of Tricks and put it in my car."

The three men clambered down the bank and, in Indian file, wandered slowly along the waterside. The Tamar was at its best on this perfect morning. From a sky of deep azure, the sun poured down upon the wide water, crystal clear; so clear of any kind of pollution, indeed, that it was almost as though the three men were looking at the river bottom in these shallows through a piece of sheet glass. Shale and granite slats, at crazy angles, lay scattered here and there on the clean gravel of the river bed, some three or four feet below the surface of the water.

"Beautiful water, this, you know, Merry," the scientist remarked. "Sometimes I wonder we ever catch trout in it at all. The clearness of it is almost like a spring. It must make us visible to a trout fifty yards away."

"Perhaps that is why they feel safe, Doctor," was the sergeant's retort. "I like it because one can wade, and see one's step in advance. Now, take Hungerford. After you have waded a few yards in the stream there, the water round you looks as though someone had emptied a churn of milk into it."

"That is true of parts of the Test, too, Merry," Manson added. "No, I will say that you cannot find better trout water anywhere than in these Cornish streams. Even the Devon waters get coloured, and impregnated with the loose bottom of the river."

The three men had now walked up as far as the Meeting Pool, almost at the end of the beat which the colonel had fished. A sudden splash, a few feet in front, startled them. As they looked up a slender dark-backed, form slid again beneath the waters.

"Sea-trout?" asked Manson.

The superintendent shook his head. "No, Doctor," he said. "It is a bit too early for sea-trout. Just an ordinary one. Must have weighed well over a pound. A whopper for here."

"Yes. Manson made a mental note of the spot where the fish had risen. "That's the one drawback to the fishing here; the trout are on the small side. Average is, I suppose, about three to the pound, eh, Superintendent?"

"I should say that is about right," the officer agreed.

"What makes them so small, do you think? The water is sweet, there is a good flow, and plenty of timber for shade. Why should they keep on the small side and not grow up into three or four pounders like Berkshire and Hampshire?"

"Well, Doctor, it's the flow that does it. There are a lot of trout here—too many, if you ask me. And they breed well. A trout, now, has to have food if it's going to grow large. That is where our fast Cornish streams are bad. They run so swiftly that food doesn't grow on the river bed. And then, the bed being shale and gravel, there is no soil for the roots of any weeds or grass to get a hold in. Take a look at the water here; there isn't even so much as a bed of reeds or a single clump of aquatic flora. Fish must have feed to grow any size."

"True. Have you tried planting any green stuff?"

"Lor bless you, yes. But it doesn't grow. When it gets big enough to offer resistance to the stream, the current swishes it out of the gravel. No, the only way to increase the size of the fish here is to reduce the number of the fish. Then the remaining ones would have a little more share of the scanty food there is."

"But not so much sport for the fisherman?"

"As you say, Doctor, not so much sport."

At the top of the Meeting Pool the scientist stopped. "Unless you want to do anything, Superintendent, we may as well cut across the fields and get back to the car. There is nothing further here that can help me at the moment."

The car put the trio down at the entrance to the Tremarden Arms. The superintendent turned in the direction of the police station, but was stopped by Manson. "You had better come up, Superintendent, and have a drink. I dare say you could do with a beer, eh?"

"It would not come amiss," was the reply, as the Cornish chief mopped a brow. "It's going to be a scorcher a bit later on."

In their room, Merry poured out three glasses of ale. He passed two of them round. "Well, here's good health, Super," said Manson, raising his glass.

"And good luck, Doctor." The superintendent took a deep draught. Eyeing the remains appreciatively he put his glass on the mantelpiece above him.

A chink caused him to look up, and he moved the glass forward away from contact with a jar at the back of the mantelpiece. "What the deuce have you got there, Doctor?" he asked.

"Where? Oh! In the jar? That is some of the contents of the colonel's lungs. I'm going to test it later on." He crossed to the mantelpiece and looked down at the jar. "Not that there is likely to—"

The words broke off suddenly. The superintendent, glancing up at the pause, saw the scientist staring hard at the jar.

"Merry!"

Manson called the sergeant over. "Do you see what I see?" he asked.

The sergeant directed his gaze at the exhibit, noting the foreign particles floating in the liquid. But it was not until he looked into the jar from above that he noticed the layer of sediment at the bottom. He glanced across at the scientist, a query in the look. Manson nodded a reply.

"But, Doctor," the sergeant was puzzled, "wouldn't you expect to find it. Impurities in the water, taken in with the breath, would naturally sink to the bottom after the jar has been standing for a time."

"That is just the point, Merry," was the retort. Taking the utmost care not to disturb the contents, Manson lifted up one of the jars to the light and peered closely at the deposit. With equal care, he placed it on the table. From the Box of Tricks he produced an empty jar and a length of thin rubber tubing of the kind used with the old-fashioned baby's feeding bottle. "Siphon the liquid out, Merry," he said; and the sergeant took charge of the apparatus.

Probing again into the Box of Tricks, the scientist lifted out an electric "Bunsen" burner, and his microscope. He dipped a glass rod into the sediment now left in the jar after the siphoning and transferred a little of the matter to a microscope slide. Then, plugging in the flex of the "Bunsen" burner, he placed the jar and stand over it, and switched on the heat. While the sediment was evaporating dry, Manson inspected the fragment on the microscope slide. In its enlarged form through the eyepiece it magnified into some kind of crystals. Making a note of his conclusions, Manson placed it aside.

Similar examination was then made of the now dry sediment from the Bunsen jar—with like result, except that there was matter among it decidedly not crystal form; but rather mushy, and reflecting a greenish tint. Manson stared hard at this, but beyond a muttered "Curious," he made no comment. He was careful, however, to empty the now dusty sediment into a seed envelope, and to label it exactly, placing the receptacle, when sealed, into the Box of Tricks.

The superintendent, who had followed the experiment with lively curiosity, now sought enlightenment.

Manson shook his head. "There is nothing I can say positively just yet, Superintendent," he replied. "But I think we will have a talk over the case this afternoon. There are several things which we ought to discuss in the light of what has transpired from our inquiries. And I think that the Chief Constable should be present. Perhaps you can arrange that."

"Where would you like the chat, Doctor? Here, or in the station?"

"If Sir William doesn't mind, it would be more convenient to have it here."

The three men then parted for lunch.

* * * * *

Sir William Polglaze was not the man to bear animosity; and when, shortly after lunch, he walked into Doctor Manson's sitting-room, he shook hands warmly and, glancing at the table still holding the impedimenta of the pre-lunch experiments, asked, jocularly: "How's Tricks?"

"That, Sir William, is exactly what I want to talk about. Take an armchair; and what about a cigar and a liqueur, eh?" He passed over his case and, pouring out a trio of Benedictine, handed them round to his guests. Cigars lit, he commenced the consultation.

"I think, Sir William, that my investigations have now reached a stage when we should start some inquiries into the people who encircled the colonel," he said. "And that is a job for you and your Force. When I have finished laying certain aspects of the case before you, I think you will see the reasons for such inquiries.

"You will remember that the official view of the colonel's death at first was that he had fallen in the river at the spot we have seen on the bank, and that in doing so he had hit his head on a boulder at the edge of the water, and had entered the water unconscious. You will know that, from the beginning, I had not agreed with that theory. The post-mortem which convinced you, served only to strengthen my contrary opinion."

The Chief Constable nodded; and a rueful smile accompanied the nod.

"I do not know whether the Commissioner told you his reasons for taking my view; but perhaps I had better run over them briefly. It will make my subsequent remarks more comprehensible. Very well, then. Dr. Tremayne's report said that the blow on the head was accidental, and had occurred as the colonel went into the water. The unconscious Colonel would have died within a few seconds of entering the water. The state and colouring of the bruise, as the Home Office Expert confirmed, was consistent only with it having been inflicted from half to three-quarters of an hour before death. The water content and the state of the lungs of the colonel again, were inconsistent with Tremayne's conclusions.

"Very well. I began investigations on the assumption that the affair was not an accident. Not, mark you, because Tremayne had been said to be wrong. I had hoped that the doctor would have confirmed my earlier suspicions. They had begun before the post-mortem. The state of the bank at the fatal spot had intrigued me considerably, particularly the marks made by the colonel in his descent. You will remember that there were scores, or indentations, in the ground at intervals—parallel scores, as though made by a pair of sliding heels."

"I saw them, Doctor. They were quite plainly marked."

"Too plainly marked I thought at the time, Sir William. That was the first mistake the person responsible made. Most murderers DO make mistakes, thank goodness."

"And this mistake, Doctor?" The Chief Constable leaned forward. "I confess I do not see it."

"To-day, Burns here, Merry and I, carried out a certain experiment at the spot. I feel sure it convinced the superintendent."

Burns nodded vigorously.

"The result of that was merely to demonstrate what I was sure of at the time of the tragedy, and which I had to convince you people—namely, that nobody, however hard he was jerked over the edge, could go full length down that bank dragging his heels in parallel scratches, broken at intervals, with an appreciable distance between. The falling body would. . . . What would it do, Superintendent?"

"The body would begin at once to roll after striking the ground," was the prompt and emphatic reply.

The Chief Constable stared. Then: "By God, of course it would, Doctor!"

Manson bowed. "That is, of course, what I had realised from the first. Now, having at last established that fact, let us turn to the reason for the marks. What, Sir William, would in your view, produce such heel marks, bearing in mind that they could not have been made by a falling body?"

The Chief Constable jerked himself forward. "By jove, Doctor, I'm beginning to see what you're getting at. The man was dragged down the bank by the shoulders with the heels trailing. That's it of course. Damn us for blind bats!"

Sergeant Merry chuckled out loud at this tribute to his chief. Manson, however, gave no sign of gratification. Instead, he wore an air almost of despondency. "That was the conclusion which I came to—unfortunately," he said.

"Unfortunately?" echoed the superintendent.

"Yes, unfortunately, Superintendent, *BECAUSE I WAS WRONG*. I committed an offence which I am always condemning in others; I theorised without first probing for the facts. It was not until to-day that I paid close attention to those heel-marks. Then the superintendent, and Merry and I explored them fully. We took casts of them."

As he spoke, the scientist produced the sets of casts and placed them on the table, laying a magnifying glass beside them. "I want you, Superintendent, to examine these casts and tell me from what manner of heels you think they came."

Superintendent Burns, taking the glass, scanned the first of the casts. The scores which had been cut in the ground were now of course, projecting, embossed on the casts. The result was that they obviously lent themselves to more accurate observation than when the marks were indentures in the ground, half hidden by the grass of the bank. They were, in fact, far more distinct than had been the original marks on the bankside.

The superintendent, after some moments, put down the glass and scratched his head. "That's a queer thing," he said, and turned to the second cast. Spending only a few minutes on that, he finally passed the glass over the third set. Then he sat back and looked at Manson.

"Well?" asked the scientist.

"I should have said that each of the marks was made by the same foot, though that, of course, is impossible."

"*Why* is it impossible, Superintendent?" Manson's voice was sharp.

"Well . . . er . . . isn't it? The man had two feet."

Manson eyed him ironically. "You know, Burns, I cannot understand you. Why go out of your way to find an alibi, merely to disprove your first, and perfectly correct, impression. *Of course* the parallel marks were made by the same heel."

"What! The two side by side?" asked the Chief Constable.

"Even those two, Sir William," Manson corroborated. "If you will come to the table I will show you why." He took the first of the casts. "Now, if you look carefully, Sir William, at the impression on the left, you will see, about one-sixteenth-of-an-inch from the centre, a small additional ridge—just a suspicion, as it were."

The Chief Constable peered through the glass, then felt gently with his finger. "Yes, I can get that quite distinctly, Doctor," he said.

"Now, if you will look at the impression on the right, you will see, again, that same ridge—in exactly the same place—to an hundredth part of an inch. And if, again, you will look at the impressions on the remaining casts you will find it repeated."

The Chief Constable confirmed that curious fact.

"Now," continued Manson, "it *MIGHT* happen that the two shoes of a man's feet *MIGHT* have two projecting nails at exactly the same spot; but the chances are several millions to one against. I was, therefore, forced to accept the view that all the scratches were made by one boot-heel. The inevitable conclusion to be drawn from that was that it was certainly not the colonel's heel that made the marks, for I don't suppose that he, having fallen and scratched one impression, would climb back and fall a second time in exactly the same way to duplicate the scratches in parallel. I had a look at the fishing brogues which we took from the colonel's body; they are in the cupboard there. There is not a projecting nail in either of the heels.

"That was sufficient, even for me! Someone had made those marks by drawing the heel of their right foot down the bank, and then repeating the action alongside the first scratches; and so on twice more down the bank. I asked myself why."

The scientist looked at his audience.

"To make it appear that the colonel had fallen there," hazarded the superintendent.

"Of course!" retorted Manson. "And that brings us to another link in the chain of logical reasoning. A great thing is logic and logical reasoning. It should be the very first item in the curriculum of all schools except the infant classes; only it is not. The result is that one of the most important things in education is withheld from the student—training in how to think. I asked myself why should anyone want to make us think that the colonel had fallen into the river at that particular spot? There is only one answer to that—because he did *NOT* fall at that spot."

"Upon my soul, Doctor, it seems obvious, put like that." The Chief Constable stared in surprise at the idea that he had, himself, failed to see so unmistakable a fact!

Merry chuckled. "Just the scientifically trained mind, you see, Sir William," he said. "It's also due to a very suspicious mind. That's the worst of the Doctor; he possesses a strongly suspicious mind, don't you, Doctor?"

Superintendent Burns chuckled at that. It was one of Manson's idiosyncrasies, invariably used by him to press home a point to his superiors and inferiors, to use the phrase: "I've a very suspicious mind, you know."

"Well, it's a damned good job, he has," the Chief Constable commented. "Go on, Doctor."

Manson continued his hypothesis. "Having, then, arrived at the logical deduction that the colonel had not fallen into the river at that spot, I searched round for actual proof—the sort of proof that I could put before a jury, with certainty of it being accepted." He paused and looked round at the company.

Superintendent Burns leaned forward and stared hard. "That, Doctor, is the line of country we want. I can understand that. Did you find any?"

"I found three pieces of concrete evidence, Superintendent, to prove without doubt that the colonel did *not* fall into the river at the spot where we are invited to believe that he fell in. *What is more, the evidence proves conclusively, to my mind, that he was not drowned in the river at all.*"

Manson's statement came like a bombshell to the other three men in the room. For a moment there was complete silence. Then, the superintendent broke in. He leaned forward, looking, perhaps a little uncomfortable, for he felt that he must have missed something in the investigations. "What—" he hesitated for a second, and then continued: "what were they, Doctor?" he asked.

The scientist eyed him. "Come, come, Superintendent," he said, "you should know. You saw them. We even discussed two of them during our river walk this morning."

"Discussed them?"

"Certainly. Did we not, Merry?"

The sergeant answered with a vigorous nod. These little evasions of the Doctor tickled him immensely and he never failed to enjoy sharing in them. Manson, he knew, delighted to reduce the non-scientific mind to confess complete inability to see what to him was perfectly obvious; and then to point out the simplicity of the explanation.

"Well, I'm hanged if I can see any proof, Doctor," the superintendent confessed at length.

Manson continued his tantalisation. "Now, Superintendent, come. Just think back for a few moments while I pour out some more beer. We were walking along the river bank and talking. We continued the talk in this very room. Goodness, now, I've nearly told you!" The scientist tilted a bottle over the superintendent's glass.

A deep drink, however, did not help that officer. "No, Doctor, I give it up," he said. "I don't see any proof."

"Ah well, I'll have to tell you, then."

He spoke rapidly for a couple of minutes, and the superintendent gasped. "Of course . . . of course, Doctor! Damn it! . . . of course," he said.

"There you go," was Manson's comment. "Elementary, isn't it? That's how my reputation goes! Nothing at all out of the way."

* * * * *

The reader is invited to decide for himself what are the pieces of concrete evidence, outlined by Doctor Manson, which prove that Colonel Donoughmore did not fall in the river at the spot stated; and did not, in fact, fall in the river at all. Nothing has been withheld in the way of evidence.

They are really quite simple if the principles of organised and logical thinking, so emphasised by Doctor Manson, are combined with close attention to detail.

* * * * *

"You've given us two pieces, Doctor," the Chief Constable pointed out after the explanation had been digested, "but not the third?"

"That," was the answer. "Oh! That was the second mistake that the person we want made. You will remember that on the day we found the body, the sergeant, Franky, and I walked to the scene of the alleged fall. The colonel's rod was lying at the top of the bank. We were coming away when Franky drew my attention to it. I let the line run through my fingers. It was a fully-tapered dry-fly line. The colonel, you will remember, was a purist in fishing. He fished always dry-fly. Well, attached to the cast was a fly—a WET FLY, even worse, a nymph, definitely an underwater fly. No purist would use such a fly, and particularly on a dry-fly line. A wet-fly line, as you all know, has no tapering.

"There was, however, a chance that the colonel talked one kind of fishing and fished another—secretly. I went through his fly box and his fishing bag. Not another sign of a wet-fly could I find. I told Franky and the sergeant to search the ground in the vicinity for a box of wet-flies or any loose wet-fly, even to search the river-bed at the spot of the alleged fall. I went carefully through the pockets of the colonel's waders. There was no trace of a wet-fly. The colonel hadn't one.

"Someone had tied that fly on the colonel's cast to mislead us. And what is more, he had tied it to a cast unlike any other that the colonel had in his cast tin."

"That settles it." The Chief Constable held out a hand to the scientist. "A day or two ago, Doctor, we had a little disagreement over this case. I said that we had to accept Dr. Tremayne's post-mortem. I would like to withdraw. I apologise. It's a darned good thing you refused to listen to me. Otherwise, we would have left the swine who has done this in security. Every help you want in tracking him down I'll see you have."

Manson took the hand in a warm grasp. "That is very nice of you, Sir William," he said. "But quite unnecessary, believe me. My job is to find loopholes. If you people didn't leave loopholes I wouldn't have any job; and the police, you know, cannot be experts in every branch of investigation."

"Now, we've got to find the man." The Chief Constable, once convinced that the tragedy was not an accident, became the war-horse! "Any idea whom he may be?" His voice had the inflexion of one who believes in miracles!

"No, Sir William, not even the germ of an idea. The only way we can start is, I think, by the process of elimination."

The superintendent started as though he had been stung. An idea had leapt into his mind. "It occurs to me, Doctor," he began.

"Yes?" queried Manson.

"We've proved beyond doubt that the colonel did not fall or get pushed into the water at the spot we thought. Then where did he fall in?"

"I wondered if you were going to ask that," was the reply. "I do not know."

"Any idea?" The question came again from the Chief Constable.

"No, not the least. There are, however, one or two useful clues to start with. For the moment, however, I want to discuss the elimination process, because, as I said before, that work can be done by your police here concurrently with anything to which I devote my attention. We can save time that way. Now, what strikes you as regards that, Superintendent?"

"That's more in my line, Doctor," was the answer. He turned to his Chief Constable. "There's one queer thing which I think wants explaining," he announced.

"What's that?"

"The fact that nobody saw the colonel on that day except Emmett. There is something there that doesn't seem to me to square-up at all. Emmett says he saw him poaching in his (Emmett's) beat at 11.15 o'clock. They had a row, and the colonel, according to Emmett, then walked back into his own beat. We questioned Emmett on how he fixed the time, and everything fitted together like a fishing-rod. Now, at 11.15, Sir Edward Maurice reached the colonel's beat. He walked the full length of it, looking for his cigarette case. He saw no sign of the colonel. Where had the man got to?"

The Chief Constable nodded. "You mean that if Emmett saw him walk to his beat, Sir Edward must be telling an untruth when he says that he did not see the colonel. Therefore, he may have had something to do with the colonel's demise."

"Well, either that or Emmett was lying when he says the colonel walked back into his beat. There was a row, you know, and if Emmett lost his temper and struck him, knocking him into the river, the colonel might have been 'out' before Sir Edward reached the scene. In that case, Sir Edward would not have seen him. And Emmett would have had to have made an alibi. The spot of the 'accident' isn't more than a minute or two's walk from Emmett's water."

"But the Doctor says that the colonel wasn't drowned in the river, and we've decided he didn't go in there, anyway," protested Sir William.

"The colonel might, of course, have seen Sir Edward coming, and have concealed himself behind a bush. Or he might have been in the water near the bank, fishing. Sir Edward would not be likely to see him if he was," Manson suggested.

"True," admitted the superintendent. "But then, Sir Edward passed along there again in the afternoon, after four o'clock, and still did not see the colonel."

"Quite. But the colonel was dead, then," pointed out Manson.

"Well, anyhow, I think Emmett is a suspect," insisted the superintendent. "He was fishing next to the colonel, and he was heard to say that he had threatened to throw him in the river. I would have felt inclined, Doctor, to concentrate on Mrs. Devereux, on the other side of the colonel. We know that there was feeling against the colonel on her part. But she wasn't on the water, so that puts her out."

"Why?" Manson snapped. "Nobody is out, Superintendent, until they are *proved* out."

"If I may point out one thing," Sergeant Merry interrupted, "I made a note during our interview with Major Smithers, which I think needs some elucidating." He turned the pages of his note-book and read out the passage:

> "Then about two o'clock, I saw Mrs. Devereux. At least, I suppose it was Mrs. Devereux. She had a rod and was standing at the edge of the Avenue, the other side of the Pylons."

"If Mrs. Devereux was not on the water, who was it that Major Smithers saw?" the sergeant asked.

"Or *SAID* he saw," added the superintendent.

"Or said he saw," Merry agreed. "On the other hand, Sir Edward on his walk-up must have traversed parallel to part of Mrs. Devereux's beat, and he says he saw nothing of her."

"What do you say to all this, Doctor?" the Chief Constable interposed.

"It is precisely this that I mean when I say we shall have to work on the process of elimination, Sir William. We must get these suspects sorted out and reduced. That is what I want you people to do. You will, of course, Superintendent, pry into any motive. Emmett didn't throw the colonel into the water because he was poaching his fish. Sir Edward, so far as I can see, didn't do it because he didn't like the look of the colonel's face. If Mrs. Devereux was on the water—we *must* probe into that—she didn't kill him because he pursued her, if he did pursue her. She'd be angry, but gratified at the compliment. Any woman would be. Is there some motive for violence of which we do not know? We'll have to search into the lives of all of them. That is routine work for the detective force. Meanwhile, I will work along certain lines which I have in mind to find in what part of the water the colonel was pushed."

With that parting shot from the scientist the conference broke up.

CHAPTER X
Mrs. Devereux

Mrs. Janice Devereux had a line in that fount of information, the *London Telephone Directory, A—K*. It announced to all and sundry that she lived in Palace Court, Buckingham Gate, London, S.W.1; that her telephone number was Tha. 0123.

Palace Court was an imposing block of luxury flats at the rear of Buckingham Palace; and the rents of them were as imposing as their appearance. The flat occupied by Mrs. Devereux was on the first floor of one of the sections of the block—"houses"—the proprietors of the flats called them. Its rent was one of the highest.

From its doorway, Mrs. Devereux sallied forth daily on her social round. She was a member of several Bridge Clubs, and had an extensive acquaintanceship of friends of considerable standing; but not *THE* standing. It was a source of irritation to her, and had been for a long time that, though she hovered continually on the fringe of Society, spelt with a capital "S," she had never managed to cross the border into that select circle. She hoped and believed, however, that her coming marriage to Sir John Shepstone, wealthy dilettante, would, at last, prove the Open Sesame.

Meanwhile, Mrs. Devereux had made a point of visiting those functions where Society usually accorded its gracious patronage; and it may be said in passing, that she was generally among the best-dressed of the butterflies which fluttered in the sunshine of wealthy idleness.

At the moment, however, Mrs. Devereux was sitting in the lounge of the Tremarden Arms partaking of a pre-lunch cocktail; and on the opposite side of the lounge, drinking a ginger-ale, Detective-Inspector Penryn meditated on her. It was his task, allotted to him by Superintendent Burns, to investigate the lady.

It was quickly apparent to him that there was little to be learned of her here in Tremarden. This was her first visit; she had been there a few days only when the colonel met his death; and the days she seemed to have spent fishing by day and playing Bridge by night. She had seemed fairly popular, but was accounted by the men as something of an adventuress. So far as fishing was concerned, she fished with anything that a fish was likely to look at once too often. In fact, there was a rumour that she had hooked one trout on a worm!

In this dilemma, Inspector Penryn sought London's aid, by telephone. Scotland Yard passed him over to the "Society Index." That Department had supplied the details which the inspector was turning over in his mind as he sat in the hotel lounge. To them had been added the fact that the lady had come to London from India, where her husband had been an officer in the Indian Army. No source of income, other than the pension due to her from her husband's death, was known.

Inspector Penryn had seen a copy of the notes of the interview which Doctor Manson and the superintendent had had with the woman, and had gone carefully through the examination. A keen investigator, with a quick, alert mind, one phrase in the report had struck him as unusual; it was Mrs. Devereux's reply to Doctor Manson's suggestion that her absence from the water on that particular day was due to the presence on the next beat of the colonel. "I did not like the colonel. I hated the sight of him. I never did like him; and I don't know any woman who did," she had said. The inspector thought the outburst decidedly peculiar in the choice of words, especially when taken in conjunction with her subsequent explanation that she meant that she had not liked the colonel from the first day she had met him in the Tremarden Arms. One does not use the phrase, "I never *DID* like him," the inspector argued, of a man one has known only nine days. He wondered whether Mrs. Devereux was speaking the truth, or whether she had known the colonel before her visit to the hotel. Should the latter prove to be the fact, the inspector communed, then the vehemence of her feelings towards the colonel might put a different complexion on the case. He decided to visit the neighbourhood of Buckingham Gate, and see if there was anything to be gained there, leaving his sergeant to check up the lady's alibi with the Devonshire Tea Rooms in Tavistock.

His inquiries produced little result. The lady, he learned from the staff at the flats, lived a decorous life, receiving only one or two men friends. One of these, it was known, was her fiancé, Sir John Shepstone. Another was a tall, soldierly looking man of past middle-age. He had, however, been seen only twice, and that quite recently. It was at this point, when he seemed to be making little progress that a fortunate chance provided Penryn with a totally unexpected angle on the woman.

The inspector was one of those men who had drifted into the Police Force after finding that a University career did not attract prospective employers as a reason for providing him with a salary. It had the advantage, however, of qualifying him for membership of the Universities Club in London. Dropping in at the club for lunch, after his visit to Mrs. Devereux's flat, the first person he saw was Major Ruddock, with whom he had been a fellow student at Emmanuel College, Cambridge. Over lunch, the two talked of past and present times. It was as they were about to part that Penryn remembered that the major had for some years held an appointment in the Indian Police. He took a long chance.

"I suppose you never came across a Mrs. Devereux during the time you were in India, Jack?" he asked.

Ruddock looked up in astonishment. "Devereux?" he queried. "What, Janice Devereux? Good Lord, yes! Lively young woman she was, too. Married to an Indian Army officer, Lieutenant Ronald Devereux. In the artillery if I remember rightly. Got himself killed. Queer you should ask me that," he said, ruminatingly. "I thought I saw Janice in town the other day. Now, you start asking me about her."

A thought struck him. "In the Force, aren't you? What do you want with Janice Devereux? Aren't thinking of marrying her or something, are you?"

"Not I!" Penryn laughed. "A bachelor life for me, same as you, Jack. No, she's popped up in a case with which I have some connection. A fellow fell in the river while fishing, and was drowned. Scotland Yard think it's a curious case, so we are investigating the alibis of the people who were on the river the same day. Mrs Devereux is one of them. Old Donoughmore. . . ."

"Who did you say?" Ruddock stared.

"Donoughmore. Dashed old Colonel. Why?"

"Well, damn me for coincidence. I see Janice Devereux in Town, first time I've seen or heard of her for years. Then you ask me about her. Now you poll up with old Donoughmore. Damn it, Penryn, Colonel Donoughmore was the C.O. of a command to which young Devereux was attached."

"The deuce he was! Did he know Devereux?"

"Couldn't say, old fellow. Shouldn't think so. Devereux was mostly in the Plains, you know, and Donoughmore was higher up. And Colonels don't know Junior Lieutenants, m'lad."

"Where was Mrs. Devereux?"

"Mostly up with us. I knew her pretty well."

"Did the colonel know her?"

"Again I couldn't say. He must have known her by sight. And we all went to dances in the same club, you know."

"You said that Devereux was killed. How come?"

"Shooting. He went out on a couple of days' leave. He was an adventurous young devil. Year before he had been mauled by a tiger, which he'd missed at short range. The thing got behind him and leapt. Clawed his right arm pretty badly. He got a wigging from old Donoughmore. He was off duty for weeks with it. Anyway, this last time he didn't come back—not even with a wound. Apparently, he tried to cross a torrent in a native boat. It capsized and he was swept away. A couple of boys tried to reach him and were drowned as well. His body was never recovered. Janice Devereux left India shortly afterwards. I thought she had gone to the French Riviera."

"But I take it she would have known Colonel Donoughmore by sight?"

"Oh Lor! Yes. Damn it, she must have seen him in the club."

"What kind of a man was Donoughmore?"

"Bit of a bully. He was C.O., and let everybody know it. Not a popular fellow, either, with the men or the women, though he fancied himself as a lady killer."

Inspector Penryn left his club in a reflective mood. He wanted to think how this unexpected information fitted into the jigsaw puzzle of the Tamar tragedy. He turned into Oxford Street and boarded a bus for Richmond. He could think best on a bus, and he wanted to see Richmond again, anyway. He had been wont, in his younger days, to sail a boat there. From a front seat on the nearly empty bus he argued the pros and cons with an imaginary companion.

"Supposing she had known the colonel in India, what's that to do with his going into the Tamar, anyway? After all, she had been away from India for several years, and there had been no reunion greetings when she had met the colonel in the Tremarden Arms."

"You don't think that will do?" The inspector frowned at his imaginary companion. "You don't see any need for Mrs. Devereux not to have acknowledged the colonel as an old acquaintance? Well, why should she acknowledge him?"

"No reason at all; any more than she should say that she had never seen him before she came to the Tremarden Arms. There is no reason why she should not have known him. Or is there?"

"True," the inspector conceded. "She must, at any rate, have heard of him in India. Why hide it?"

"She lied in that case, you see—" from the companion.

"I see what you're getting at. If she lied about not knowing the colonel, then she might have lied about not being on the water."

"Didn't one of the guests say he saw her there?"

"He says he supposed it was her."

"Once a liar always a liar."

The bus lumbered up the hilly main street of Richmond, and the inspector, with a nod of appreciation at his invisible friend, descended and walked to the river bank.

In the evening, before catching the night train back to Tremarden, he visited the *Daily Examiner*. There he secured the information he wanted. Press cuttings from the extensive library of the paper revealed that Mrs. Devereux had made the acquaintance of Sir John Shepstone during the previous winter at Mentone, on the French Riviera, where Sir John had a villa out near the Italian border at Mentone-Garavan.

The inspector was early at his office next morning. After preparing his written report for the superintendent, he rang his bell and a sergeant answered.

"How did the Devereux alibi go, Bates?" he asked.

"Absolutely cast iron, sir," was the reply. "I saw the proprietress of the Devonshire Tea Rooms, and I saw the waitress who served Mrs. Devereux both times. I questioned them very closely and separately. Each of them described the woman. There is no doubt about the description fitting Mrs. Devereux."

"What about the scarf and the teacup?"

"Identified, Inspector. The waitress remembered seeing the scarf after the customer had left, about 12.45. It's funny how she forgot it, because it was lying across the back of a chair on the other side of the table from her. Mrs. Devereux was the only person at that table for lunch. Anyhow, nobody could mistake the scarf—yellow, with black dogs and horses all over it—the sort of thing once seen never forgotten. The proprietress says that Millie—that's the waitress—gave it to her to take care of; and when Mrs. Devereux walked in, at a quarter to five, Millie told her at once in a whisper: 'That's the lady who left the scarf!'"

"And the tea-cup?"

"Happened just as she said. Waitress says that Mrs. Devereux had paid for the tea and stood up to go. She swept the cup and saucer off the edge of the table. They broke to pieces on the floor. Mrs. Devereux apologised and insisted on paying for the damage."

"Hm! That seems to dispose of that, then, Bates. All right. Keep on hand in case I want you. Is the Super in?"

"Yes, sir. He's in with the Chief Constable and the Scotland Yard man."

Penryn decided that it would be as well to give the result of his investigations to the three men at once, when it could be considered by them collectively. It would save time. Knocking at the door, he peeped round the jamb at the conference.

"Ah! Come in, Penryn. We were just talking about you," greeted the Chief Constable. "Anything come of the Devereux inquiries?"

"So far as this end is concerned the alibi is sound, sir." He related the result of the sergeant's talk with the tea-room people. "As regards the wider inquiries, which I have made in London, I am not so sure as to what they are going to mean to Doctor Manson."

The inspector paused, to give effect to his coming pronouncement.

"Mrs. Devereux knew Colonel Donoughmore before she ever came to Tremarden," he said.

The effect on the three men was instantaneous.

"What!" roared the Chief Constable. "Why she said she had never met him."

Superintendent Burns swore that he had never believed the damned woman. Manson alone spoke quietly: "Let's hear all about it, Penryn," he said.

Briefly the inspector sketched in all the details of his talk with his club friend. "There is no doubt whatever that, if she did not know the colonel personally—and she is certain to have done so, in my view—she must have known of him, and who he was. She spent two years in India and her husband was in Colonel Donoughmore's command."

"And what do you see in the fact that she said she had never met him, Inspector?" asked Manson.

"That there is some reason connected with his death that would implicate her if it was known that she was acquainted with him before Tremarden," was the inspector's prompt reply.

Manson nodded. "There is something to be said for that point of view," he admitted. "But you must not take it for granted. For instance, Mrs. Devereux is engaged to be married to a wealthy Baronet. Her denial of any acquaintance with the colonel might be due to a desire not to be mixed up or associated in any way with the colonel's death. She might assume that, if we knew that she had known the colonel, we would ask her questions about that acquaintance. That would be quite understandable."

"In certain circumstances, yes sir," retorted Penryn. "But that does not explain why, when she came to the hotel she did not acknowledge the acquaintance. She didn't know then that the colonel was going to be killed."

He paused as a thought suddenly struck him.

"Or did she?" he asked emphatically.

Even Manson was startled by the remark. He looked long and sharply at the inspector. Then: "That is an accusation, Penryn," he said. "Is there any ground for it that we do not know. I mean, have you anything that you have not told us?"

"No, Doctor. But I have been thinking pretty deeply over this case since Major Ruddock told me about the Indian business. And, frankly, I am suspicious of the lady. Major Smithers says he saw her on the water. She denies that she was ever there. She does not, by the way, know that the major says he saw her there. She gives us an alibi. *I think it is too good an alibi.*"

Manson was listening to the inspector with marked attention. As the officer paused he nodded to him to continue. "Go on, Inspector," he said. "You are interesting me very considerably."

"Well, gentlemen, I have had a lot of experience with alibis. And I have found that a person with an alibi is, more often than not, a guilty person. The innocent person seldom has an alibi *because he has never prepared one beforehand*—he has had no reason to do so. For instance, if I asked the Chief Constable here, for an alibi for the afternoon on which Colonel Donoughmore died, I would be very much surprised if he could give me a satisfactory answer—one which could be checked and accepted." He looked across at the Chief Constable.

Sir William thought for a few moments. "I remember that I went out in my car that afternoon," he said.

"Where?" asked Penryn.

"Just for a drive, Inspector."

"Did you see anyone you know, who could vouch that you were at any given spot?"

"No. I don't remember seeing anyone I knew."

"Did you call anywhere, sir?"

"No. I just drove out, stopped by the roadside once to refill my pipe, and then turned for home."

Manson chuckled and took up the questioning. "So, if the inspector, here, said he believed that you went to the river, had a row with the colonel and pushed him in, you could not prove that you were elsewhere, Sir William?"

The Chief Constable looked staggered at the suggestion. He realised that he was now, himself, in the position of being asked to account for his movements, that many men had been in at his hands and at the hands of his officers. He glanced from one to the other of the two men, and his tone became much less assured than usual. "Dammit, Manson, I couldn't," he said. "I . . . I . . . I really c-c-ouldn't."

"Stammering over the reply—that's usually a very bad sign," commented Manson to the others. "I suppose you DIDN'T kill the colonel, Sir William?" he asked suddenly.

"ME!" roared the Chief Constable with a fine disregard for grammar. "Me—of course I didn't!"

"Well, PROVE it, sir," said Inspector Penryn. "By an alibi," he added.

"You see what I mean, sir," he went on. "Here is a woman apparently hiding something between her and the colonel. She has an alibi which is good from midday to about five or six o'clock in the evening. And somewhere between those times the colonel gets killed. I say I view so perfect an alibi with suspicion, the more so in view of the fact that one of the persons on the river says he saw a woman on the bank. And the only woman who had any right to be there—she had a rod the major said—is the woman with this beautiful alibi."

The inspector sat back, wiping his brow with his handkerchief. He had, he felt, gone a little too far with the Chief Constable.

Sir William turned a comprehensive gaze on the police chiefs. There was a rueful, but at the same time, humorous glint in his eyes. "Well, Doctor, what do you say to all this?" he asked. "Do YOU want to pull me in?"

Manson returned the smile. "No, Sir William. I think we will acquit you on this count. But—" and his face became serious—"as to the other aspect, Inspector Penryn has thought along the very lines that I myself would have put forward had I had the knowledge that he had gained. It is a very well-reasoned argument; and I would like to say so in front of him. We must, I think, take serious notice of it. And if there is any chance of the alibi being a prepared one, then it must be investigated very thoroughly."

"Have you any idea of the actual time the colonel died, Doctor?" the Chief Constable asked. "That seems to be a crucial point."

"I haven't, Sir William. That is a very difficult thing to decide in drowning cases, or where water is concerned. Normally, the heat of the body is lost almost twice as rapidly in water as it is in the air, and the temperature of the water is reached in about 14 hours. The temperature of the colonel's body, according to Dr. Tremayne, was slightly higher than that of the water in the Tamar. That would make the colonel's death in normal circumstances about five o'clock the previous night. But several things might affect the position. The colonel might have engaged in a struggle, which would have increased his temperature at the time of death; and he was wearing heavy waders and waterproof coat, which would have retarded cooling—it might be to the extent of three or four hours. But I think we can say, as an estimate, that Donoughmore died not earlier than two o'clock, and not later than four o'clock. Both these times are well-covered by Mrs. Devereux's alibi."

"We can narrow things down a little more, can we not, Doctor?" said Inspector Penryn. "Mrs. Devereux did not leave the tea rooms after lunch until 12.45, and she was back at tea at 4.45."

"So she would have four hours in which to get from Tavistock to the Tamar beat, and back to the tea rooms." Superintendent Burns supplied the calculation.

"And the hours we are most concerned with—2 to 4 p.m.— you will notice are right bang in the middle of her time," commented the Chief Constable. "Could she get there and back and do the deed in the time?"

"How far is Tavistock?" asked Manson.

"Thirteen miles from Tremarden and about ten-and-a-half from the nearest point to the Tamar beats."

"That is 21 miles, there and back. There doesn't seem any difficulty about covering the distance. Any cars for hire in Tavistock?"

"Yes, Doctor."

"Well, perhaps we had better leave the inquiries to Inspector Penryn, who has done so well up to now. There is, however, one thing you might do, Inspector."

"Yes, Doctor?"

"Have a word with Major Smithers and see whether he can fix the time he saw the woman at the end of the Avenue, and whether he can identify the woman more closely. Also, whether he saw her subsequently."

"I'll do that, sir."

"I'll have a word with the Tavistock police, Penryn, and get them to give you any help you may require," said the Chief Constable.

CHAPTER XI
THE MAJOR

"ACTUALLY, all I can say, Inspector, is that I saw a woman on the beat which adjoined mine. I assumed, naturally assumed, that woman to be Mrs. Devereux. If it was not, then I have no idea who she could have been."

"How far away would she be when you caught sight of her, Major?"

"Difficult to say now, Inspector. I didn't notice particularly. I had fished half up my beat, walking upstream, and decided to have a rest and a smoke. It was when I turned and waded slightly downstream, and across to the bank, that I caught sight of her, quite casually, if you know what I mean; just mentally noted having seen her."

Inspector Penryn was sitting with Major Smithers on a bank of the upper Lyner. The sun was shining hotly down through the timbering along the bank, turning the water, as it were, into a lacey design as light and shadow was reflected from the trees on to the surface of the stream. The major was munching sandwiches, and eyeing with a frown the speckled forms lying in his creel. The catch was a good one; normally the major would have regarded it with no little satisfaction. The presence of the inspector, however, had robbed the fishing of its pleasure. Major Smithers desired nothing so much as to forget the colonel and his death; and it had been with mixed feelings that, a few minutes earlier, he had looked up to see the inspector approaching along the bank.

He might have felt differently, perhaps, had he realised that Inspector Penryn had shown not a little consideration, at inconvenience to himself, in thus visiting the major at the riverside. His first intention after the conference with his chiefs had been to call at the hotel and interview Major Smithers there. The thought had then crossed his mind that, possibly, neither of the parties, in the circumstances, would care to be seen chatting with a police officer in full view of the other guests. He had, accordingly, waited until the major had set out to fish; had given him an hour, and then slowly walked along the bank till he came upon the angler.

"Quite," he commented to the major's description of his fleeting glance at the woman he had seen on the bank. "There was not, of course, any reason why you should have taken particular notice of anyone on a beat where you would naturally expect to see somebody or other during the course of the day. I think you told Doctor Manson that the time was about two o'clock?"

"As near as I can say, Inspector, yes. It might have been a trifle later. I did not note the time, of course. It was not before two o'clock—I know that. And it certainly was not after two-thirty, because I remember looking at my watch some time later, and it was just two-thirty then."

The inspector noted the statement in his book. "And I think you said she had a rod?" he asked.

"She certainly had. That was the first thing I noticed. It's funny how an angler will see a rod before he sees anything else. But, in any case, why worry me, Inspector? Why not ask Mrs. Devereux? She ought to know what time she was on the beat."

Penryn was silent for a fraction of a minute. He was thinking rapidly. So far, the major was equally suspect with Emmett, Sir Edward and Mrs. Devereux herself. His story of seeing a woman might be only another attempt at an alibi. How far he (the inspector) could go in telling one suspect anything about another was exercising the inspector's mind, while the major waited for an answer to his remark. But then, he argued, he had known the major for a considerable time now, and had fished with him. As far as one could judge men from acquaintance with them, the major was not, in his opinion, the man to go about killing superior officers. It wasn't done in Army circles, argued Penryn. He decided to take the risk.

"Well, the point is, Major," he said at length. "We *have* asked Mrs. Devereux. This, by the way, is in strict confidence between you and me. Mrs. Devereux says she was never on the water on that day; and she has turned up with an alibi to say where she was. And it is as excellent an alibi as ever I have come across."

The major looked up quickly, but met a glance from the inspector devoid of any expression other than that of interest in the topic under discussion. "I see," he said. "And you think, perhaps, that the woman on the beat was a figment of my imagination!"

The major had not seen years of service in Military Intelligence without being able to see through a brick wall, as it were.

Penryn cursed himself under his breath. But he smiled cordially at his victim. It was a smile with a chuckle behind it. "That would be *touché* to you, Major, if it was correct," he said. "But it is not correct. What I am trying to get from you is some kind of description, in order that we can have a go at tracing the woman. If it wasn't Mrs, Devereux, then it must have been some other woman. Is there any chance that you noticed, even casually, what she was wearing?"

"Not a hope, Inspector. As I say, I simply noted her mentally in passing. I do not suppose my eyes were on her more than a fraction of a second. I saw a rod and a woman. I knew that Mrs. Devereux had that beat, and I said to myself: 'There is Mrs. Devereux.' The figure looked like Mrs. Devereux—although that may have been due to the psychological fact that I expected to see Mrs. Devereux, if I saw anybody at all."

"That's what I am trying to get at, Major. Supposing the woman had been totally unlike Mrs. Devereux, would the fact have registered in your mind? Would you have said, for instance: 'Now, who the Devil is that'?"

Major Smithers considered the question. "I see what you mean, Inspector, and it is very ingenious," he replied. "But I don't know whether I can answer. If I had kept her in sight for even a minute, I should have said that it would. But in the passing glance which I caught, I should say it is extremely doubtful. Anyway, if Mrs. Devereux has shown that she was not there, then, obviously, it could not have registered with me, because I would be prepared to say, as I did indeed say, quite definitely, that I had seen her at that spot."

The inspector left it at that, and tried another tack. "It's a dreadful business, the whole thing, Major," he commiserated, "and a very uncomfortable one for me, knowing Franky so long, and Sir Edward and you. It's a pity the whole thing could not have been allowed to go down as the accident we at first thought it was. Of course, when suspicion arose, we had to take up the investigation."

"I'm inclined to agree with you that it WAS a pity, Inspector," was the reply. "I am afraid that my sympathies are all on the side of the person who rid us of the presence of the colonel. I cannot feel any regret at Donoughmore's passing. I knew quite a lot about him, and I think his death will be blessed, rather than mourned, by a number of people. Perhaps I should not say that—nil bonum, you know—but the fact remains that he won't be missed except, perhaps, by the village maidens."

Penryn's brain jerked again into alertness at the asperity in the major's voice. There seemed, to his mind, something suspiciously like a personal note behind the epitaph. He might be wrong—"I'm getting suspicious of everybody," he said to himself—but it might be worth while probing a little deeper. "You had known him for some years, had you not, Major?" he asked.

"I wouldn't say I had known him, Inspector. He had come down here for several years and since, like myself, he had usually picked the best trouting months, we were generally here together. Sir Edward was usually here also."

"Where did he get his money, do you know? Franky's place isn't cheap by any means, and he usually stayed a couple of months or so, didn't he?"

"He had his army pension, of course, and perhaps he had saved a bit, though I doubt it—in India. I know of one or two occasions on which he made considerable sums of money by what I, personally, would call fraudulent means, but which I have no doubt he called smart business. That is what I meant by saying that he wouldn't be mourned; and I've an idea that he made a business of the 'means' behind the 'fellow fisherman' guise. I cannot, of course, say that that is true. There are only two cases that I know of."

"Would it be too much to ask what they were, Major?"

"No, I can't tell you that, Inspector. It concerns other people, and has nothing to do with this case. I only mentioned it to show you the character of the man."

"And the village maidens, Major. Any of them in Tremarden?"

"Quite a number, I should think, Inspector. And some who were by no means maidens, if the truth is known."

"That's why old Trepol was so anxious to offer a free coffin for the colonel if he had fallen in the river and drowned himself, wasn't it?"

The major smiled for the first time during the talk. "Oh, old Trepol's bark is a good deal worse than his bite. *YOU* know that. I don't think there was much between his girl and the colonel. The number of people to whom old Trepol has offered free coffins is legion—and they are still alive."

A smile passed between the two men. The inspector knew Trepol as well as he knew the major—if not, indeed, better. "Nevertheless," the inspector said to himself: "I'll have a word or two with the girl. She *was* with the colonel in the ruins at night." Aloud he said: "Well, Major, you'll want to get on with your fishing, and I must be getting back to the station. Thanks for the help you've been. Perhaps if you remember anything else you'll give me a ring, or let me come along and see you."

"I will, Inspector."

Penryn wended a way back to Tremarden in a thoughtful frame of mind. His inquiry, he felt, was not getting him any forrader; on the contrary, it seemed to be putting him further and deeper into the mystery. Who, for instance, were the people who had been the victims of the colonel's frauds; for that is what Major Smithers had virtually accused the dead man of perpetrating. They must have been pretty bad frauds to have aroused so much feeling in the major, for, the inspector ruminated, he was not the man to be easily moved. Were they, the inspector wondered, sufficiently serious to have goaded the victims to take revenge on the colonel? And were the people concerned local people, or outlanders, as the Cornishman calls strangers? If they were locals . . .

The inspector's soliloquy was broken by the sudden appearance over a hedge of a line full of clothes, jerked up at the end of a clothes prop.

Anne Trepol was hanging out the family washing.

Penryn grunted. "Might as well get a talk with her while her old father's away," he said to himself. He walked through the gate and along to the back door.

The girl looked up at him from the other side of a washtub, her arms deep in soapsuds. Anne Trepol was eighteen, but a large eighteen, and a buxom one, with spacious curves which she never troubled to conceal overmuch at any time, but which were now hardly concealed at all. The inspector looked her over with disapproval at the brazenness.

"I want to talk to you about Colonel Donoughmore, Anne," he said.

The girl made no reply, but began again to rub the clothes in the tub. Going to be difficult, the inspector decided. A tactful man, he made a new approach. "The colonel was very good to you, Anne, wasn't he? Now, we think he may have been killed, and I'm sure you wouldn't like anyone who killed him to get off scot free, when you might be able to tell us something that might help us to catch him."

"How do you know the colonel was good to me?" Anne demanded.

"Well, Anne, we know you used to meet him. You've been seen in the old ruins, you know."

"That would be the Devereux woman who told you that, I know. She wanted the colonel herself, I suppose. She flew at me that night, and said as how the colonel wouldn't do me any good and I had better not meet him any more. I reckon she killed him herself, she was always rowing with him."

"Rowing? How do you mean, Anne?"

"I've heard them in the hotel when I've been helping as a chamber-maid, when the hotel has been full."

The inspector nodded. "Of course, Anne. I had forgotten that you went in there sometimes. How were Mrs. Devereux and the colonel rowing?"

"Well, once he was in her bedroom and I heard her say, 'Don't drive me too far, my friend, or I'll have to find some way out.'"

Penryn looked up, startled. "Did the colonel say anything to that?" he asked.

"Yes, he said, 'You'll be well advised not to, my lady. I'm not such a fool as to leave things so you could get away with anything. It's in black and white.'"

"When did this happen, Anne?"

"Last week-end. It would be on the Friday, when the coach-load of people came to the hotel."

"Was anything else said?"

"I don't know. I was in the room next door and then Mrs. Baker came in, and I had to go out."

"Were you down by the river on the day the colonel was drowned, Anne?"

"Me? No. I wasn't near the river that day. *I wasn't, I tell you.*"

Inspector Penryn looked hard at the girl. The vehemence of her reply seemed to him to be concealing something she feared to have revealed. She had, he thought, a frightened air. "You

see, Anne, Mrs. Devereux wasn't on the river that day, though
we thought she was. So she couldn't have hurt the colonel. But
Major Smithers says he saw a woman down there. . . ."

"Major Smithers! Him! He's another one who hated the colonel. He couldn't say a good word for him. The colonel told me
all about it. It wasn't the colonel's fault that him and Sir Edward
lost money on the shares. He couldn't help it. How could he?"

"Shares?" The inspector spoke sharply. "What shares,
Anne?"

"Shares what the colonel sold to them. How could he help
it if the companies didn't pay any money. The colonel told me
all about it. He gave me some of the shares, too, he did. And he
said, they'd be worth a lot of money some time."

Penryn felt himself wading in deep water, to use a fisherman's term. Was this to do with the frauds that the major had
talked about half an hour since? Shares . . . lost money . . . companies didn't pay anything. He decided that he ought to see the
shares which Anne held.

"Of course, the colonel couldn't help it, Anne," he said.
"Shares are always going up and down, and lots of people lose
money every week buying them. I hope your shares *will* be worth
a lot of money, Anne. Perhaps I could tell you if they are worth
much money now, if I saw them. Have you still got them?"

The girl nodded. She turned, ran upstairs, and came down
a minute or two later with a bundle of engraved papers. "That's
them," she said.

Penryn, looking them through, whistled softly to himself.
They were, according to the wording, 400 shares of £10 each
in the Grand Consolidated Gold Mining Corporation of South
Africa, Ltd. Four thousand pounds' worth of money—"and the
gold on the paper worth another five pounds, I should think,"
the inspector said to himself. He handed them back to the girl.
"I don't know much about these shares, Anne, but I don't think
they are worth much money now. Of course, as the colonel said,
they may be worth more later. You keep hold of them, and don't
let anybody else see them."

"I shall take care of that," was the reply.

"And you can't tell me anything else about the colonel, Anne?"

"No. Only about the major and Sir Edward having threatened him."

"What did your father say about you knowing the colonel?"

The girl coloured. "Him!" she said. "I didn't care what he said, nor what he did. He give me a good hiding when somebody told him and he said I wasn't to see the colonel again. He said he'd give the colonel a good hiding, too. The colonel said not to worry about that, as he was used to dealing with men, him being an officer of a regiment."

"And you saw the colonel again, I suppose?"

The girl scowled. "Of course I did," she agreed.

"But not on the day he died, Anne? You're sure of that, are you?"

"I never saw him that day," was the reply.

Penryn hurried back to the Tremarden Arms, turning over in his mind the strange story of £4,000 worth of shares given to a chamber-maid, and other shares over which Sir Edward Maurice and Major Smithers had, according to Anne, lost money. Was there, he wondered some link between those losses and the tragedy of the Tamar? He turned in at the hotel, walked up the stairs, and into Doctor Manson's room. The Doctor was bending over his microscope. He glanced up as the door opened. A questioning look on his visitor's face caused him to push the microscope back. "Anything wrong, Inspector?" he asked.

"Do you know anything, Doctor—" Penryn spoke very slowly—"about the shares of the Grand Consolidated Gold Mining Corporation of South Africa, Ltd.?"

Manson stared at him in bewilderment. "Grand Consolidated Gold Mining Corporation of South Africa?" he repeated. "Never heard of them, Penryn. Why? Anything to do with us?"

"I don't know, Doctor—yet. But it might help if you can find out anything about the company."

"I dare say I can find out, Penryn." The scientist pulled the telephone towards him and spoke into the mouthpiece. "This is a police priority call, please. Get me Whitehall 1212, and I want a personal call to Inspector Thompson—What? Half an hour? Very well."

"Thompson is the Yard's City expert, Penryn," he explained to the superintendent. "If he knows anything about your company I will telephone you. That all right?"

"It will do me fine, Doctor," was the reply.

* * * * *

Inspector Penryn lifted the telephone receiver. By force of habit he glanced at the clock, a routine precaution in case the call should require timing for future reference. It was less than twenty minutes since he had left Doctor Manson. "Hallo!" he said. "Inspector Penryn."

"Manson here," was the reply. "Grand Consolidated Gold Mining Corporation of South Africa is a moribund company. Two years ago it was concerned in a share-pushing fraud. The mine was a genuine concern at its start, fifteen years ago, but gold petered out. Then, two years ago, a report was circulated that a new vein of gold had been found. An inspector's report was attached giving glowing prospects. Nothing was disclosed to the Stock Exchange, but the shares were sold privately, in thousands, at the price of £50 a £10 share, mostly by circular and through the whispered offers of people who were prepared to let a few friends in 'on a good thing.' Something like 150,000 shares were sold, Thompson says, before the fraud leaked out. There was no gold; there had never been any gold. The inspector and his reports were both frauds, and were circulated after a man named Mallinson and two companions had bought the original shares from their holders for two shillings apiece, which was one and elevenpence more than they were worth. Mallinson vanished to South America, and is still living there on the proceeds—about £750,000 profit. The shares to-day are not worth £1 for the whole issue. That any use to you?"

"I'm coming round to see you, Doctor. I'm going to talk," was the reply.

CHAPTER XII
THE COLONEL

FRAN BAKER, crossing the lounge of his hotel after seeing that his guests were well supplied with lunch, was button-holed by Doctor Manson.

"You and I, Franky, are going down to the Rostrum to catch a fish. Come along."

Franky looked from the Doctor's rod to his gaff. "Ef so be it is a salmon yew want, Doctor, you're a bit early. Beant any salmon up yet."

"Then, Franky, we'll have a few spins for another fish, and hope for a run," he said.

The two rolled comfortably to the river in the Doctor's Oldsmobile, and, leaving it parked in the farmyard, strolled slowly down to the water-side. Arrived there, Manson made no attempt to fit his rod together. Instead, he sat on the granite "rostrum" and motioned the hotelier to sit beside him.

"Franky," he said, "I brought you down here because I did not want to talk my kind of fish language in front of the hotel people. I'm spinning in waters I do not know, but I think, perhaps, you DO know them. Together, you with that knowledge and I with my bait, we might get over a fish."

Baker made no comment. Doctor Manson produced his case, applied a lighted match to the hotelier's cigarette and his own, and settled comfortably down in the Rostrum. Then he spoke.

"How long has the colonel been coming down to the Arms, Franky?" he asked.

"This would a'ben his fourth year, Doctor," was the quiet reply.

"Did you know anything about him before?"

"Only what he had told me beforetimes, Doctor. Whensobe he first came, he seemed a nice kind of man, y'see. He made good friends here and was popular in the place."

"And what did he tell you?"

"Well, I disremember a lot of it. He said he had been a C.O. in India and had retired a year before, and wanted a place to visit for the fishing."

"Did he say what he did for a living?"

"No, Doctor. We reckoned he was on his pension. And, of course, gentlemen in the Army usually have a bit of money—in the peace-time army I mean, like old General Bearton, over at Honiton. He was in India, as you well know."

"Quite. When did the colonel begin to get unpopular?"

"About half-way through his second year. One or two people he had known before wouldn't talk to him. I think they had caught him fishing in the ends of their beats. Then, once, he accused a young journalist fellow from London of fishing for salmon without a salmon licence. He reported him to the bailiff. It seems that the colonel went down to the water to fly-fish for salmon and found the young journalist there spinning. I'd given him the beat for salmon and the colonel had no right there, anyways, except in the trout water. Well, the colonel was annoyed and asked him if he had taken out a license for salmon. The young fellow replied: 'No, I haven't taken out a licence. What the hell has it to do with you anyway? More than one pool, isn't there?' You see the colonel mostly fished for trout. So he told the bailiff."

Franky grinned. "He had to write and apologise to the young fellow. You see," he added slyly, "the young man was quite right in saying he hadn't taken out a licence for salmon. I had taken it out for him, and charged it on the hotel bill. Well, the young fellow spilled the tale in the hotel and that didn't help the colonel with the other guests."

"And, of course, with the same people coming down every year, they'd remember it against him," mused Manson. "Yes, I see that. When did Sir Edward and the major first meet him?"

"The first year they were down here. They were all friendly together. Always divided a stream's beats between them, and usually took a luncheon basket for three."

"The same next year?"

"Yes, Doctor. All through the season. And the night before the colonel left—he lived in Surbiton, Surrey, then, so I was told—the three had a champagne party. Very good friends they were. That was in September. When Major and Sir Edward came down next year they weren't on speaking terms with the colonel."

"The major had a nice little estate at that time, hadn't he, Franky? Was it not in Devonshire?"

Baker nodded.

"And then he came to live in the Tremarden Arms?"

"That's so, Doctor."

"He had sold the estate?"

Another nod from the hotelier.

"Lost his money, didn't he?"

Baker nodded again.

"Anything to do with the colonel?"

There was no answer, but the Doctor, his eyes on Franky's face, saw the shadow that passed over it. "I know all about the share deal, Franky," he said gently, "or at least nearly all about it."

The shadow passed from the hotelier's face. He looked up in relief.

"Well, then, Doctor, that is all there is to it. Major and Sir Edward thought Colonel had 'frauded them of their money, and they were very sore about it—especially Major. He had reason to be—God knows," he added after a pause.

Manson let a few moments pass in silence. Franky's remark had come as a shock to him. So, Sir Edward was in it too, he mused, silently. Then: "How did the thing start, Franky?" he asked. "Do you know?"

"Yes, Doctor. Major told me the story the first night he came to live in the hotel. Seems it began half-way through the season, when they were all such good friends. Major, he said the colonel was all up in the air like, one evening, saying he was on the point of making a fortune. It was more or less a secret, so he said. Major and Sir Edward twitted him a bit and then he told 'em all about it. That's what the major said to me, anyhow. Him, that's the colonel, had a financial friend who knew about a gold mine in South Africa that hadn't got any gold in it. But it seemed like that the colonel's friend knew that there *was* gold in it. He said that a new thing had been found—is it a vein?"

"Yes, a new vein of ore, Franky."

"Well, it had been found by a prospector or something like that and he had told the financial gentleman. And they were going round buying up all the shares in the mine for a shilling or two apiece. It all had to be done very quietly—Colonel said, else secret would get out and they would have to pay several pounds for the shares."

"How did the colonel know all this, Franky?"

"I don't understand the rights of finance, Doctor, but I think the colonel had a lot of the old shares when the mine was first running, and he knew because the financier man wanted to buy them and the colonel didn't want to sell at first. Anyways, Colonel told Major and Sir Edward they weren't sure whether the gold was all right or not then, but an assayer was making a secret report for the financier, and they'd know the facts in a few days' time."

"Oh, my God. A story that's been told a hundred times," moaned Manson. "Do people STILL fall for it?"

"They did know, too," Franky went on. "Colonel, he showed them the report a few days afterwards. It said that there was a rich streak on land which the old company had leased or op-tioned or something, but had never worked. Something about wrong direction, if you understands what that means, Doctor."

"Yes, Franky. The old vein, which had seemed to end, turned at right angles and was taken to have petered out. The new di-rection wasn't traced."

"There was a fortune in the mine, the report said, and the new vein could be worked cheaply, as it was near the surface. The colonel, he said he was in clover, because he had two thou-sand of the old shares, and the financier, 'cause Colonel was keeping the story secret, was letting him buy another two thou-sand at £10 each. Major said Colonel was grumbling at the price because the financier had only paid two shillings each for the shares. But the shares would be worth £50 in no time, and perhaps more very soon."

"I should know the rest, Franky. I've heard it so many times. Of course, Sir Edward and the major wanted to be let in, and the colonel wrote to his friend, the financier, and as they were friends of the colonel they, could have a few shares at the price the colonel was paying for them, only they mustn't breathe a word about it. That was it, wasn't it? How many shares did the major buy?"

Franky nodded slowly. "It was just like you said, Doctor. You might a'most have been there. Major, he bought 500 shares, and Sir Edward he bought 500, too. Mind you, it looked all right, 'cos it wasn't very long before each of them received £500 on account of the mine's dividends or something. I'm not quite sure what it was. So both of them bought some more shares off the colonel's friend with it."

"Next thing I see was the financier friend was reported in the papers as wanted for a bucket-shop, and had gone to South America with all the money he had got for the shares, and the mine wasn't worth a penny. Seems the report was a fraud and there had never been any gold at all."

"And the major?"

"He lost about £10,000 and had to sell his house—lovely little house it was, too, Doctor. He'd been born in that house. So had his father. And all his money went 'cept his pension. And that wasn't the worst. The shock of losing all they had sent his wife funny, and after a time she died. Major said Colonel had killed her and some day he'd send him the same way."

"What happened when they met the colonel at the Arms next year?"

"Ah!" Franky's face clouded as he gazed mentally back. "Colonel looked to be in a terrible state. He said as how he was sorry. His friend was a damned fraud, and that he himself had been hit and lost a packet. Major, he listened and then said, 'Well, it couldn't be helped—he'd been a damned fool and lost a lot of money,' but he wasn't out, not by long chalks. And after that he ignored the colonel."

"And Sir Edward?"

"He's a very rich gentleman, as you know, Doctor. I don't think he felt the loss very much, but he was pretty wild about the major's money, and wanted to hound the colonel out of the hotel. But they couldn't prove that the colonel had known that the shares were wrong 'uns. At least, not then," the hotelier added, as an afterthought.

"What do you mean, not then?"

"Well, Doctor, it seems that after the colonel had gone—he went early that year—two men were talking one day with Sir Edward in the lounge of the Arms, and spotted in the letter-rack an envelope addressed to Colonel. One of them said: 'Donoughmore? Ah! He's a smart guy. Met him in a hotel at Okehampton last year, and he told us he'd made £10,000 in a month.'"

"'Ah!' said Sir Edward, 'that wants a bit of making these days. Did he say how he did it?' 'Yes,' says the other man. 'He's in the City, and he said he'd just unloaded a packet of shares on to a couple of suckers at ten times their value.' 'I see,' says Sir Edward, in a nasty voice; and he told the major. Major says, 'Suckers is the right word, Edward. We asked for it.'"

Franky spread his hands. "You see, Doctor, it was in my hotel it all took place. And Major and me have always been good friends. And I knew his wife."

"And this was the first time they had seen the colonel since they knew the truth that the colonel was a sharepusher?"

"Yes, they agreed, so Major said, not to let him know they knew. Major wouldn't have it known that he'd been such a fool. He told me it served him right for trusting anybody in speculation without making financial provision for his wife, in case anything went wrong. He said he was nearly as bad as Colonel. He had ruined his own wife."

"There is only one more point, Franky. Sir Edward called the colonel a sharepusher. Did he know that for a fact?"

"Oh, yes, Doctor. He went up to London and got a private detective to find out all about Colonel. The detective said he had been selling shares for years. He said he was a man who went to hotels, made friends with wealthy people, and then 'let them have shares'—these were the words the detective used, Sir Edward said, but nobody had complained, and there was no direct proof. Sir Edward, he saw the committees of two clubs Colonel was a member of, and Colonel was asked to resign."

Doctor Manson lay back against the granite slabs of the Rostrum when Franky had finished. His eyes stared across the swiftly running water of the rapids as they entered the salmon pool. Franky watched him for a time. Then: "I don't think that it puts you over a fish, do it, Doctor?"

"Fish?" Manson pondered bewilderedly for a time. "Oh, I see. The colonel! I don't know, Franky. We've had one or two rises, but the fish is coming short. What do you do in a case like that, Franky?"

"Give him a rest, Doctor, and try same pool later on . . . with a different fly, mebbe."

"Like most of the advice you give, Franky, very sound," was the reply. "We'll try it. Come along, it's getting near time for a cup of tea."

CHAPTER XIII
FRED EMMETT

SOME FIVE MILES out of Exeter, on the London side of the city, there stands, amid farm lands, a large flour mill. On the opposite side of the road is a cattle cake mill. Next to the flour mill is an extensive piggery, with hundreds of Medium-Whites lolling in "garden" pens in front of their stys. From above the roof of each sty a revolving cowl whizzes round, drawing out the smelly air that comes from the presence of Mr. Pig's sleeping quarters. Adjacent to the cattle mill are acres of poultry pens, divided and sub-divided into smaller enclosures; and each enclosure confining a separate breed of fowl.

Stretching across the front of each of the mills is a painted sign. It blazons to the onlooker that the mill is owned by Frederick Emmett and Sons, Ltd. The description is not quite accurate;

the Emmett part had been deceased for some years at this time and the "Son" now reigned in his stead.

For nine months of the year Fred Emmett ground grain into flour. He turned the by-products into cattle food. He fed the middlings from the grindings to the pigs—and used the manure from the pigs for land, on which he grew grain to feed to his fowl. Nothing was ever wasted in Emmett's mills; the result was that Fred Emmett could spend the remaining three months of the year fishing and shooting in Tremarden.

Sergeant Merry found all this out for himself when, on his tour of investigation of the Tremarden Arms suspects, he reached Emmett. Emmett's workpeople, gathered in the roadside pub, announced enthusiastically that "Master Fred" was the best employer for whom any man or woman could hope to work. His business rivals, sadly outstripped, were eager to confess that a better man had beaten them. Everybody agreed that Fred was worth a mint of money, hadn't a care in the world, and was friendly to all men. His bite, they agreed unanimously, was even less dangerous than his friendly bark.

In fact, try as he would, Merry could find nothing which would suggest any kind of motive through which Mr. Emmett would be likely to push the late, and unlamented, Colonel Donoughmore off this mortal coil.

Back in Tremarden, his search bore no better fruit. Nobody had ever heard Emmett say anything against the colonel. He had twitted him now and again, and said he'd knock his damned block off. But then, said the local sportsmen, Master Emmett was always going to knock somebody's block off; but never did.

The only thing which Merry could find that was worrying Emmett was that he had lost his spectacles. He couldn't see his fly on the water very well without them; a circumstance which had decreased his creel to an unfortunate level. He blamed the colonel for the upset, which had resulted in his mislaying the spectacles in a place he could not, for the life of him, remember, and said that he wished now, that he *had* thrown the damned man in the river, because it would probably have saved the man getting killed on that day and then he, Emmett, would not have lost his glasses.

Merry gave it up. As he said to Doctor Manson: "If I was one of those book detectives, I'd know Emmett was the murderer, him being the only one against whom there is no suspicion. You see, the man who says he's going to throw a fellow in the river always says it in books because he thinks that that makes him out to be innocent, since only a fool would say he would do it if he meant to do it."

"Quite!" said Manson, with a face which threatened to burst into a contortion of merriment.

"But not being a book detective, but only a real one, I'm puzzled, you see, Harry," Merry went on. "I'd as soon suspect a fellow with no alibi or motive, but with access to the dead person, as I'd suspect one with so darned good an alibi as to be supernatural. I'm suspecting Emmett because he sounds too good to be true."

"Quite," replied Manson, again. "Now, I suspect everybody, Jim. I've got a mind like that."

"I know you have, Doctor," was the reply. "One of these days you'll be having somebody sueing you for slander or libel, or something, if you go on having a mind like that. You'd dash-well have to produce some ground for having your suspicious mind pointing its suspicion at them."

He fell silent for a few moments. Then, a chuckle came from between his lips.

"Now what's the matter?" asked Manson.

"I was just thinking of the time when I first came across your suspicious mind," was the reply.

"Can't recall it, Jim. When was it?"

"When you insisted on questioning old Giles and his Dean about the possible whereabouts of your missing bottles of beer. And I'll never forget the Master's face as he gathered that you had begun investigations of the disappearance with him."

Manson laughed with his Sergeant and friend over the incident.

Giles, you see, had been the Master of Emmanuel College, Cambridge, where Manson and Merry were undergraduates. The idea of questioning one's college Head in connection with missing beer from Hall could only have occurred to anybody with an extraordinarily suspicious mind!

CHAPTER XIV
FOOTPRINTS

CHIEF DETECTIVE INSPECTOR Harry Manson, D.Sc., and detective Sergeant Merry, B.Sc., lowered themselves into two chairs in a way-side café on the high road five miles outside Tremarden, and called for tea.

For two hours they had trudged a devious way over fields, guided by mysterious marks which the scientist had drawn on an Ordnance Survey map of the district. They had peered into ditches and skirted round ponds. The result was, as Manson admitted, nil.

The colonel hadn't died in any of them.

"Where the heck *DID* he die, then?" Merry asked between gulps of tea.

"Beyond the fact that it wasn't in the Tamar, I don't know," answered Manson. "And what is more, I haven't the faintest idea. I know, and so do you, the conditions required for his death, but I do not know where we can find those conditions."

The two men had devoted the afternoon to following the two pieces of concrete evidence which the Doctor had outlined to Superintendent Burns to prove that the colonel did not drown at the spot suspected. They had reached the café at the end of the search, and had pulled in for refreshment.

"Well. . . ." Manson looked at his watch. "We had better be making our way back. I want to walk down the river bank."

The burly figure of the café proprietor bore down on them. "You gents want anything else?" he asked.

"No thanks," Manson answered. "You make tea like a Yorkshireman," he added, with a smile.

"Ah am an' all," was the reply. "Joe Smithwaite's the name. Sithee, we knaws how to put tea i' pot oop theer. That'll be two bob, and thank ye very much."

"I suppose if we go across the fields here, we can reach the river?" asked Manson.

"No, sir. Tha can't go that way. All private property, like, and private fishin' on river. T'water belongs to Lunnon gents, and, sides, it's all cornfields. Now what you gennelmen *CAN* do is to take the bus down t'road for about three miles and then tha can cut down right of way which'll put thee on t'riverside. Then, tha walks reight down t'river past Tremarden Arms fishin' water."

"That will do us excellently. What time is there a bus?"

"Due most any minute now, sir. Ask Joe—he's the conductor—to put thee down at Tremorres's farm and tha'll see the path. It's t'one fishermen use."

Ten minutes later the bus dropped the couple at the footpath; another five minutes and their eyes saw the glint of the Tamar. In a further five they were at the bank, looking at dozens of widening rings on the surface of the water, as trout came up for the late afternoon rise of fly.

"Whereabouts are we, Harry?" asked Merry. "I don't recognise the spot."

"Looks like Number Four beat. . . . Yes, there's the board. This will be where the major was fishing on the day of the colonel's death."

Together, the couple turned and began to stroll downstream, drinking in the beauty of the afternoon, the warmth of which was steadied by a light breeze which rippled the water gently on the wind-ward side of the stream. They had strolled some twenty minutes when Manson looked ahead and stopped. "Now this would be the spot, I should think, from which the major saw the woman he took to be Mrs. Devereux. What did he say? That she was standing at the edge of the Avenue, the other side of the pylons?"

Manson sat on the bank, his legs dangling over the water and gazed towards the pylons. "Yes," he decided, "he could have seen a woman quite easily from here. And he is right in saying that he could not recognise her. It's too far away for that. Well, that is one point for the major."

They resumed their walk in the direction of the flow of the river. A few minutes brought them within reach of the pylons, two tall, square spindled towers that bridged electric power cables across the water to carry the light that now flooded cottages at the pressing of a switch, where once paraffin and a wick had provided the only luminant. Merry saw nothing of the light of progress, but only the ugliness that had destroyed the beauty of the river scenery. He said so.

"But think, Merry," retorted Manson. "Think of the advantages that it brings to these isolated areas. The harnessed power, the . . ."

His voice broke off suddenly. Merry, looking up for the reason, found the scientist staring, incredibly, down at his feet, and followed his gaze. After one glance his eyes stared with the dazed look of a man dealt a sudden blow on the solar plexis.

Bulging out from the river and widening from a narrow neck, was a circle of muddy water. At a rough estimate, Merry calculated, it measured ten feet in diameter and twelve feet in depth from the river bank. A piece of barbed wire guarded the neck, where it joined the Tamar.

Deep indentations of hoofmarks, round the shelving edges showed its purpose plainly enough; it was a drinking pool for cattle; one obviously dug out for the purpose, and set below the water level so that the river might feed it, and keep it supplied with water. The water was still muddy from the wading of cows, now grazing some distance away after their cooling stand in the pond. At the landward extremity, the pond was covered with a surface weed, light green, in contrast to the darker green of the grass in the field.

Manson walked gingerly down to the water edge. Pulling a piece of the weed towards him with a branch, he examined it. He answered Merry's glance of inquiry with a nod. The sergeant, feeling in an inside pocket of his coat, produced an envelope, and squeezing the weed free of surplus moisture, he slipped it inside, replacing the envelope in his pocket.

"Footsteps?" he asked, as the two men stared at the pool.

"I should say not a chance, Merry," was the scientist's reply. "The place has been trodden down by cattle. We'll have to look, of course; but it's a forlorn hope."

The pessimistic view of the scientist was justified. Though the two men scanned, on hands and knees, the circumference of the pool, no print of human feet, identifiable as such, could be found. The only possible footstep visible was on the dried mud, along one side of the neck of the pool, and it had been so washed by the lapping water, flowing through the neck, as to be useless for any purpose of possible identification.

Similar disappointment resulted from the examination of the area surrounding the pool; the ankle-deep grass, on land baked by rainless days, showed no traces of any comings and goings. Manson let his gaze wander over the field and along the river bank. Fifty yards away, the Avenue began its shadowed length of the water. The scientist measured the distance with his eyes. "The major saw a woman at the entrance to the Avenue," he said. "At that distance the shortening of vision might easily be some forty or fifty yards. That would bring the real position of the woman to, roughly, level with this pool. Do you agree?"

Merry nodded. "That would be about right, Harry," he confirmed.

"It doesn't make sense, Merry."

"Why not?"

The scientist threw out his arms. "All open . . . full view of everyone, and everything." He surveyed the scene again, letting his gaze pass from the river, past the pool, and along the direction from which they had lately walked. His eyes stopped at a little cluster of three trees, the lower part of their trunks half hidden by a mass of thick bramble bushes. "I wonder?" he said, and walked towards them.

One glance was sufficient to justify his premonition. There were signs, in plenty, of a struggle. The long grass in the centre showed it; a number of twigs from the lower tree stems were lying where they had fallen, broken off by violent contact with some force or other.

Manson commenced a methodical examination of the scene. It was obvious, however, that the hard ground, covered with long grass, was not likely to provide any evidence beyond that, plain to see, that more than one person had been engaged in violent exertion. The grass was torn, and trodden in a circle of some three yards wide. The two eyed it. Manson bent down and examined the nearest blades.

"Any indication of how long ago?" asked Merry.

Manson nodded. "I think so," he said. "Doctor Johnson, you know, said that one green field was like another green field. There was a lot of ignorance in Doctor Johnson. He took the view that grass is just grass. Robert Gibbings knew better. 'There is no greater competition for existence anywhere than in a meadow,' he wrote. 'Even human footsteps will encourage those grasses which prefer a firm tilth, to the detriment of those which like a looser soil. Hence, the clearly marked line of a footpath where the grasses which thrive happen to be a dark colour.' But not the kind of footsteps we've had here," Manson added.

He was examining the bruised blades through his glass. "You know, Merry," he proceeded, "there's a man named Waldie at Reading University who devotes all his life to grass. No quadruped is a greater connoisseur. He knows every blade and he'll tell you the amount of minerals, carbohydrates, proteins and fats possessed by each. And he'll tell you, too, at what week in the year they start growing and what week they finish growing. And I'm quite sure he could tell us to within an hour just when this bruising took place. I know a little about such matters myself, and I should say the struggle occurred two or three days ago. The blades of grass you notice are beginning to recover from their wounds and are recovering slightly to their upright condition. Now, if anyone had just laid on them, they would have recovered before now and they would not have been broken and bruised."

He pulled aside a low hanging branch of one of the trees and peered through the opening thus caused. In a patch of firm ground, beside one of the bramble bushes the distinct print of a boot lay revealed. That it was there was one of those fortunate chances which sometimes occur in crime detection. There had been no rain for days; everywhere the ground was baked hard, and the chances of footprints were a hundred to one against. But the shade of the bramble bushes had kept the clayey soil sufficiently moist with dew to take an impression. Then the hot, dry atmosphere of the days which had followed, had cemented it firmly, almost as though it had been baked in a kiln.

The print was that of a man's boot. "Size eight or nine," Merry suggested. "And as good an impression as ever I have seen," he added.

Glass in hand, Manson bent over the print. The enlarged vision, represented by the magnification, revealed several peculiarities not immediately obvious to the unaided vision. On the left side of the sole—it was a left boot—a patch had, at some time, been cobbled on. Through the patch a hobnail had been driven, to match a similar nail on the opposite side, and a further row of three round the toe and four at the heel.

"I don't like it, Merry." The scientist's face was very grave.

"Looks very much like a fisherman's brogue," was the sergeant's verdict.

"That is just what I meant."

"We ought to have a cast of it, Harry. What do we do about that?"

For reply the scientist emptied an inside jacket pocket of a collection of letters and papers. He selected a letter on foolscap paper and, opening it out, placed it carefully over the footprint. With a pencil, he marked, roughly, the outline. Then, with a pair of pocket scissors he cut out the pattern. Carefully shaving the edges, a little at a time, he gradually fitted the pattern into the print until it lay, closely, in the impression. Satisfied of its accuracy, Doctor Manson, using his wallet as a support, meticulously drew in the print's peculiarities, exactly as they appeared in the impression, measuring with his pocket calipers the size of the patch, and the positions of the hobnails.

"We will have to have a cast, if possible, Merry," he said. "But anything may happen before we can get back here with the plaster. A cow may wander in and put her foot on it . . ."

"Or the owner may come along and obliterate it."

"Quite. We have now, at least, something which can, quite feasibly help us if the worst happens. Meanwhile, we'll break off a few branches and cover the print over. It may guard it against chance destruction. Then, I think, we had better hurry to the hotel and back here with the plaster."

The plan was, however, to be delayed by a further, and equally unexpected, discovery. As Merry turned away, a glint of light from the tangled grass at the edge of the bushes caught his eye. He bent down and picked up a fragment of glass. He was about to throw it away again, when the thinness of the glass took his attention. Closer examination caused him to drop hurriedly to his knees. Parting the grass circumspectly, he retrieved a second piece, about the size of a sixpence. Manson, who had turned away and commenced the walk back to the hotel, turned at his Sergeant's whistle. A beckoning wave of a hand caused him to retrace his steps. One look at the fragments of glass was sufficient to tell him the importance of the sergeant's discovery. "Spectacle glass, of course," he said. "We'll have to search the spot thoroughly, Merry. This may put a noose round somebody's neck."

Together, the men combed the copse as though with a toothcomb, parting carefully each blade of grass from the next and peering beneath it. It was nearly an hour before they were satisfied that no further recoverable particle remained to be salvaged. There were then about twenty pieces of glass in the envelope into which they had been dropped as they were recovered, some of the pieces little more than splinters. Manson regarded them in the mass. "I should say we have nearly enough for a pair of spectacles, Merry," he announced. "Certainly, there will be enough for the grinding of them to be decided with certainty."

The sergeant stood up, and dusted his trouser knees. "This," he said, "looks as if we are getting somewhere at last. A fisherman's brogue print and a pair of spectacles."

"Not necessarily," interrupted Manson. "We haven't proved they are brogue prints."

"No. But it's most likely, is it not?"

"Yes, I think from the place and the circumstance we might concede that point," the scientist agreed. "And if we find a fisherman who is minus a pair of glasses, we shall have to put him under very vigilant surveillance."

They began the walk back to the road which had been interrupted by Merry's discovery. The sergeant shuffled uncomfortably for some moments. Then he spoke his thoughts:

"Emmett told me that he had lost his spectacles, Harry," he said, slowly.

"Yes . . . I know, Jim."

The pair walked on in silence.

CHAPTER XV
THE COFFIN MAKER

SUPERINTENDENT BURNS looked up as Sergeant Barrett entered his room and announced his presence with a cough. "What is it, Sergeant?" he asked. "I'm busy."

"Sorry, sir, but there's a man in the outside office who insists on seeing you, personally. Says he knows something about the colonel. He won't tell us anything."

"Who is he, Sergeant?"

"Name of Cobley, sir. He's a labourer on Tremorres's farm." The superintendent put down his pen and pushed back the paper on which he had been working. "All right, Barrett, show him in. And you had better come in yourself, and bring a notebook. Take down anything he says—if he says anything worth taking down."

"Very good, sir."

He left the room and returned with a stockily-built man, dressed obviously in his Sunday best for the occasion of his visit. "Mr. Cobley," the sergeant announced.

"Mornin' to 'ee," said Cobley.

"Good morning, Mr. Cobley." The superintendent waved him to a chair. "The sergeant here says you have something to tell us about Colonel Donoughmore's drowning. Is that right?"

Cobley scratched his head. "Well, zur, I doan't be zure about it," he said. "Policeman Lewis, now, he said ef be anyone saw a woman on the river on day Colonel was drowned, he was to tell 'ee." He waited anxiously for confirmation.

"That's quite right, Cobley," the superintendent agreed. "Did you see a woman there?"

"Ay. A shouldn't a cum ef a hadn't."

"Where did you see her?"

"Wud 'ee know Varmer Tremorres's big field of oats down theer by 'lectric wires?"

Burns nodded.

"I was workin' at top of field when I see her runnin's down the path to road."

"What time was this?"

"It'ud be about one o'clock. A was a'goin' to have some dinner."

"Did you recognise her?"

"Ay, I reckoned it were the Trepol girl."

The superintendent started as though he had been stung. "Ann Trepol!" he ejaculated.

"Ay, that were her."

For some seconds the two officers stared at the visitor. Whoever they had expected the man to identify, it certainly wasn't Ann Trepol. They had hoped that he would have given them a description of, say, Mrs. Devereux; the superintendent still cast doubtful eyes on the Tavistock alibi. But Ann Trepol. . . . !

The superintendent leaned forward and spoke quietly, but gravely, to Cobley. "That is a very serious statement, Cobley," he said, warningly. "Are you quite sure that it was Ann Trepol whom you saw?"

"Ay, A reckoned as how it were her, cos why? Cos I saw Master Trepol no longer'n two more minutes."

"What!" The superintendent stared incredulously as he spoke after this second shock. "Willie Trepol?"

"That's what a said."

"And what was Mr. Trepol doing when you saw him, Mr. Cobley?"

"Goan down path arter his girl, as a works it out."

Sergeant Barrett leaned across to the superintendent and spoke quietly. Burns nodded in reply and then addressed himself again to Cobley. "Now, Mr. Cobley, that field is a pretty big field, isn't it? And you would be a pretty good way from the path. Are you sure that it was Mr. Trepol you saw there?" He held up his hand as the man began to speak. "Now, think carefully. Anybody might be misled. Why, I went across the market place only yesterday evening to speak to a man I thought I knew. He looked like my friend, but when I got to him I saw that he was a perfect stranger. There I was, thinking of my friend, and was led to be sure that I saw him. Now, think carefully and decide if you feel sure about it."

Cobley shifted uncomfortably in his chair. "Well, zur," he said, "it be true enough I never seed into'm faces. But a ses to meself, that be old Trepol and his darter. And when Policeman Lewis says as how anybody who so be saw a woman on river must come aloan' an tell 'ee, ah came."

"That is so, Mr. Cobley. You did right. Only, you see, we have to be quite sure that it was Mr. Trepol and Ann you saw. Shall we say that you saw two people there, who were a long way off, but who you took to be Mr. Trepol and his daughter? Will that do?"

"Sure sartin, zur."

"All right. Then Sergeant Barrett will write down what you have said and read it over to you. Then you can sign it. You had better give Mr. Cobley a sovereign for his expenses and a drink, Sergeant."

"Very good, sir."

"And ask Inspector Penryn to come in, will you?"

Mr. Cobley, taking his sovereign, hurried round to the Tremarden Arms to spend it. Unfortunately, in his eyes, the drinking had one drawback—he could not tell his story of the river bank. The sergeant had made that very clear. "Only the Super, and you and I know of it, Cobley," he said. "If I hear it from anywhere else we'll know you have been talking, and then—well, we've got some pretty bad cells here," he added darkly, and quite illegally! So Cobley drank with lips as sealed as those of Prime Minister Baldwin! And the liquor did not taste so good as he had hoped it would have done!

In the room at the police station which Cobley had vacated, the superintendent looked inquiringly at Inspector Penryn. "What do you make of it, Penryn?" he asked.

"Hanged if I know, sir. Funnily enough, I asked Ann Trepol when I saw her, if she had been down at the river bank that day. She denied it." The inspector broke off suddenly. "Damn it," he said. "What's that, Penryn?"

"Come to think of it, she seemed remarkably keen on denying it. I remember how I noted, curiously, her vehemence. Just struck me at the time as being curious; as though she thought we might tell the story to her father. But now . . ."

"I think we had better have her here, Penryn. Send somebody for her. And we'd better have Trepol as well. Only, don't let them see each other."

Ann Trepol came into the room scowling, and swinging her hat in one hand. "What do you want me here for?" she demanded.

Burns ignored the scowl, returning a pleasant smile. "We shall not keep you very long, Ann, if you are a good girl," he said. "But there is something I want you to tell me. You remember that the inspector here saw you at your home and you showed him some shares?"

A nod from the girl.

"You told the inspector, Ann, that you had not been to the river bank that day. Now, was that true?"

"Of course it was true."

"Now, think, Ann. There is no reason whatever why you should not have gone to the river if you wanted. You've been there often enough before. And nobody suggests that you were catching Franky Baker's fish. But somebody has said they thought they saw you there round about one o'clock. Now, tell me, Anne—and it won't go any further, if that is what you are afraid of—were you there at all, at any time that morning or afternoon?"

"No, I wasn't. I've said so, and I'll say it again. I tell you I wasn't there." The girl flew into a passion. "And I'm not staying here any longer."

"All right. We don't want to keep you. Show Ann out, Inspector—through my private door."

"Well, that's that," he commented as Penryn returned. "Is Trepol here? Good. We'll see what HE has to say."

He said little!

"Good morning, Willie," the superintendent greeted him.

"Mornin', Super." The voice came in glum and melancholy tones. Long years as an undertaker had given Willie Trepol a countenance and voice remarkably appropriate to his solemn calling. "The sergeant said you wanted to see me. What service can I do ye?"

"We don't quite know, Willie. But we are hoping that you may be able to help us—over the colonel's death, you know. Now, we are trying to find the time he died. That means we want to find the latest time he was seen. We understand that you were down by the river that morning, about one o'clock. Did you see the colonel anywhere around?"

"Me?" the voice came up as from the bottomless pit. "I didn't see the colonel at all. I was never down by the river to see him. Who says I was there?"

"Nobody says so, definitely, Willie. But a farm worker down there says he *thought* he saw you somewhere by the Pylons at one o'clock, lunch-time, that day. No reason why you shouldn't be there, of course. You've done a bit of fishing there in your time. We thought you might have seen the colonel. If you had that would have helped us to fix a time when we knew the colonel to be alive."

"Gentlemen, I had no wish at all to see the colonel. And I saw nothing of him, except in the morning, about ten o'clock, or somewheres about that, when I saw him outside the Tremarden Arms. He'd got his fishing stuff with him."

"And you didn't see him again?"

"I didn't."

"Then that's all there is to it, Willie."

"They be saying in the town that he were killed, Super. Would that be right?"

Trepol, the two men thought, waited the answer in an attitude almost of strain. It communicated to the feeling that it was anxiety altogether out of keeping with the fact that he had never been associated with the colonel, not even on speaking terms.

"Quite true, I'm afraid, Willie," the superintendent replied. He eyed the undertaker with a glint in his eyes. "Are you carrying out your promise?" he asked.

"Promise?" Trepol looked puzzled. "What promise would that be?"

"Come, Willie! Didn't you say, in the Tremarden Arms, that if the gentlemen made it a funeral for the colonel you'd give him a coffin free?" The superintendent chuckled. "It's certain sure a funeral."

Trepol's face grew even more elongated and mournful. "It don't always do, Super, to take what a man says in a bar as what he means like. The colonel was an outlander and I didn't like'n anyhows."

He paused, and an expression that might have been mistaken for a smile flickered over his face. "I'm fitting him with a coffin, anyways," he went on. "Twenty pounds it'll be. An' it's a good strong coffin," he added, half under his breath.

"Well, Willie, so far as I know, you've always given satisfaction that way," the superintendent said. "I've never heard of a customer complaining."

There was no answering smile from the undertaker at the joke. He turned round with a "good morning" and left the room.

"That settles it, Penryn. Cobley has got a sovereign out of us, the rascal."

"Looks that way, sir."

"I hope he drinks himself sick."

"He won't, sir. Not on a sovereign, he won't! Not old Tom Cobley!"

CHAPTER XVI
Ill Fittings

WHILE THE superintendent and Inspector Penryn had been engaged on the problem of elucidating the story of Cobley, Doctor Manson and Sergeant Merry were turning their attention to a more material investigation, though, perhaps, not less hypothetical. The sergeant, after a preliminary discussion with the scientist, had returned by police car to the main road turning at which he and Manson had left the bus. From there he had walked, carrying a bag containing Plaster of Paris, a bowl, and a table spoon. His task was to obtain a plaster cast of the bootprint beneath the bramble bushes.

Meanwhile, Doctor Manson, had visited a stationer's shop. There he had purchased a large double sheet of blotting paper, a small tube of colourless cement, of the type used for repairing glass and china, and a box of drawing pins. Back in his room in the Tremarden Arms he fastened the blotting paper down to his table with the drawing pins, and placed the tube of cement alongside.

Then, on to the virgin-white surface of the blotting paper he carefully shook out from an envelope the pieces of spectacle glass which he and the sergeant had salvaged from the trodden grass by the river side. Sitting at the table, the scientist began the task that was to take him nearly two hours to complete. With infinite patience he commenced to sort out the pieces into their place in the murder jigsaw. The task, at the outset, seemed an impossible one. A number of the pieces of glass were hardly more than an eighth of an inch across. But Dr. Manson was not the man to shirk the seemingly impossible, so long as there was any chance, even the slimmest, of success.

Piece by piece, he sorted out the fragments, fitting them together. Often he had to call into use an optician's eyepiece in order to ensure that the breaks in the two slivvers he had placed together really made one. Twice he was placed in a quandary by pieces which seemed to fit perfectly on to two, or more, other fragments.

Since it was hardly likely from the concavity of the lenses that both eyes would have exactly the same sight correction, it was, the scientist knew, of the utmost importance that there should be no mistake in fitting the pieces if the final result was to prove, or disprove, any theory to which they might lead him.

At last all the particles had been placed in two arrangements, one on each side of the scientist; and he then began the delicate task of fixing them into two concerted wholes, or as near two concerted wholes as they would go. With a sharpened match-stick, he applied to the edges of each segment a thin coating of cement, fitting, one at a time, the pieces corresponding to the breaking-line. It was a task of the utmost delicacy and patience, requiring that the cement joining one piece should be hardened and set before any attempt was made to add a further piece. The task completed at last, Dr. Manson sat back and looked at the result with no little satisfaction. It showed the two elliptical lenses, plainly identifiable as left and right eyeglasses.

When he was satisfied that the cement had hardened sufficiently to allow the lenses to be carefully lifted, he turned them over, so that the concave surface faced upwards. Before he had time to continue his inspection, the door opened and Merry entered the room. He caught the Doctor's look of inquiry, and answered it. "Just like we left it, Harry. It makes a good cast. Not perfect, mind you; but good enough for identification, I think." He produced the cast from his bag and handed it across. Manson, turning it over in his hands glanced with lively interest at the plainly marked patch and the embossed, projecting, hobnails. "I agree, Jim," he commented, and placed the cast in a cupboard.

"Anything from the glass, Harry?" the sergeant asked.

Manson nodded towards the table, and Merry crossed over and looked down at the reconstructed lenses. "And what do they tell?" he asked. "Any link with Emmett?"

Manson gave a non-committal "Possibly. The age is all right," he said. "As to the rest I do not know as yet."

"The age all right? How come?"

"Well, Jim, the answer is easy. There are four general conditions of eyesight which require spectacles. There is myopia, or near sight, which requires the weakest concave lenses. Then, there is hypermetropia, or long distance, and for this the strongest convex is needed. Thirdly, there is presbyopia, or old sight, which usually becomes manifest after the age of forty-five or fifty. Now these lenses are certainly in the latter class. And Emmett is getting towards the fifties, isn't he?"

"He is. And what do we now do with them?" pointing to the lenses.

For reply the scientist picked up the telephone receiver and asked the hotel switchboard for Baker. "Is there a good occulist in the place, Franky?" he asked. "Or an eye surgeon?"

"Sure there is, Doctor. Merryweather, in the Market Square, is a good man; and then there is Mr. Welles, in the corner house on the Okehampton Road. He was an eye-surgeon in Harley Street until he retired."

"Good. He'll do. Can we get him on the phone? Right, I'll hang on."

"This is a piece of luck, Jim. We'll ha . . . Hallo, is that Mr. Welles? . . . This is Chief Detective Inspector Manson, of Scotland Yard, Mr. Welles . . . What's that? . . . Yes . . . Well, that's extraordinary. Of course I remember you, now. Drop in at the Tremarden Arms to-night, and renew the acquaintance. Meanwhile, can you help me out of a difficulty? I have a pair of spectacle lenses here, reconstructed from smashed pieces. If I send them round, can you give me the prescription to which they are ground? You can? That is excellent. I'll send them at once. And I'll expect to see you here to-night. Until then . . ."

"Here you are, Merry. Pack them into this box and drop round with them. Ask him if he would be kind enough to telephone me the prescription as soon as possible."

The two men left the room—Merry on his errand, and Dr. Manson for a cocktail in the lounge of the Tremarden Arms. Fred Emmett was already imbibing one, and Manson joined him at the table.

"Been fishing, Emmett?" he asked.

"Only for an hour or two, Doctor. There wasn't much doing."

"No. Sport seems to have dropped a bit. No hatch of fly lately, I'm told. Who's that coming in now? Haven't seen him before."

Emmett looked up towards the hotel entrance, felt in his pocket and produced a spectacle case. Manson eyed it. "Found your glasses, then? Didn't Merry tell me that you had lost them?"

"Yes. I wired home for my spare pair. Can't see a rise quickly enough without them, you know."

"Let's have a look at them, old chap. Perhaps I can tell you what is wrong with your eyes."

Emmett passed the glasses over, and Manson gave them a passing glance. It was enough. They are practically flat, but showing a slight magnification. There was hardly a sign of concaveness. "Just a little strain in the sight, that's all, Emmett," Manson said, and handed them back.

Merry, returning, joined his chief as Emmett went upstairs to wash before the meal.

"Well?" asked Manson.

"He'll let you know in about half an hour, Harry."

"He won't lead us to Emmett, Jim, anyhow. Emmett is wearing a spare pair of glasses, and they certainly do not compare in any degree with the ones we have."

It was half-way through the meal when the eye specialist's reply was brought to the Doctor. He opened the envelope, brought by a waiter, and the prescription, on the sheet of notepaper, fluttered out. It read:

<table>
<tr><td>RIGHT EYE</td><td>LEFT EYE</td></tr>
<tr><td>+1.00</td><td>+1.25 +0.75/100.</td></tr>
</table>

Prescribed for a patient with old sight but whose long
sight would seem to be normal. Close sight rather bad.

"As I thought," commented Manson, passing the note over to Merry.

The result of his hours of labour over the broken glasses afforded Doctor Manson no little satisfaction. He realised that it should now be a matter of no difficulty to track down the owner of the smashed spectacles, and in that way to turn the evidence and the signs of struggle in the copse to good effect. The experiment was an example of the value of the scientist and his assistant, to crime detection. Manson had, at the beginning of his studies at the university years ago, taken up science as a hobby. He had been blessed with a sufficiency of income to make him independent of the necessity to earn a living. Consequently he had become a dilettante in science; that is to say, he had not been confined to the specialisation in any particular branch which, in science particularly, the need for making a livelihood demands. So Manson had ranged throughout the whole field, gathering knowledge here and there, strange knowledge sometimes, which seemed hardly likely to be of any material use at the time it was assimilated. Nevertheless, he forgot nothing he had read; it was pigeonholed in his brain for recall when, if ever, it was wanted.

The diverseness of his knowledge was remarkable. He could tell a painter exactly what colours he had mixed to obtain an effect in a picture and he proportioned the order in which he had mixed them. He could tell whether a piece of handwriting had come from a right or left handed person. Give him a spectroscope and he would tell at once the names of the minerals which chanced to be in the particular part of the moon, or sun, at which the apparatus was pointing; or a parcel of bones, and he would sort them, unhesitatingly into their positions in the body, whether it be human or animal. Given a speck of blood, he could identify its late owner, be he man or a bird or an animal, and in the case of human blood he could "group" it. His geology was equally expert; a crystal—he could identify whether it be sand, silicate, sugar, salt or anything else; and his knowledge of microscopical investigation was unique.

The result of all this perambulatory knowledge was that small things turning up during investigation, which the ordinary man-hunter would cast aside as of no importance, assumed in Doctor Manson's mind an instinctive query, sometimes because it was so out of place as to be *outré*, such as, for instance, a few grains of silicates in the pockets of a man who worked in the West End of London. Or an ear of oats lying on a path, when Manson, whose eyes took everything in as he journeyed, knew that no oats were growing in the neighbourhood. It was this scholarship in science that had at once forced upon Doctor Manson the realisation that the glass was spectacle glass, and that, could it be recovered in sufficient quantity, it could be identified with the wearer. He was now anxious to test the latter theory.

Tremarden woke to life again at two o'clock after its luncheon siesta. Shop blinds went up, doors opened, and shopkeepers stood outside exchanging confidences with the man at the shop next door. Seeing the resurrection, Doctor Manson sallied forth, a small parcel in one hand. Skirting the hotel corner, he made a beeline for a shop on the other side of the Market Place and asked to see the manager. To that executive he disclosed his official position, at the same time producing from his parcel the boot-cast from the riverside. "I want to know," he said, "if you can identify the boot of which this is an impression. It has lately been repaired, as you will see, and the patch on the left side should be easy to remember. It might be, and probably is, a fishing brogue."

The manager eyed the cast intently. "Yes, it should be remembered," he agreed, "but I do not think it was done by us. However, if you will wait a few minutes I will take it over to the repair shop. They will know if we did the repair."

The quest proved abortive. "Quite definitely we did not do it," the manager reported. Thanking him for his trouble, Manson proceeded to the second of the addresses on his list, repeating his request to the shopkeeper. Again he was unsuccessful, and he had reached the sixth repairer without any satisfactory result. This man, however, eyed the cast with interest. "Somehow, sir, I don't think it would be a fishing brogue," he said. "We should not put hobnails in the heel, or for that matter in anywhere else, of a fishing brogue since, in wading, if the wearer trod unexpectedly forward on a piece of granite sloping away, the nails would send his feet sliding from underneath him, and throw him off his balance and into the water. Would the wearer be a Tremarden man?" he asked.

"That is what I want to know." Manson smiled at the inquiry. "All I can say is that the boot was being worn in Tremarden three days ago."

"Well, I assure you, the owner did not have it patched or nailed here, sir."

And with that the scientist had to be content. "You will have to get a constable or somebody to carry it round the locality, into the villages and see if the patching was done there," he told Superintendent Burns later.

When he came to the spectacles, however, Manson had rapid and satisfactory results. There were only two firms in the town who tested eyesight and corrected it with glasses. And it was at the first of them that he found the owner of the damaged spectacles. Once again explaining his official position, he passed the prescription over to the manager of the establishment, at the same time showing him the reconstructed lenses.

"That's a clever piece of reconstruction, if I may say so, sir," was the comment. He consulted a drawer of filed cards and turned back to the scientist. "Yes, we tested the eyes and made a pair of glasses to that prescription," he said. "As a matter of fact, we are just completing a new pair to the prescription for the same customer."

Manson felt the glow of the experimentist at the successful end to his search. "And the customer is . . . whom?" he asked.

The manager hesitated. "I am not sure that I am at liberty to give the name of a customer," he said. "My principals would not, I think, view such a practice as desirable."

Manson eyed him sharply. "I am not making idle inquiries," was his reply. "I am asking for the name of the person for whom these glasses were made, and I am doing so in the interests of justice. There is no suggestion, at the moment, that we have anything against this person, but the presence of the fragments of glass which I have shown you in their reconstructed form, is a stumbling block to investigations we are pursuing. When we get that obstacle out of the way we shall be able to proceed. The glass may, and most likely was, lying where it was found by pure accident. We want to prove whether that is so, or not. The only way it can be proved is by asking the person to whom the glasses originally belonged. I could, of course, call on you in the name of the law for the name, but I don't want to expose you to that."

The manager conceded the point with, however, no great show of enthusiasm. "The spectacles," he said, "were made to the order of a Mr. William Trepol, of this town."

"You mean the joiner and undertaker?"

"I mean Mr. Trepol, the undertaker," the manager agreed.

"I suppose Mr. Trepol is having new lenses fitted into the old frames?"

"That is so."

"And the frames are having to be straightened slightly?"

"Yes."

It was not until he carried this piece of news to Inspector Burns that Doctor Manson heard of the denials of Trepol and Ann Trepol that they had been on the riverside on the day of the colonel's death. The notes of the interviews made by Sergeant Barrett were read over to him; and the superintendent waited anxiously for his views.

"I am afraid that he, at any rate, is lying, Burns," was the scientist's verdict. "I don't know about Ann; she might not have been there. But Trepol was certainly at the spot."

"Might not the glasses have been there for several days, Doctor? I mean to say, they *could* have been dropped previously, could they not?"

Manson shook his head. "Not a chance, Burns. Merry saw the glint of the first of the pieces of glass we retrieved on top of the trodden grass. They were, in fact, at the spot where the bruising of the undergrowth started. If the glass had been broken or dropped there previously, the struggle, which the signs show took place, would have trodden the fragments of lenses into the earth, not to mention the fact that they would have been ground into tiny particles."

"That seems definitely to settle it then, Doctor. I suppose we had better get Trepol back again."

The undertaker, glumly gruff, and this time also a little short-tempered, repeated his denials. "I've told you already, Superintendent, I wasn't down on the river that day. I had no call to go down."

"Where would you have been about one o'clock, dinner time, Willie?" the superintendent asked.

"In my shop, planing some boards."

Doctor Manson took up the questioning. "Mr. Trepol, you suffer with your eyes, do you not?" he asked. "I mean that, while you can see very well at a distance, you cannot see so well close to?"

"I wear my spectacles, sir?" was the reply.

Manson took a wallet from a pocket and, extracting a card passed it over to the man. "Read me what it says on there, Mr. Trepol," he asked.

The undertaker peered at the card, his eyes only a few inches away. "Try your glasses," Manson suggested.

"I haven't brought them with me."

"In point of fact, Mr. Trepol, you have broken them, have you not? And you are having a new pair made up in this town?"

"What if I am? It isn't against the law to break a pair of spectacles, is it?"

"How did you break your spectacles, and where?" Manson's voice became sharper and more imperative in tone.

"Dropped 'em in the workshop."

The scientist produced a box from his pocket. Opening it, he lifted out, one at a time, the lenses he had reconstructed from the broken pieces. He placed them on the table side by side. "Here are your glasses, Trepol," he said. "My Sergeant and I picked up the pieces from under those trees by the pylons down on the river bank, near the path along which your daughter and you were seen at one o'clock on the day that Colonel Donoughmore died. I say that they dropped from the waistcoat pocket, where you kept them for convenience, during a struggle which you had with Colonel Donoughmore in that copse. What have you to say to that?"

He saw the man's face pale, and the look of fear which came into his eyes. The man himself sat silent . . . thinking.

"WERE you down on the river bank that day, Trepol?" The scientist asked the question insistently. But it was two long and painful minutes before the man spoke. Then:

"Ay, I suppose it will have to come out now," he said. The hand he raised to wipe away beads of perspiration from his forehead trembled. "Well, I was there, and I saw the colonel. Damn him," he added in an outburst of fury. "I was hoping to keep it quiet for my girl's sake. . . ."

"She was there too, was she?" from the superintendent.

"She was. I told her I'd beat the hide off'n her if she said a word about her or me being there."

"How did you come to be there, the two of you?"

"You'll have heard, Super, that my girl had been seen with the colonel a night or two. I gave her a hiding when I found out, and I promised her another for every time I heard of her being with him. He wasn't up to any good with Ann, him being a rich man and one of the gentry, as it were. Then, one day, when I was a' driving a coffin along the top road I saw her and the colonel across the fields, talking by the gorge. So I give her another hiding when I got her home.

"When I goes for dinner at twelve o'clock on day the colonel died, there was nothing ready, and Jim Reddy said he had seen Ann on her bicycle going down t'wards Tremorres's farm. I guessed as how she was going to the colonel, cause I'd seen him setting out that way to fish at ten o'clock. So I goes down there, too. When I gets to the path over the fields I sees Ann's bicycle in the hedge."

"What time was that?" asked Manson.

"As near as I can say about half-past twelve. Soon as I got to the end of the path I see's Ann's frock through a break in the bramble bushes. I goes in the copse and there she was with him. I tells her to get off home and I'll settle with the colonel. Ann says she'll go when she pleases, so I fetches her a cut across the ear, and pushes her out of the copse. Then I tells the colonel what I has to say about his leading my girl wrong ways."

"Did you hit him, Trepol?"

"Ay, I hit him all right. He called me a blasted something I didn't know, and tried to push me out of his way. I says as how I wasn't going till I'd had it out with him, and ef so be I caught him with my girl again, I'd call in the police agen him. He got ravin' mad then, and came at me with his salmon priest. He might'a killed me, way he was aiming, so I hit him with my fist and knocked him down."

"Hit him on the point of the jaw, didn't you?" asked Manson.

Trepol looked surprised. "Ay, like I used to knock 'em out in the ring, as the Super here well knows. But how did you know I hit him on the point?"

Manson smiled. "Never mind that, Trepol," he said. "What happened then?"

"Well, he gets up, and I says there'll be a few more like it if he speaks to my girl again, and he went off without saying anything."

The man ceased talking. He wiped his brow with his hand-kerchief. Superintendent Burns moved his chair forward and looked him in the face. "You're quite sure, Trepol, that he *DID* walk away?" he asked. "He didn't by any chance, stay down, I suppose?"

"He didn't. I said he got up."

"And you didn't push him into the river?"

Trepol dropped his head in his hands, but not before both men had seen the look of fear in his eyes again. They thought he was about to faint. He recovered in a few seconds, however, and looked up. "If so be you mean did I kill the man, Super, you'll know that you haven't any right to be saying that. You've known me years enough to be sure that I wouldn't kill anybody."

"What did you do when the colonel walked away?" asked Manson. His question was directed as much to side-tracking the superintendent as to bringing an answer.

"I just turned round and went home," was the reply.

"How soon would that be after Miss Trepol left?"

"No more'n two or three minutes."

"And you got back to Tremarden, what time?"

"It would be, near as I can say, just afore half-past one."

"Could you prove that, if you had to?"

"Ay. I was talking to Mr. Westlake about a cupboard he wanted putting up in his kitchen and he said it were one-thirty and he'd come back after he had had his lunch."

The scientist looked across at the superintendent. Burns shook his head, and rose. "All right, Trepol," he said. "It's a pity you didn't tell the truth when you were first asked. You would have saved us a lot of trouble. You can go, now."

Trepol walked slowly towards the door. He had opened it when Manson halted him. "Did you by any chance see anyone else while you were down there; either on the river bank or the path?" he asked. "No, sir. I saw nobody."

"Did you pass anybody on the road at all?"

"No. Not a soul."

"You are sure of that?"

"Ay," and he went out, shutting the door behind him. Superintendent Burns stared at the door and then at the scientist. "That looks like the man we want, Doctor," he said. "I'd never have thought of Trepol."

Doctor Manson returned the look. "Neither would I," he said, with an enigmatical smile.

CHAPTER XVII
SHUFFLING THE PIECES

THE CHIEF CONSTABLE slipped a monocle into his right eye, and through it surveyed the group sitting in his room. On his right, Inspector Penryn, wore an air of despondency as he gazed at a collection of notes which he had compiled on sheets of official foolscap paper, fastened together with a pin. Next to him, Sergeant Merry toyed with a pocket magnifying glass with no expression at all—Merry, we mean—not the glass! Superintendent Burns's gaze rested hopefully, not to say optimistically, on the figure of Doctor Manson. The scientist was lying back in an armchair, his eyes fixed on something nobody else could see in the darkest corner of the room, his restless finger-tips tapping one against the other. His was the only countenance to register complete repose.

It was the first full-dress debate on the colonel's death since the investigations had got into full swing. "I've called the conference," the Chief Constable said, "because Doctor Manson wants a complete picture of the inquiries as far as they have got. So far he has had only extracts from the various officers concerned."

"And, also, I want to point out various things I have discovered so that we can see how they fit in, in relation to the other features of the case," interposed Doctor Manson.

Sir William conveyed, with a wave of a hand, his agreement. "Would you, then, like to start the discussion, Doctor?" he suggested.

"I think we will start with the facts, first, Sir William." Manson was blandly emphatic. "It is always better to have the facts as a basis. There is only one fact, one real fact, and that is the spot where Colonel Donoughmore met his death. You will remember that, at the last talk we had, I said that the colonel did not fall in the river where we were led to suppose he did. And I gave you my reasons why."

Heads nodded in agreement.

"Superintendent Burns then asked me: 'If the colonel didn't fall in there, where *DID* he fall in?' And I said that I did not know—then. Well, I know now." He paused—and Merry chuckled. He liked these dramatic pauses of the Doctor before the thunderbolt was launched. The Chief Constable broke the silence.

"Well, Doctor, where *did* he fall in?"

Manson spoke slowly and with emphatic articulation.

"Colonel Donoughmore was killed a few yards away from the pylons crossing the river. He was knocked on the head, and he either fell, or was thrown, in the cattle drinking pool fed by the river at that spot. Nothing is more certain in fact than that. You will want proof? Well, listen."

The scientist leaned forward and detailed the points by which he had arrived at his conclusions, enumerating them one by one on his fingers.

(They included the clues given in Chapter IX, which the reader, if he has not already elucidated them, is again invited to do so, in the knowledge of the subsequent investigations.)

"That, so far, is the only fact we possess," Manson went on. "How the body came to be in the round pool we do not know, though I can surmise several methods. With them, at the moment, however, we are not concerned. What we want to discuss is the person who had a motive . . ."

"And the opportunity?" interrupted the Chief Constable.

"Let us stick to the motive, Sir William. Logical reasoning can take only one step at a time. Motive, after all, is the first step in murder. If the motive is strong enough, the opportunity can be made. Now, who of our obvious suspects had a motive?"

"All of them. Every man jack of 'em had a motive," Superintendent Burns snorted. "Each one of the six."

"The six being?" inquired Sir William.

"Emmett, Sir Edward, Mrs. Devereux, the major, Trepol, and the girl."

The Chief Constable protested. "Five I'll grant you, Burns. But I can't see any motive in the case of Ann. The colonel was her friend. He had been exceedingly kind to her, and generous as well. She's *LOST* something by his death. Where is her motive? What do you say to that, Doctor?"

"I agree with you so far as we have any evidence at present, Sir William—subject, of course, to anything we may find out in the future."

"That cuts it down to five, then. Now, let us look at the five. Take the major. How strong is his motive. What do you say to that, Inspector?"

Inspector Penryn considered his verdict. "I can hardly imagine a stronger motive, sir," he said. "The major had lost nearly everything he had, except his pension. His home—even—and his parents had had that home, and he had been born there. The shock of the loss of his home and fortune killed his wife, and now, homeless, he is living in a hotel. Also, he had told Baker that he would send the colonel the same way as his wife some time. Now, in view of that, Major Smithers, as I see it, had an extraordinarily strong motive."

"Agreed." The Chief Constable looked round the company and received confirming nods.

"There is just one point I would like to raise on that," said Manson. "You remember the peculiarity of the marks made down the bank where we were asked to believe that the colonel fell? You do? Then you will recall that there was an indentation made by a projecting nail in the boot used. Have you, Burns, or you, Inspector, examined the fishing brogues of Major Smithers?"

"Afraid I didn't, Doctor," from Penryn.

"Nor I," admitted the superintendent.

"Well, I did," retorted Manson. "Not only was there no sign of a projecting nail or a missing nail, but Major Smithers wears crêpe-soled brogues—and always has done."

"Well, that's the major." The Chief Constable ticked him off the list. "Now what about Sir Edward Maurice?"

"Not much in the way of motive there that I can see," said the superintendent. "It's true that he was another victim of the share swindle, but Sir Edward is a very wealthy man. He lost less than a tenth of his fortune. I see no motive there for murder."

"His greatest friend was the major," interjected Penryn. "And his greatest friend was ruined. Given what appeared to be a foolproof opportunity, he might avenge his friend."

"True," commented Sir William. "Anything further against Sir Edward?"

There was silence.

"Right. Then we'll take Emmett."

Sergeant Merry broke the silence that followed the Chief Constable's question. "Well, of course, he had a row with the colonel on the water and he DID threaten to throw him in."

"And admitted it in the hotel before we discovered the death," commented Burns.

"That might be viewed as a very good idea in casting away suspicion," put in Doctor Manson, grimly. "Who would expect the man who did it to admit the fact before the corpse was discovered? I am only pointing out snags in *assuming* innocence," he hastened to explain.

"A quarrel over poaching isn't a good enough motive for murder, do you think?" asked Penryn. "Though, of course, as against that, Emmett might have thrown him in during a struggle and the colonel might in that way have been accidentally drowned."

"If the colonel had fallen in where we assumed at first, I should have viewed Emmett with grave suspicion," Superintendent Burns contributed. "The argument might very well have led to blows in the heat of the moment, and the colonel might have gone down into the water. But the evidence of the wound, and the fact that the colonel was not drowned at the spot, removes that possibility."

"On the grounds that the most likely murderer is the one least likely to have done it, I should plumb for Emmett," said Merry, jokingly. "That's the detective story method."

"Now we've got Trepol." The Chief Constable leaned forward. "I don't like Trepol's part in this. He lied right and left about being down on the river. And only the Doctor's damned good work on those lenses threw him down. The motive there is plain; the colonel was messing about with his daughter. And he now admits that he went down to the river to have it out with the colonel. He says, at last, that there was a struggle in the copse place. All the marks were there, as the Doctor says. His glasses were broken there. And the colonel died there."

Superintendent Burns urged agreement with this view. "I feel that there is a very strong case against Trepol," he said. "How do *YOU* feel about it, Doctor?"

Manson surveyed the ceiling for a few moments as if collecting his thoughts. His fingers were beating their invariable tattoo. Then, his eyes dropped and completed a circle of the faces of his companions. Placing his finger-tips together, he conjured his thoughts into words. "Let's take the objections first," he said. "The colonel's death we have placed as between two o'clock and four o'clock. Trepol, according to his statement, saw the colonel about one o'clock. He left Tremarden at twelve-thirty. That makes the times about right. He was back in Tremarden, in his workshop at one-thirty, and produces a Mr. Westlake to prove it. They were discussing cupboards at one-thirty by Trepol's clock. Now I don't pay too much attention to that. Clocks can be put backwards or forwards. There was an excellent example of this in a recent West End play, and it gave clock alibis away for all time very nicely. The point to bear in mind about that is whether Westlake can be sure that Trepol's clock was, in fact, right. It should be easy. He ought to remember whether, when he arrived at lunch, the time was earlier or later than he expected, having regard to the time Trepol had told him it was. But, if the time was correct, then you will have to eliminate Trepol, because there is confirmatory evidence of his absence from the scene at the time of death."

"What evidence?" Sir William asked.

"The wound on the head, which was anterior to the drowning. The wound was inflicted half to three quarters of an hour before the colonel was drowned. *But the bruise on the chin, which Trepol admits having caused, was inflicted at least twenty minutes before the wound on the head. The condition of the two bruises at the post-mortem proves that beyond doubt.* If, therefore, Trepol's fist caused the chin bruise, and Trepol was back in his workshop at one-thirty o'clock, *he could not possibly have caused the other bruise.* Ergo, he could not possibly have killed the colonel."

The scientist paused for comment. The only one came from Sergeant Merry. "There is a further confirmation which the Doctor has, perhaps, overlooked," he suggested.

Manson looked across inquiringly.

"If Trepol was back in his workshop at one-thirty o'clock, and he left two or three minutes after his daughter, then she was not the woman the major says he saw at the end of the Avenue at two o'clock. Ergo, again, Trepol could not have been there at the time of the tragedy. Who WAS the woman?"

"Mrs. Devereux, if you ask me," retorted Superintendent Burns.

"Right!" The Chief Constable wrote the last of the names down on his pad. "We will look now into Mrs. Devereux. Motive, gentlemen, please."

"Unknown," replied Manson. "We have not found a motive. But I have no doubt that there is a possible motive. What do you think about that, Penryn? You know more of Mrs. Devereux than any of us."

"I think there is something fishy about Mrs. Devereux, Doctor," the inspector replied. "She knew the colonel before she came to Tremarden. She must have known him on the day she reached the hotel and saw him. Yet she gave no sign of recognition. Why? They dined at different tables and never so much as a glance passed between them. That is the evidence of the waiter. Again, I ask why?"

Manson eyed the inspector. "One explanation springs to the mind," he said. "She might, I only say might, have given no sign of surprise or recognition *because she knew she would meet the colonel there.*"

The Chief Constable jumped. "Do you mean that it was an arranged meeting?" he asked.

"It might well have been," the scientist retorted. "It seems to me the only possible explanation if they had known each other before."

Penryn nodded his head slowly, as he met Manson's gaze. "In which case, of course, the meeting as strangers might have been arranged. The fact that they knew each other is pretty evident from Ann Trepol's story of their quarrel over something or other. The girl just couldn't have invented that." Penryn consulted his notes. "Here is the passage I mean," he said.

Mrs. Devereux: Don't drive me too far, or I'll have to find a way out.
The colonel: You'll be advised not to, my lady. I'm not such a fool as to leave things so that you could get away with it. It's in black-and-white.

"Find a way out of what?" asked Penryn. "There, to my mind, is the motive."

Manson was thinking. The wrinkles were again creasing the high, broad forehead. "There is one phrase in the colonel's retort that strikes me as curious," he said, after a few moments. "And that is: 'You'll be advised not to, *my lady!*'" He stressed the words. "Now, what did he mean by that? Was it, for instance, a phrase such as the working classes use? Such as: 'You wait till I get you home, my lady,' or 'All right, my fine lady.' Or was it a veiled reference to Mrs. Devereux's approaching marriage to Sir John Shepstone? I would have liked to have heard the tone of voice in which the colonel said it."

"You mean that, if he used the words in the latter sense . . ." The Chief Constable paused.

"That the motive may be associated with Mrs. Devereux's approaching marriage," the scientist completed. "Was the colonel the type of man to use 'my lady' in the working class way?"

"I thought she rather gave herself away when she said she never had liked the colonel," commented Burns. "Her later explanation of the words was a little lame."

"Suppose we agree for a moment that the colonel's 'my lady' *did* have reference to her approaching marriage with Sir John, how do we stand then?" The Chief Constable let his monocled eye rove over the company.

Superintendent Burns took up the point. "Well, sir," he said, "taken in conjunction with the phrase 'Don't drive me too far, or I'll have to find a way out,' might it not be inferred that the colonel had it in his power to prevent her from becoming 'my lady?'"

"It might," Manson agreed. "But I must point out that it is all theory. However, let's proceed with it, for once. What, then, could the colonel hold over her to prevent the marriage? We might as well carry the theorising forward to that extent. Something may emerge which will give us a line on which to work."

"The colonel knew she had a lover." The suggestion came from the Chief Constable.

"She may have been concerned in something shady," put in Merry.

"I don't think the former would count with Sir John," Manson complained. "He knew that she had been married before. The second suggestion is likely, perhaps. Something shady might affect Sir John—particularly if it is concerning money. But I do not see that we can get any further with motive at present," the scientist decided. "We shall have to make inquiries into the woman's life at Mentone and Monte Carlo. She lived there after leaving India, and it was there that she met Sir John. I'll have a word with the Yard's Society man. He will know of a 'regular' at Monte who can spin any gossip there is going. Then, I should point out that we have not yet examined the personal belongings of the colonel in his town flat, or at his bankers. That should help. He said, did he not, that 'it'—whatever 'it' is—is in black-and-white?"

"That's an idea." The Chief Constable frowned. "We ought to have thought of that."

"I did, Sir William." Manson smiled slightly at the idea that so important a point could be overlooked. "The flat is sealed awaiting examination. I propose to look after that part of the case myself."

"Any more ideas?" the Chief Constable looked round. "None? Well, that disposes of the motive end. Now, we come to opportunity. Perhaps we had better take the names in the same order. Emmett is first. Could he have done it, motive omitted."

"I doubt it," declared Penryn. "If the original spot had been the place where the colonel died, I would have said 'yes' to Emmett. He would have been the only person near to the colonel for a couple of miles. But up at the Pylons! How would Emmett get there and back unseen?"

"How did the person who brought the colonel's fishing-rod down from the Pylons to the colonel's beat get there with it unseen?" asked Manson.

"By George! That's true!" The Chief Constable stared. "Might it have been Emmett on the way back to his beat after the murder, Doctor?"

"Not unless he had another pair of brogues, Sir William. Remember the projecting nails."

"That is so. Well, we will assume that Emmett had no motive, so far as is at present known, and no opportunity either, eh?"

Unanimous nods registered agreement.

"Now there is the major. I feel that I should say here that I take a very grave view of the major. We know that he had good cause against the colonel; and he was fishing close to the spot which we now know was the real scene of the death. His beat, as we all know, came almost to the Pylons; in fact, the copse was definitely in the field on his beat. We know that the colonel, Trepol and Trepol's girl were all there at some time. *Smithers says he saw nobody except some woman—he took her to be Mrs. Devereux—at two o'clock. Yet, there seems to have been a procession of people there.* Even a farm labourer saw two of them. Ann Trepol was there somewhere about one o'clock. We have only the major's word that there was a woman there at two o'clock, round about the time that the colonel was killed. And I ought to emphasise the point that if a woman was there at two o'clock *she is a mighty fine alibi for the major.*"

Superintendent Burns ended the silence which followed the Chief Constable's statement of the case against the major. "If I might point out, sir?" he asked.

"Yes?"

"If the major was at the top end of his beat—he'd start at the bottom, being a dry-fly fisherman, and would be half-way up at one o'clock—he would be wading, and for a considerable time would be wading below the height of the bank. It is feasible that he would not see anyone who might be walking about in the field. Eh, Doctor?"

Manson nodded agreement. "I should say probable rather than possible. But I agree that there is strong suspicion attached to Major Smithers. He is the only one of whom we have definite evidence that he was actually near the scene of the murder."

"Now we have Sir Edward Maurice?" the Chief Constable pointed out. "The only motive we have ascribed to him is that the major was his friend. What opportunity had he?"

"He was on the next beat to the major, and could possibly have seen the colonel. On the other hand, he may only have guilty knowledge." Inspector Penryn proceeded to elaborate his thesis: "Suppose the major had confided in him that he had killed the colonel, or suppose that he had come on the scene and actually witnessed the deed. I have no doubt that the colonel having done what he had, Sir Edward would do all that he could to protect his friend. Now, we have no clue to the identity of the person who made the false marks on the bank where the colonel was thought by us to have fallen in the stream. But Sir Edward has told us at the end of his day's fishing he walked back along the river to the farmyard to his car, and did not see the colonel or anybody else. *Might he not have taken the colonel's fishing rod back with him, and have made the bank markings at the same time?* And he could very easily have slipped the colonel's landing net into the hotel lounge umbrella stand. Who better than a fisherman could carry a net into the place. He's *expected* to be seen with a net."

"Again—his brogues have no nails which would fit the marks," pointed out Burns.

The Chief Constable came out of the brown study into which the inspector's ideas had sent him. "That is dashed interesting, Penryn," he said. "Now about the brogues. Suppose he had a spare pair? Ought we to drag the river there for boots which may have been thrown in, Doctor?"

Manson inclined his head. "Yes, Sir William, it should certainly be done. I had not, I must confess, thought of that."

"The only objection I have to the implication of the major and Sir Edward is this:" Merry leaned forward and pointed a finger impressively at the company. "How could either of them have known that the colonel would be up at the copse or even near the Pylons? That was Mrs. Devereux's beat, and for all they knew, Mrs. Devereux was fishing it. If, then, they did not know that the colonel was there alone, so to speak, it seems to me there is no evidence of opportunity against them. The major would hardly be likely to go about murdering people under the eyes of a Mrs. Devereux who might turn up at any moment."

A surprised ejaculation caused the others to turn their glance in the direction of Doctor Manson. He was looking what, in anybody else, might have been called startled. "Something struck you, Doctor?" asked the Chief Constable.

"Yes—and it has struck pretty hard, Sir William," was the reply. He smiled at his waiting colleagues. "I'll speak of it later. Go on, now, to Trepol."

Superintendent Burns put the case for opportunity on the part of the undertaker in a nutshell: "He was there. He quarrelled with the colonel. He hit him. He could have done it, except for one thing."

The superintendent paused and looked at Doctor Manson. "Trepol has an alibi for one-thirty o'clock onwards. The bruise he made on the colonel's chin is an alibi for about half an hour earlier. If the pathological deductions of Doctor Manson and the Home Office expert are correct—and I have no doubt that they are—Trepol was miles away from the scene when the colonel was killed."

"Well and truly spoken, Burns," said Manson. "The same goes for Ann Trepol. Now, we are left, I think, with Mrs. Devereux. Any developments in the testing of her suspicious alibi?"

"Not so far, Doctor." Penryn replied to the query. "I have three of my best plain-clothes men on the job, and they are being helped by the Tavistock police. They are trying to trace her between the times she left the tea rooms at 12.45 after lunch and 4.45, when she came back to tea."

Manson nodded. "It is important because of the very interesting point which Merry raised a few minutes ago. He asked, you remember: 'How would Major Smithers and Sir Edward know that the colonel would be at the copse? For all they knew, Mrs. Devereux was fishing her beat. Now that is a very vital point in the investigations and one which I ought to have seen before now. What Merry said is quite true. But he might very well have added that, for all the colonel *himself* knew, Mrs. Devereux was fishing the beat. How, then, did he come to be at the copse at all? How, indeed, *unless he had been invited to be there*? Now, who would be the person to invite him there, and when he was there to kill him? There are, as I see it, two possibilities, and two only; either someone who knew Mrs. Devereux was not fishing that water, or . . ."

Manson looked, one by one, at the company listening with keen interest to his reasoning.

"... *Or the one and only person to whom whatever happened there would not matter, if proof could be forthcoming that she wasn't there at all! In other words, Mrs. Devereux, who could invite the colonel on to that beat, and to whom, we can logically assume, knowing the things we do, the colonel would respond.*

"This investigation, gentlemen, has now become to my mind, the investigation of Mrs. Devereux's alibi."

CHAPTER XVIII
JULY THE 15TH

DOCTOR MANSON and Sergeant Merry arrived together at the Yard after an all-night journey from Tremarden. A sleeping compartment in the train, with breakfast, had left them refreshed after the journey, and after a chat in the Doctor's laboratory they parted Merry to probe out Mrs. Devereux's life on the Riviera, and Manson, with the aid of Inspector Rawlings, to go through the late Colonel's belongings with the fine comb of the Law.

At Tremarden, at the same hour, Mrs. Devereux had set out with rod and line to fish the very water where, three days before, the colonel had met his death. Seeing her on the river, where he had himself gone to visit the copse in order to have a picture of it in his mind, Superintendent Burns, somewhat aghast, meditated whether any woman could possess the nerve to fish the water where, if the evidence accumulating in her dossier at police headquarters was correct, she had killed a man so recently. He had half a mind to talk the case over with her; but on second thoughts put the temptation aside, lest he might say something which would put the woman on her guard. He was in the difficult position of not knowing exactly what was in the mind of Doctor Manson; and again, anything that either of the two scientists found in London might be negatived by an unwise phrase or remark he might make to Mrs. Devereux in

Tremarden. So, beyond passing the time of day, and wishing her "Good Killing"—he chuckled within himself at the grim humour of the fisherman's greeting—he said nothing.

At Tavistock, Sergeant McRobbie, with a staff of four men, was scouring the town for traces there of the fishing woman on the day of the colonel's death.

On the river, Mrs. Devereux, flicking a wrist, tightened her line, and an unseen force carried it straight upstream for ten yards before she was able to reel slowly in. Into her landing net she guided a three quarters of a pound, speckled trout. Holding it in her left hand she gave it a sharp blow at the junction of head and neck with her "priest," and it lay still and limp. "There!" she said, and the satisfaction in her voice was purely animal. She might, as a sportsman would have done, have played the fish for a few minutes for the satisfaction of giving it a chance to get away. But Mrs. Devereux, as she had told Doctor Manson, did not fish for sport. She angled to kill fish. Manson had never forgotten her confession.

At the time that Mrs. Devereux killed the trout in the paragraph above, the scientist himself was letting Inspector Rawlings in front of him into the residence of the late Colonel. The apartment was one of the twin-roomed service flats in Albemarle Street, that resort of the not-too-well-off who covet a fashionable address; some for reasons of pride; others because it invites confidence in the nefarious ways by which they earned a living.

The rooms in which Colonel Donoughmore had passed his days were well-furnished. Deep, club armchairs stood on either side of the fireplace. A refectory table occupied the centre of the dining-room, and a well filled bookcase stood opposite the oak sideboard-and-cocktail cabinet combined. At the end of the room, opposite the door, a heavy oak desk stood solidly on guard, as it were, over its dead owner's secrets. It was to this desk that Doctor Manson turned after a cursory examination of the bookshelves and letters and papers pushed behind a clock on the mantelpiece. It was locked.

"All right, Doctor. That won't cause us any trouble." Inspector Rawlings produced a bunch of keys. The second one turned the wards of the lock, and the inspector threw the top open. He smiled at the scientist's interested look at the keys. "We took them off the best office burglar I ever knew," he explained. "Man we called 'Keys' Denham. Died in prison. And very useful the keys have proved to us on several occasions."

"I believe it, Inspector!" Manson chuckled. "Let's hope they have unlocked a secret I want this time." He surveyed the desk with its triple rows of pigeon-holes of various sizes, all neatly filled with papers and documents, and his head unconsciously nodded in recognition of its orderliness. Manson had an orderly mind, and appreciated the habit in others. "Whatever else this man may have been, and I think he was a very nasty kind of man, Rawlings, he was at any rate a tidy individual."

"Army training, probably, Doctor. You have to be neat and methodical there."

"Yes." The scientist spoke absent-mindedly. He was already looking through the contents of the first of the pigeon-holes. "Mostly bills and receipts," he said, and replaced them. Nothing in the contents of the other holes raised any comment from him until the larger of them gave up its contents. They consisted of a dozen or so bundles of share script. Manson, after a glance, passed them over to the inspector. "Your line, I think," he said.

Rawlings eyebrows rose at the names of the companies printed across the script. "If this was his means of livelihood, Doctor, he died a poor man," he said.

"On the contrary, Rawlings, he died a pretty well-off man, I should say. He lived on those shares, all right."

"But they are useless, Doctor."

"Mebbe, but the colonel sold a few thousand of them for good money. These, I take it, are the remnants."

"You mean—he was a sharepusher?"

"Exactly. . . . Hallo! What is this?" Manson had pulled a packet of photographs from a drawer of the top row of recesses, and was staring at them with marked interest. They were unusual photographs to say the least. Instead of the usual array of faces of groups or representations of buildings or scenery, the prints showed only lines of newspaper print. They were, in fact, photographs of half a dozen reports copied by a camera from the pages of a newspaper. Each was pasted on a headed sheet of notepaper which announced that it was supplied by the Service Press-Cutting Agency, Fleet Street, London; and in the space between the reproductions a date stamp of five years ago was printed.

"Obviously the date of the issue of the paper in which the report appeared, Doctor," said Rawlings.

"Quite. What *ARE* the papers? . . . Um . . . *Times of India, The Statesman, Calcutta Times, Simla Journal*, the *Times* again and the London *Times*. Very interesting."

Settling himself in one of the colonel's armchairs, Doctor Manson read slowly through the reports. Pieced together they unfolded the panorama of the death of Lieutenant Ronald Devereux of the Indian Army, thumbnail sketches of the officer and his wife, and finally, the departure of the grief stricken young widow from India.

Manson, his perusal ended, pushed them back into the envelope which had held them. "Now, why do you suppose he wanted those?" he asked, half aloud. The wrinkles formed on his forehead, and he eyed the envelope as though expecting it to answer. Slipping it into his pocket, he rose and turned again to the desk.

Only one other item raised any interest in him, however; a desk size diary which lay in the drawer beneath the writing-pad. As he turned the pages over, expletives escaped from his lips from time to time.

At last he turned away. "I think that is all the desk can tell us, Rawlings," he said. "I suppose you can lock it again with those keys of yours?" Manson shut down the top and made way for the inspector.

"Just as easily as I opened it, Doctor." With a grin he slipped in the key and turned it. "There you are. Nobody would know that it had been opened if it wasn't for your finger-prints, Doctor."

He chuckled. "I'm surprised *you* made the mistake of handling it. We've got your prints at the Yard, you know. By the way, can we turn the flat over to the relatives now. They want to see what they can take away. Or will you want to keep it intact?"

"No. I have all that is likely to be of any use to me. Give them access, if you like."

Manson entered the Yard on his return, at the precise moment that the Assistant Commissioner walked in. He took his arm. "Hallo, A.C. I want to have a chat with you."

"Didn't know you were in Town again, Harry," was the surprised reply. "Hooked that fish of your's yet?"

"Just what I want to talk over, A.C." The two men walked arm in arm along the corridor to the Assistant Commissioner's room.

* * * * *

"Janice Devereux? Now what has that young woman been up to that a detective should want to know anything about her? Did I know her? Of course I knew her. Bless me, everybody knew her in Monte Carlo, and some of 'em wished to goodness they hadn't known her afterwards. Didn't I see the other day that she is going to marry Johnny Shepstone?"

Mrs. Watkins looked up from the depths of her brocade-covered chair at Sergeant Merry, perched, ill at ease, on a piece of straight-backed, delicate, Louis Quinze furniture, fearing to move lest an incautious misbalance of weight should break off one of the spindle legs, or something.

It was on the advice of the Yard's Society expert that he was sitting in front of the painted old woman—mutton served up as lamb, was his unspoken comment. "If it's any scandal on the Riviera you want to know about, Merry, go and see Mrs. Watkins," the expert had advised.

"She'll know it. The damn old mischief-maker can describe everybody's dirty linen piece by piece. Her tongue will wag an omnibus biography of scandal. Go and see her. Here, I'll make an appointment for you."

He picked up the phone and dialled. "That you, Mrs. Watkins?" he asked the answering voice. "Larry Waller here. I'm sending a young man round to see you. He wants to know something about someone who was at Monte. Can he come along now?"

"Of course he can, Larry. I can't give him longer than twelve o'clock. I'm lunching out at half-past. And be sure that he IS a young man. The last one you sent round was old enough to be my husband."

"There you are, Merry. You hop round—and you'll have to be careful if you want to get away without being seduced."

Merry went!

"Now what has that young woman been up to?" Mrs. Watkins demanded again.

"She hasn't been up to anything, so far as we know," Merry explained. "But somebody connected with her is concerned in a case of death we are investigating, Mrs. Watkins, and we wanted a background to them. How long had Mrs. Devereux been in Monte Carlo when you knew her?"

"Bless the boy! I had been going to Monte for the season before Janice Devereux was born," was the reply. "I remember the day she turned up in the place in widow's weeds, and with a face looking like as though the world had come to a sudden and tragic end. Bah! A pose. She had every man in the place round her within a week. Never saw a widow so much enjoy herself in her tragic loss, never before nor since."

"I suppose you mean the weeds were a sprat, eh, Mrs. Watkins?"

"What do you suppose? She was a clever woman, and she stopped clever."

"How so?"

"How so? A woman who lived in the Hotel de Paris and played roulette and baccarat in the Sporting Club wants a few hundreds more than her husband left her plus an army lieutenant's pension. I should know! Why, damn you, she went everywhere, dressed like a mannequin, and entertained. And I've seen her stake a maximum on the transversales at roulette."

"Men, I suppose?" Merry's question was accompanied by the smug look which seemed justified by the tones of Mrs. Watkins' voice.

"And she played 'em well. Mind you, I've nothing against her for that. They're fair game and a woman has to have her fun.

Men have bought me a few luxuries in me time, and Janice was a pretty woman and knew her way about. But I used to have 'em one at a time—with another always in the background." The old woman leered.

"Janice had 'em all on the stage at the same time. And they never knew when it was their turn to do the play-acting. She made mistakes, mark you. Got herself engaged to young White-haven one night, in the Abrek Nightclub. Now *THAT* was the place to spend money in Monte. If the bank couldn't break you, Abrek could. Idea of a few Russian naval—ex-Czar—officers that was. They borrowed some money off the mugs who thought it grand to entertain penniless grand dukes, and took the lease of a cellar in a back street. All very fine, it was, me lad. Waiters were the Naval officers, the orchestra leader was a nephew of one of the Czar's dukes, and what with the dim light and the vodka and champagne, you never realised until you went home to break-fast that you'd paid ten pounds for something that hadn't cost 'em ten shillings to produce.

"Abrek, eh? I asked a Russian one day what the damn word meant. It wasn't a word he told me, young man: it was formed of a syllable each of three Russian words which meant 'rob the rich to help the poor' and I never knew a place that lived up to its name better or more painstakingly. The place didn't open until midnight, when everything else was closed down except the Casino. The Russian robbers knew the victims all right—that was good psychology. There was never a night, or rather morn-ing, when Janice Devereux wasn't there. And that's where she made the mistake over Billy Whitehaven."

"Mistake?" queried Merry.

"Mistake, I said. She thought he was the other brother, who had been left £25,000 a year by his aunt. He wasn't. He was the one who lived on the other one's allowance. She dropped all the other men like a hot brick till she found out—I told her." The old harridan chortled with glee at the recollection. Then she started up all over again, "I'm telling you, young man, not much stands in the way of Janice Devereux when she wants something. She gets what she intends to get. There was one incident—well, I was told by the Court Chamberlain of Monaco that she was in prison there for one night. It was hushed up, so I heard, and only one or two knew about it."

"She seems to have been a bit of a goer," said Merry with a smile. "But she's finished up all right. Sir John Shepstone seems to think the world of her. Wonder what would happen if somebody came between them—that is, if she is still the same kind of woman?"

"You can bet your breeks she's still the same kind of woman. That sort don't change. And this, mark you, is Janice Devereux's last chance. She's no chicken now. I think she'd do murder before she lost Johnny Shepstone."

Merry had hard work to keep down the exclamation that rose to his lips. Instead, he laughed quietly. "Murder!" he said. "My dear Mrs. Watkins! Little Janice Devereux! Murder! Do women do murder?"

"For their men, yes. It's about the only thing for which they would murder," was the reply.

"Did you know anything about her husband?"

"Only how he died, while shooting. He was dead, of course, when I met Janice. He was a good-looking young man, mind you, according to the photograph she gave me. I've got it somewhere, still."

Mrs. Watkins rummaged through the drawers of an escritoire to emerge with a photograph. A cabinet size head and shoulders, it showed Lieutenant Devereux in uniform with sun helmet, and Mrs. Devereux in cream silk with floppy hat. Merry eyed it with interest. "Do you mind if I borrow this, Mrs. Watkins?" he asked.

"No, my boy. You can have it, so long as you bring it back yourself when you've finished with it, and have tea with me."

"I'll certainly do that, Mrs. Watkins. I'd love to." (I don't think! he added under his breath). "And now, I mustn't keep you any longer. Many thanks for the interesting chat."

Merry collected his hat and made for the street.

* * * * *

"Get the Photographic Department to copy the photograph and have half a dozen proofs made for us, Merry. We'll catch the 3.15 back to Tremarden."

Doctor Manson had listened with marked interest to Merry's account of Mrs. Devereux's Riviera life. Once or twice he nodded to himself, and wrote down a few words in his note-book. He made no comment, however; but detailed his own morning's work to his assistant, and the talk he had had with the Assistant Commissioner.

After lunching at the Savage Club, the two walked back to the Yard, collected the Devereux photographs and, leaving by the side entrance, hailed a taxicab.

"Forty-four 'B,' Fleet Street, and wait there," the scientist instructed the driver. The taxi, skirting the Embankment slipped up into the Strand in front of St. Dunstan's Church and two minutes' later dropped them at the entrance to the offices of the Service Press Cutting Agency.

Manson demanded a private talk with the manager. "A few days ago you sent to a Colonel Donoughmore, of Albemarle Street, a number of photographic reproductions of reports in Indian papers," he said.

The manager agreed. "That is so, Chief Inspector," he said. "Something wrong, is there?"

"No. But they have cropped up in an investigation we are making. Can you give me the date on which the colonel asked for these cuttings to be traced and copied?"

"I think so. Excuse me for a moment." He left the room to return with a file. He produced a letter, ran a finger through the contents and finally handed it over to the Doctor. "That is his letter to us. You will see that it is dated July 15th."

Manson read the letter and passed it over to Merry. It asked for all available cuttings of Mrs. Devereux from the Indian papers of April, 1933. It was a matter of some urgency, the letter said, and he would be obliged if they could make every effort to get a complete account and post them to reach the Albemarle address by July 17th.

"It was, of course, impossible to get in London numbers of the Indian papers so far back as that," the manager explained. "But we did get the consent of the London offices of the papers concerned to photograph the references to the Devereuxs in their files. These we developed and printed and sent to Colonel Donoughmore."

Manson smiled. "Service seems to be your method as well as your name," he said, genially. "I would never have thought of that neat way of getting the cuttings. I'm much obliged to you."

The pair returned to the taxi. "Waterloo," said Manson, and sat back in his seat. The taxi sped down the Street of Ink, passed that extraordinary glass-house of the *Daily Express* (if there is any truth in the old adage that they who live in glasshouses shouldn't throw stones, that newspaper ought to be exceedingly careful not to throw brickbats about!), passed the centre of interest of Aussies over here—the shop of Jack Hobbs, the greatest cricketer of all time. It swung into New Bridge Street, over that experimental bit of rubber street surface; what the experiment proved or disproved has never leaked out to the public, though it is about fifteen years since the road was laid down. Over Blackfriars Bridge, past that home of desperate fights, the Blackfriars Ring, and under the arches to Waterloo Road.

Merry woke to life here. He nudged Doctor Manson. "Do you think we could have got anywhere with the little murders round here, Harry?" he asked.

Manson looked up. "What murders?" he asked. He had only caught the tail end of his Sergeant's query.

"Wasn't it round here that Jack the Ripper made his favourite hunting-ground?"

"Oh, I see. Yes, I think that a scientist in the Yard might have solved Jack the Ripper. I'm not sure that we could not name Jack the Ripper even now, Jim," he concluded. The scientist fell into silence again. He took his seat in an empty first-class carriage of the Cornish train, with Merry beside him. The sergeant eyed his chief curiously from time to time. The train was tearing through Clapham Junction, however, before he spoke.

"Something worrying you, Harry?" he asked.

"Yes, Jim . . . a curious problem."

He paused, and then suddenly demanded of his Sergeant:

"What happened in the Tremarden Arms, on July 15th, to make Colonel Donoughmore write for those cuttings?"

CHAPTER XIX
THE ALIBI

SERGEANT MACROBBIE was a small man, lithe with the muscular suppleness of the Scot; and small boned, which was a peculiar circumstance in men of his clan. How he came to be a member of the Cornish Criminal Investigation Force was something that even he could not really answer. He had the reputation of being the only Scotsman ever to last in the Cornish police, with whom he had now been for some seven years. The explanation was said by his colleagues to be (and it might well be true) that while he could not understand what the Cornish dialect was saying about him, the Cornishmen, on the other hand, were totally unable to comprehend what the Scottish brogue was saying about them! They kept, therefore, good friends!

Habitually, MacRobbie wore Harris tweeds, and red hair; at the moment he was overdressed, since he was wearing, in addition, a worried expression; the task of finding traces of Mrs. Devereux was proving harder than finding a way through a Scotch mist in his native Lossiemouth.

He had decided, after a talk with Inspector Penryn, that his inquiries should begin with an attempt to trace the movements of Mrs. Devereux from the time she left the Devonshire Tea Rooms at 12.45 p.m., leaving the scarf to greet her return at such time as she occupied the table again at 4.45.

He was equipped for his search—mainly through the good offices of the lady's chambermaid—with a detailed description, in some degrees an embarrassing one, of the clothes which Mrs. Devereux had been wearing on that day. A piece of unexpected luck had provided him also, with a photograph of her actually in the clothes. An itinerant movie-camera man wending through

Tremarden on his way to the coast, had sought to make a pound or two by snapping pictures of promising passers-by in the street of the town, afterwards handing them a card giving the number of the exposure made, and the information that prints would be obtainable next day, at the price of a shilling each, by calling at the Swan Inn.

Mrs. Devereux had, it seems, complained to the chamber-maid of the man's importunings. The chambermaid had passed the information on to Inspector Penryn, when he had inter-viewed the girl in confidence (engendered by a vivid word pic-ture of police cells if she didn't talk!) to obtain a description of the articles of adornment which the guest had worn that day. The photographer was rounded up, his films examined, and en-largements made of the promenading fisherwoman. It was half a dozen of these prints which the sergeant and his three consta-bles were carrying for identification purposes.

MacRobbie had tackled the search, after some deep think-ing, by visiting Mrs. MacRobbie.

"Maggie," he said. "If you, bein' an ordinary kind of woman, had three 'oors tae spend in Tavistock betwixt denner-time an' tea-time, hoo wid ye spend it? What wid a woman dae tae wile awa' a' that time?"

Mrs. MacRobbie had considered the question, slowly and dourly. "She wad be a body wi' nae responsibeelitees to be hevin' a' that time tae waste?" she suggested.

"Aye, an' wi' plenty o' bawbees tae spen'."

"Ah!" Mrs. MacRobbie surveyed her braw figure in the glass over the mantelpiece. "Well, Jamie, if I hed the bawbees tae throw awa on sich flippances, I'd hae ma' hair deen in the London wye. An' I might, ye ken, go buying knick-knacks in the stores. There are ane or twa I could dee wi'," she added, hopeful-ly, an eye on her husband.

Jimmy shook his head. "A'm nae promissin' onythin', ye onderstan'. It's a' in the way o' bisiness. An' whit wid ye be daein' when ye's haen yer hair deen up and bought a few wee knick-knacks?"

"Gae and hae ma tea," his spouse said quickly.

"Ye dinna wint tae hae tea until a quarter tae five, ye onderstan'. An' ye've an oor an' a half tae a quarter tae five."

"A'd gae tae pictures, then."

"Ay. A hadna thoucht o' that. Mebbe she did ane or a' o' them," he added, after a pause.

"She? And wha wid she be?"

"The lassie ah'm trying to find." He caught the look in his wife's eye. "It's a' in the matter of the law a'm tellin' ye," he added hastily.

The sergeant sent his men on a round of the hairdressing salons and beauty parlours of Tavistock. He had himself taken the nearest establishment to the tea rooms. The manageress, looking round a corner at the opening of the door, hastily pulled the curtain across a cubicle and stepped out.

"Wid ye be knowin' a Mistress Devereux?" the sergeant demanded. "It's a matter o' law, ye ken," he added, showing his warrant card.

The woman denied any knowledge of a customer of that name. "What would she come here for?" she demanded.

"Mebbe tae hae her hair din up," the sergeant suggested. "It wid be four days agone at ane o'clock."

The manageress examined her book. "No," she announced. "We have had nobody of that name in the place."

The sergeant produced his photograph. "This wid be the leddy," he said. "Wid ye hae seen her at all?"

A shake of the head was the answer. "We've never had her in here, Sergeant."

"Ah, weel, it mun hae bin somewheres else she wint, then," he added. "Guid day tae ye."

The same tale was told by the three constables under the sergeant's orders. They had, they reported, visited every salon in the town, large and small. Neither had dressed hair, lifted the face or manicured the nails of a Mrs. Devereux; and none could identify the photograph, or recognise the description of the clothes which they were given. Wherever Mrs. Devereux had spent her time in Tavistock, it was certainly not in a beauty salon.

"Verra guid, then," said the sergeant. "Och aye, it luiks like the leddy wint tae the shops or, mebbe, tae the peectures. Ye maun tak a' the leddies shops. Ah'l be gaun aboot the peectures."

The party set off again on a tour of the shops. The second task was not so simple as the investigation of the beauty salons. There are three Department Stores in Tavistock, and each department, and nearly every assistant, had to be interviewed, and give an opinion on whether the woman in the photograph had been served by her on the day in question.

The smaller shops retailing women's garments and fancy goods then had to be similarly visited. Once or twice the sergeant thought the quest had been ended. At one fashionable establishment the woman looking carefully at the picture said that she thought she had served the lady with a *crêpe de chine* garment.

"Did ye now?" said the sergeant, who had been fetched to see the assistant.

"Yes, I'm almost certain it was her," the girl replied.

"Wid ye be able, now, to say whit the leddy was wearin'?"

"Yes, Sergeant. She was wearing a tweed coat and skirt and she had a yellow scarf round her neck with dogs on. That is, if it is the lady you mean."

The sergeant jumped. "Oo aye," he said. "That wid be her, nae doot." He stopped suddenly, as if at a thought. "She was wearin' a scar-r-f, ye say? Ah! Wid ye remember whit time it was when ye saw her?"

"Quite well. It would be half-past five. We were just about to close."

The confident statement came as a blow to the sergeant. During the hours for which he was searching for Mrs. Devereux, the scarf with the dogs was reclining in the tea rooms waiting her return. He turned again to the girl. "Ah'l no say ye're no richt," he said regretfully. "Ye did'nae chance tae see the leddy wi'oot the scarf, aboot ane or twa o'clock?"

"No. I'm afraid not," was the reply.

"Och! It's a peety, a verra great peety."

With this the sergeant decided that he had reached the end of the first stage of his inquiry. It seemed to him that he might now conclude that Mrs. Devereux had not spent the four hours between 12.45 and 4.45 in Tavistock. Where, then, *HAD* she spent them? He decided that his next move must be to discover how she had left the town, and where she had travelled. He started on this new hunt in equally methodical form. Tavistock detective officers made a tour of taxicab drivers, armed with a description of Mrs. Devereux. "Had his cab," each taxi-man was asked, "taken a fare to any spot between Tavistock and Tremarden, between the hours of one o'clock and two o'clock?" The latter had been agreed upon as the latest time at which any journey could have been made by Mrs. Devereux if she had, indeed, gone to the riverside.

Three of the cabs had, it appeared, gone in that direction with a woman fare. One had known his customer, and was able to give the destination. A telephone call to the address elicited the information that she had, indeed, travelled home by taxi at the time stated. That, the Tavistock officer, agreed, disposed of her. Only circumstantial evidence of the other two could be obtained, but there seemed little reason to doubt that they had no connection with Mrs. Devereux. The taxi-men stated that they had driven only a short distance from the middle of the town.

Sergeant MacRobbie's tour of car hire firms produced no more satisfactory results. It was Constable Treherne who suddenly thought of another form of locomotion. "Perhaps she hired a bicycle," he suggested.

"Mon, ye're a wonder," the sergeant said; and off on the trail went the party again. It was dark before this new line of investigation had concluded, and the sergeant and his men returned to Tremarden.

Doctor Manson and Sergeant Merry were in the inspector's room when the sergeant made his report next morning.

"The leddy, Inspector, seems juist tae hae vanished intae the air," he said. "I could na' find her in the toon, and I could na' find her oot o' the toon. I'll tak ma aith she didnae gae oot in a motor-car, nor on a bicycle, nor on the railway, 'cept, forbye, the 6.30 train frae Tavistock tae Tremarden."

"Who recognised her on that train, Sergeant?" Manson asked.

"A porter on the local platform the same, ye ken, whae saw her come i' the mor-r-n."

"And he's certain that she did not leave earlier?"

"Ay. An' for why? The man was on duty on t' platform all the day. It was too dark to proceed wi' the last wee chance," the sergeant continued. "But I'll be a' taekin' of it, the noo."

"And what chance would that be, Sergeant?" asked Manson.

The sergeant answered the question with another. "Wid she hae gone doon tae the river by bus?" he asked. "Ye ken I had thoucht o' that. But wid a body weeshin' tae avoid bein' traced travel to Tremarden on a public bus?"

Manson nodded his head. "Good for you, Sergeant," he said. "There is much to be said for both arguments. It depends on the person concerned. He or she may think that there is less chance of being remembered in a crowd than travelling alone in a vehicle, the driver of which may the more easily recollect the circumstances and identity of his fare. How do the buses run from Tavistock?"

"Every three quarters of an hour," Penryn answered for the sergeant.

"There is ane leaving at five meenites tae ane o' clock," the sergeant pointed out.

"Making the next one twenty to two," said Manson. "If I were you, Penryn, I should ring the company and find out who was the conductor on those two buses on the day, and where we can get hold of them. Perhaps a chat with them might bring some result."

"I'll do that now," the inspector said, and rising, he left the room.

He returned with the answer in five minutes' time. "The conductor of the five minutes to one bus was a man named Robson," he announced. "He is now on the bus which will be passing the Tremarden Arms in half an hour's time and the bus leaves on the return journey through here from Tavistock at 12.55."

"The same bus, then?"

"Exactly, Doctor. The same bus."

The chief claims to fame of Tavistock are, firstly, that Sir Francis Drake, that piratical old filibuster, was born there in 1540; and, secondly, that there is usually enough arsenic in the place to kill off the entire population of the British Isles—one of its industries, and a little known one, is the extraction of arsenic!

The road to it from Tremarden is a switchback track of leafy lanes. Leaving the market place the bus slid steeply down the road and into the valley in the trough of which runs the river in its rocky bed. The road crosses the river by an ages-old bridge of granite rough-hewn stones, and then begins to climb again between granite-stone walls. Then, once more, it rolls along lanes until, approaching the Devonshire town, there comes into view in the distance, the rugged, terrible moors that are called Dartmoor.

Nothing grander, or more varied in scenery, can be found in the south-west of England; but it was not with the scenery that Manson, Burns and Merry were concerned. They boarded the bus in the market place; it was not until some little time that they made their first move. Inspector Penryn, seeing the conductor free, for the time being, of duties, produced a photograph from his pocket, and drawing the ticket-puncher's attention to it, asked a question.

Robson eyed the photograph held out by Inspector Penryn. "Well, sir, I couldn't properly say if she was on the bus that day," he announced. "I mean to say, it's four days ago, you know, and the bus is mostly full. I don't have much time, you see, to go about inspecting the faces of the passengers."

"This lady, Robson, would have been dressed a little differently from your usual fares," Doctor Manson suggested. "She is an uncommonly good-looking woman. She speaks in a superior voice—if I may describe it that way—and she wore a tweed suit. Also, she had tiger-red coloured finger-nails, though she might, of course, have been wearing gloves," he added as an afterthought.

The conductor considered this new aid to identification, without satisfactory results. "No, sir," he said. "I don't remember—"

He stopped suddenly, and Manson glancing up, saw him looking out of the window as though puzzled. The bus was passing the lane along which Manson and Merry had walked to the river after their cup of tea in Joe Smirthwaite's café. Suddenly, Robson turned to the scientist. "Now, I wonder, sir. Would the lady have left the bus by this farm lane here?"

Manson experienced that thrill of satisfaction which comes from the success of a perfectly prepared set of circumstances. He had carefully timed the talk with the conductor to ensure that the vital question should be asked when the bus was actually passing the spot where a person, wanting to reach the river, would naturally have alighted, and when, therefore, the conductor would be most likely to have such a person in his memory. From the conductor's manner he had been prepared for the question, which he now answered in a voice suddenly gone hard and menacing.

"I should think it most probable that she did," he said.

"Then I think I know the woman you want, sir. She *did* ride down on the bus from Tavistock and I remember that a woman did leave the bus here. His face brightened. "Now I come to think of it, sir, I sort of wondered at the time what she would be wanting to get off at a place so far from the town, like. She was wearing one of them beret hats with a feather in, I remember now."

Manson looked an inquiry at Penryn, and received an answering nod. "Good, Robson," he said to the conductor. "That sounds like the woman we want. You observe things very well when your mind is prompted. I suppose you did not see what happened to her after she had left the bus? Which way she went, for instance?"

"No, sir. Afraid I didn't."

"Well, we'll have to guess that, now."

"Do I understand that you come back along this way to-day at the same time you did on the day that this woman travelled?"

"Yes, sir."

"And the journey and circumstances will be exactly the same?"

"Barring accidents, yes."

"Very good. Now, we shall be coming back with you. Oh! There's one thing more. Do you know whether the rota of conductors in all the buses is the same as on that day?"

"Yes, sir. So far as I know. The drivers and conductors ought to be the same unless any one of them has been moved on to a special." The remainder of the journey the three men devoted to arranging a programme which, in Manson's opinion, might correspond with the theoretical movements of Mrs. Devereux on the day of the colonel's death. The programme was carried out with studied exactness. At five minutes past midday the three entered the Devonshire Tea Rooms in Tavistock, ordering lunch. By a piece of good fortune they were able to sit at the same table which had, on the earlier occasion, been occupied by Mrs. Devereux. At twenty minutes to one they paid their bill and rose. "I think your walking-stick, Inspector," said Manson; and Penryn hung his stick by the handle over the back of the chair on which he had been sitting. At 12.45 they left the tea rooms.

Walking quickly along the street they reached the bus station and climbed into the vehicle. Robson greeted them with a nod of recognition. Manson consulted his watch. "Five minutes to spare," he announced, "but we walked very quickly. She would not have made the distance in so quick a time."

When it started its journey, punctual to the minute, the bus was not more than half full. As it pursued a winding and roundabout way through the country lanes, however, it quickly picked up passengers, and throughout the journey there was a continual changing personnel with almost every stop. It was half an hour when Manson. who had been watching the passing countryside, gave a signal, and the three rose to their feet. Pressing a button in the roof of the bus, he walked to the doorway and as the bus stopped, descended to the road. It was 1.25 o'clock.

As they did so, there was an ejaculation from Robson. Manson turned quickly round with a smile. "Remembered something else?" he asked.

"Yes, sir. Seeing you get off here suddenly reminded me."

"I rather hoped that it might," said the scientist with a smile. "What is it?"

"I remember now where the woman went," was the reply.

"Where?"

"She turned up the lane there, sir." And he pointed to the lane which Manson and Merry knew led to the copse and the river-side.

"Thanks, Robson. That's very useful."

"So far so good," commented Manson, and led the way up the lane. A sharp walk of some minutes landed the three by the side of the cattle drinking pool. Penryn surveyed what the three now recognised as the scene of the colonel's death. "And what do we do now?" he asked.

"We survey the scenery until after two o'clock," was the reply. "We can usefully occupy the time by visualising what happened here on that day. The colonel was fishing somewhere near here, probably from the little knoll there." The scientist pointed to a clear spot on the riverbank.

"What!" Penryn said, startled. "Fishing here?"

"Certainly." Manson looked surprised. "Of course he was fishing here. If my theory is correct, he came here to fish on the invitation of Mrs. Devereux herself. And he never went away again—at least, not on his feet."

The scientist walked across to the copse and from there surveyed his two companions. He walked into the copse itself, looked down at the remains of the footprint which still showed, and then he stepped close beside it and glanced towards the pool. The result brought a surprised exclamation to his lips. *From the spot, he had a clear vision, completely unobstructed, between overhanging branches, of Penryn and Merry standing beside the pool.*

He stared steadily for a few moments, whistling softly. "I wonder . . . I wonder," he said; and, still whistling, retraced his footsteps to his companions.

"Now, Merry," he said, after consulting his watch. You remember the major's story of seeing a woman's figure at the entrance to the Avenue, there? I'd like you to go to the spot where the major says he leaned against the bank and saw his vision. When you get there, watch."

The sergeant departed. Manson watched until he could no longer see him, and then, consulting his watch, walked to the Avenue. Near the entrance he paused, but seeing nothing, walked forward. He had traversed some hundred yards before he was able to catch a glimpse of Merry, and before the sergeant could answer his wave, Manson, turning, took stock of his position. Instead of being in the entrance to the Avenue, he was a good 150 feet from it, and in a line with the pool.

He retraced his steps, and, watch in hand, stood as though playing a part, and waiting for the cue to make his entrance. At half-past two, calling to Penryn and Merry, he started back along the path. Arrived at the main road, the three turned right and still led by the scientist, strolled in the direction of Tavistock. They had walked no longer than ten minutes or a quarter of an hour, when a bus came up behind. Hailing it, the three climbed aboard. Manson remaining in the entrance, prepared to pay the fares demanded. "By the way," he said to the conductor, "you were conducting this bus on Monday were you not?"

"Yes, sir." The man eyed the scientist inquiringly.

"Can you remember whether at the spot at which we hailed you, or somewhere close to it, you picked up a woman on that day?"

"I can, sir." A broad smile came over the busman's face. "We didn't pick anybody up round here, nor on this side of Tavistock. Mind you, we were hailed times enough. Only the bus was full up, see?"

"I see," agreed the scientist. "Now, what time is the next bus behind?"

"About an hour, sir."

"Then, if you would not mind signalling the driver, I think we will wait for that bus."

The three men clambered back on to the road, and recommenced their walking. "That, I think, must have been rather a nasty setback for Mrs. Devereux," Manson opined. "It upset her plans and lengthened an alibi which she wanted to be as short as possible."

He made a mental calculation. "Yes, I think the theory still hangs together all right," he decided. "We should be in Tavistock by about 4.15. Now, what are we going to do for an hour?"

He repeated the question to Penryn. "What, if you were Mrs. Devereux, would you have done. Put yourself in her place."

"Get as far from this vicinity as possible and in the quickest possible time," was the prompt reply.

"Right! Then we will continue walking—slowly. A woman could not move very quickly—at least, not the woman of whom we are thinking. Nor would she walk far."

They had covered some half-a-mile when Manson called a halt. For the last five minutes he had been scanning each side of the road, apparently in search of something or other. He now crossed to the grass verge, where the bank was broken for a width of about six feet, and where a track ran up into a copse. A gate barred the way to the copse, but a stile afforded passage way for the pedestrian. A wide, projecting bottom step had been built to assist progress over the stile. Manson sat on the step. "I think," he said, "we might wait here for the bus. I do not think that Mrs. Devereux would walk much further, and this spot, lying as it does, back from the roadway, would give her the seclusion she undoubtedly would want. If you two will find places to sit on the stile or on the grass banking, we can wait comfortably."

Merry produced a box and the three men lit up from one light. There was nothing superstitious about these hard-headed man-hunters! After he had lit his own cigarette the sergeant, with a flick of his fingers, sent the match spinning into the grass at the edge of the gate. Manson followed it with his eyes. A little flicker of flame sprang up. "Carelessness, Merry," he commented, and walking across, picked up the still lighted stalk and extinguished it between finger and thumb. Bending down, he beat out the few blades of dry grass which had become ignited. As he did so, and parted other blades of grass, a cigarette stub was revealed, lying at the bottom of one of the gate-posts. The scientist eyed it curiously.

"Now, that is a strange thing to find here," he said.

Penryn smiled. "Strange? I should not have considered it so, Doctor," he said. "When we have finished these cigarettes we shall, in all probability, toss our stumps here." He eyed the fag-end which Manson still held in his fingers. "Looks as though it has been here some time, too, Doctor. It's stained brown by the weather."

"I agree that a cigarette-end would not be out of place here, Penryn," was the reply. "It is the *kind* of cigarette-end that excites my curiosity. The paper is not stained by the weather; it is, in fact, its natural colour. This was a Russian cigarette, and an expensive one at that. About fifteen shillings a hundred, if I remember rightly—and the brand is Melikoffs. I know it quite well." He produced his magnifying glass and inspected the stub-end closely. "If you look through this, you can just make out the name," he added.

Penryn confirmed the name after a moment's perusal through the glass. "It's got purplish lipstick markings on it, too," he said.

"I should not have thought that Melikoffs were the kind of cigarettes the people who walked along this road, and so far from the town, would smoke," the scientist went on. "Especially the sort who would occupy their time sitting on this gate. That is why I said it was a strange thing to come across." He put the stub into his wallet. A smile from Penryn he answered with his own. "Never let unusual things pass by, Penryn," he said. "Not until you are sure that they will not be of some service to you. Now, Merry will label this and put it away in our curiosity cupboard, and there it will stay for six months. It may be nothing; frequently the exhibits find their way to the dustbin. But not always. We did just this very thing, once with a peculiar-coloured stone that was quite foreign to all the other stones in the vicinity. It got a man seven years a few weeks later. If we hadn't kept it—"

A noise in the distance caused him to break off. "That," he said, "sounds like the bus." He stepped out and looked down the road. "Yes, it's coming along. Now I would like to practise a little more psychology. We'll stay here until the bus is pretty well on to us, then step out and hail it."

The trio carried out the manoeuvre. The startled driver jammed his foot on the brake and the vehicle pulled up with a screeching of the tyres. As they climbed aboard Manson noticed that the conductor stared at them and then across at the opening in the bank. Finally, turning again to the three, he scratched his head. Manson smiled a satisfied smile to himself. "We reminded you of something, conductor?" he asked.

"Funny you should ask that, sir," was the reply. "You coming out o' there, sudden-like, sort of startled me. Only ever been stopped there once before, and that were exactly the same way. Only . . ."

"Only that time it was a woman, eh?" the scientist broke in. "And on your last rota on this route?"

"That's right enough, sir . . ." He stopped and gazed at Manson. "But how would you know that, sir?" he asked.

"I didn't know it, conductor. I only guessed it. Where did she go?"

"Right into Tavistock, sir."

"Then we will go to the same place. The woman was wearing tweeds and a beret, was she not?"

"Yes, sir. Very fashionable lady. Which made it funny seeing her out in the wilds, as you might say."

The three officers settled down for the journey into the town.

It was 4.20 when the bus chugged into Tavistock. Penryn checked his watch. "A little on the early side, isn't it, Doctor?" he asked. "If she dashed to the tea-shop to make as short an absence as she hoped to with the first bus she missed, she would have reached the tea-rooms before 4.45."

Manson made no reply, but stopped and seemed to be searching the street for something. He failed, apparently, to find it, for he crossed the road and spoke to a constable on point duty. The officer pointed ahead, and a turning movement of his hand suggested to Merry and Penryn that he was directing the Doctor to a street on the left. This proved, indeed, to be the case. With Manson in the van, the three entered a side turning, where Manson stopped in front of a sign, "Ladies." He tapped at the door. To a woman who answered he revealed his official standing. "I wonder if you can cast your mind back to about this time four days ago," he said. "I have reason to believe that a woman came here at this hour and may have sought some attention from you."

"Many women do, sir."

"Quite. But perhaps this woman was a little out of the ordinary. Firstly, she was a lady. And I think that possibly she would have had mud-stained shoes and dirty hands, and . . ."

The woman broke in on his description. "Oh, yes, sir," she said.

"I remember her very well. She had been walking in the country because she'd missed the bus and she had an appointment for tea. I cleaned her shoes for her . . ."

"And probably lent her a comb and glass to do her hair?"

"I did that, sir."

"How long would she have been here, would you say?"

"Nearly twenty minutes, sir."

"Would you know her again if you saw her?"

"Oh, yes. I'm sure I should. She was a very nice lady." Manson produced the photograph of Mrs. Devereux taken by the street camera-man and handed it to the woman.

"Oh, yes, sir. That's her. Why, it's the same clothes and hat!"

"Now, Mrs.—?"

"Allison is the name, sir."

"Now, Mrs. Allison. I shall be sending along, presently, a police constable, and I would be very much obliged if you would answer the questions he will ask you. They will be the same questions which I have asked you. He will write them down and ask you to sign the statement. Will you do that?"

"Well, sir. I don't think the Council would like me to tell things about the customers."

"Never mind about the Council, Mrs. Allison. This is a police matter. I will see that the Council permission is obtained."

"Very well, sir."

Thanking her, Manson rejoined his companions. Timing themselves, they left the cloakroom entrance at 4.10 and, regaining the main street, walked to the Devonshire Tea Rooms and entered. The time was within a minute of 4.45. Penryn walked up to the counter. "I left my sti . . ." he began, but was interrupted by the manageress. "Your stick, sir. Yes, I have it here. It was on the back of your chair."

"Thank you very much. Now, may we have some tea?"

They sat down at the table where, four hours earlier, they had eaten lunch; and the inspector gazed at Doctor Manson. "By Gad, Doctor," he said. "You had that worked out almost to a second. How the hell did you do it?" He paused. Then: "You know, I wouldn't like to be any man whom you were after."

Manson was human enough to feel pleasure at the genuine admiration in the voice of the inspector. "How?" he echoed. "Just a little logical reasoning in a very suspicious mind, Penryn. And as a result . . ."

"Mrs. Devereux's alibi has gone," said Penryn.

CHAPTER XX
A ROD—AND A FLY

DOCTOR MANSON was a puzzled man. In an armchair in his room at the Tremarden Arms he stared through the windows, along the blossom-flamed gardens of the hotel. The wrinkles were back on his forehead, and the fingers were tapping restlessly on the arms of the chair. He was as near perturbation as Doctor Manson could ever be.

On the table in front of him were his examination logbook, his notes of the colonel's death, and various memoranda which, from time to time, he had made. They were augmented by copies of interviews taken from witnesses who had so far told their stories; and the written results (just to refresh his memory as he put it, though nobody could ever remember the time when Manson's memory needed refreshing) of his and Merry's investigations, as well as those of Superintendent Burns and Inspector Penryn.

He had been reading through the collection and collating them into a mental precis. An hour's hard work on this task had produced the wrinkles and the doubts shown in the restless fingers. The Assistant Commissioner of Scotland Yard would have recognised the signs as denoting that something had gone wrong with the scientist's jigsaw placing: he would have diagnosed that somewhere in Manson's brain there was a piece that would not fit, and until it did the pattern could not be completed, at least, not so as to satisfy the precise mind of the scientist.

There were, in fact, three pieces that Manson could not join in the pattern. Presently, he walked across to a side table and gazed down at them. First, he eyed a boot-print cast. From that his eyes moved to an artificial fishing-fly housed in a pill-box fitted with a glass lid; and finally, they came to rest on the colonel's fishing rod. He roved from one to the other. If he was hoping that they could of themselves solve his difficulties, he was disillusioned, for after a few minutes he returned to his chair to resume his mental deliberations.

Presently, he seemed to arrive at some decision, for he lifted the telephone receiver and asked to be put through to police headquarters. The answer came a few minutes later, in the entrance of Inspector Penryn and Sergeant Merry. It was to Merry that Manson first spoke.

"Merry, find out from Franky where Mrs. Devereux is fishing this morning," he said. "Then, go down to her and ask her some questions. Any questions will do so long as you get her up from the river. I want her to cease fishing quite naturally, as any fisherman would do when asked to chat. And I want you to watch her and see exactly what she does, and how she does it. That is the important thing. Nothing else matters, not even what she says in reply to your questions. Just watch her, and describe to me when you come back what she did."

He dismissed Merry to his task with a wave of the hand and turned to Penryn. "Now you, Inspector, I want you to tell me again with all the detail you can what your Indian friend told you about Mrs. Devereux, in India. Tell me anything you can think of, without bothering whether you consider it interesting or not."

Penryn produced his note-book. "It will help me, Doctor, if I refresh myself from the report I made after the talk with Major Ruddock." For half-an-hour the inspector went over the details of the major's talk. At the end he sat back and regarded Manson anxiously. "Any help, Doctor?" he asked.

Manson answered with a question of his own. "Did Major Ruddock say anything of what Mrs. Devereux did after her husband's death?"

"Not a great deal, Doctor. I gather that she lost no time in clearing out of India, which she had said she had never liked as a place of residence. Though I gathered, too, that she had had rather a gay time there in spite of that."

"Yes, I think that she had had a gay time from what Merry's old woman said. She seems to have found consolation for a husband in a variety of lovers. However, that has nothing to do with us, except as an insight into her character. We haven't any evidence that the colonel knew about any of her Riviera lovers; and was holding it as a lever against her in connection with her forthcoming marriage to Sir John Shepstone. That's what was in your mind, wasn't it?"

Penryn grimaced. "Well . . . I had thought of something like that, Doctor," he said.

"Yes, but it must be on something that the colonel *knew* about, and could produce chapter and verse for, Penryn. And Donoughmore, so far as we can find out, had never been to Monte Carlo. There isn't a single trace of any notes in his possession even mentioning Mrs. Devereux's name. Now, if Mrs. Devereux had had any lovers in India . . . All right, Penryn, old chap. I don't see that we can get much further on this trail."

With the inspector gone, Doctor Manson sat down again at the table. He extracted a pocket-book, after reading through a number of notes he replaced the book and drawing a sheet of paper to his hand, commenced to write rapidly. The result was a tabulated statement:

July 15. Donoughmore writes to Service Press Cutting Agency.

July 17. Latest dates at which cuttings were asked to arrive at his flat.

July 18. Donoughmore goes to Town.

July 19. Returns to Tremarden.

July 27. Donoughmore killed.

The detective surveyed the table. The journey to Town and the return next day were obviously for the purpose of collecting the cuttings asked for by the 17th, he decided. That left July 15. Manson, frowning, repeated to himself the question he had put to Merry in the taxi-cab on the way to Waterloo: "What happened on July 15 to make the colonel write for the Press cuttings?"

An idea struck him. He rang his room bell; and to the maid who answered it asked if she would bring up the hotel visitors' register. With the book on his desk a minute later, he opened it at the July entries. They read as follows:

Arrival	Left	Name	Address	Nationality
July 3	July 5	Mr. Greathead	Ealing ...	British
July 3	July 7	W. G. Leathers	Whitstable ...	British
July 5	July 6	Col. and Mrs. Standish ...	Ely Place, W.1	British
July 5	July 26	Mr. and Mrs. Armstrong ...	Sydney ...	Australian
July 8	July 9	Cook's party	—	—
July 8	—	Mr. William Braddock ...	Calgary ...	Canadian
July 11	July 24	Mr. and Mrs. Arkwright ...	Long Ditton...	British
July 11	July 24	Mary Carrick	London ...	Irish
July 12	July 13	Cook's party	—	—
July 12	—	Janice Devereux	London ...	British
July 24	July 30	Miss Labrochere	Glamis ...	Scottish

The page was greeted with a frown. "There doesn't seem anything here to help," the Doctor said to himself. "I can hardly see how a Cook's party touring Cornwall can have any bearing on the colonel's sending for Indian Press cuttings. Anyway, they left next morning, so nobody there can have had any hand in the death. He made a mental note of the date, however. It would be possible to get from Cook's, if necessary, the names and addresses of the party."

Manson was about to close the book when his eye was arrested by the appearance of the page as a whole. He studied it for a moment and then closed it thoughtfully.

"Now that," he said, "is rather interesting. . . . I wonder," he added, after a pause.

* * * * *

Sergeant Merry, wandering along the banks of the Inney, came across Mrs. Devereux. She was fishing in the tail of a torrent pouring down from a steep hill lined with tall trees. As he approached he saw her hook a trout, play it for a few seconds, and then transfer it to the creel, which was slung around her shoulders. She was casting again at the tail of a deep whirlpool when he reached her. His request for a few minutes' talk was greeted with a frown.

"Now what is it, Sergeant?" she asked, angrily.

"Perhaps we had better sit on the fallen tree, here," Merry suggested. "My talk will probably take a few minutes."

"Just as you like," was the reply. Mrs. Devereux slipped the hook of her fly in the lowest of the rod's eyelets, reeled in the line tightly, and then gently placed the rod leaning against a bramble bush, taking care that it was safely poised and could not, by accident, fall or be knocked over. A few feet away a second rod reclined in similar fashion. Merry, glancing at it saw that this rod carried a wet fly. He commented on it when Mrs. Devereux, satisfied as to the safety of the rod she had just been using, sat on the trunk by his side.

"Fishing the rise, Mrs. Devereux?" he asked.

"No, just casting for a fish," was the answer. "They are not taking wet fly to-day."

For a quarter-of-an-hour the sergeant asked a number of innocuous questions bearing on the colonel's conduct and subsequent death. At the end of that time, he rose. "I mustn't keep you from your fishing any longer, Mrs. Devereux," he announced. "I see there are a few rises now. Tight lines."

Doctor Manson heard Merry's description of the scene with grim satisfaction. "That, Jim, is another pointer," he said cryptically.

* * * * *

Franky Baker was passing through the lounge of the Tremarden Arms to his bar when Doctor Manson, halting him, produced a pillbox from a waistcoat pocket. He lifted from the box the artificial fly which he had taken from the colonel's rod when it lay on the bank on the day of the tragedy. "I've come across a fly here, Franky, which I cannot place. It doesn't look to me like a machine-made fly, nor like one of the recognised ties, and there isn't one like it in any of the fly-boxes of the fishermen here, because I've looked into them all. Perhaps you can identify it for me and, I hope, can tell me who uses a fly like it."

Baker took the elegant "insect" into his right hand. He gave one quick glance at it and handed it back. "Oh, yes, Doctor, I can tell you that," he said. "I tied it myself."

Had a bomb burst suddenly behind him, the scientist could not have shown greater alarm. He dropped the box and stared at the hotelier with startled eyes. "What did you say?" he asked.

"I said that I tied the fly myself. It's one of mine. What is wrong with it?"

"You tied it, Franky?"

"Of course, Doctor. I always tie my own flies."

The scientist regarded him in strained silence. Then, hopefully: "Do you sell them, Franky?"

"No, Doctor—" with a grin. "Most everybody round here ties their own; and the visitors get theirs from the tackle shops."

Manson looked more worried than ever. "I suppose you lend one or two occasionally?"

"Nobody would borrow them, Doctor. Would you? They don't correspond to type, as you know yourself."

"There is no mistake, I suppose, Franky? It really is one of yours?"

"It's sartin sure one of mine, Doctor."

CHAPTER XXI
THE CONFESSION

THERE WAS NO outward and visible trace of perturbation in the demeanour of Mrs. Devereux as she sat in the Chief Constable's office, facing Sir William Polglaze, Doctor Manson, Superintendent Burns and Inspector Penryn. She lounged at ease, one silken-sheathed leg crossed over the other, and an air of repose surrounding her. Taking a cigarette from a gold case, she lit it from a gold petrol-lighter and, puffing a smoke-ring, waited. The men, watching her closely, could detect no anxiety in either her glances or the tone of her voice as she asked the reason for her invited presence.

The Chief Constable answered her query. "We asked you to come here, Mrs. Devereux," he said, "because we are hoping that you can throw a little more light on Colonel Donoughmore, and on his death," he said.

She flicked the ash from her cigarette into a tray at her elbow. "I cannot," she answered. "I told you all I could tell the last time you asked me. I was not, as I think you know, fishing that day."

Sir William acknowledged the checkmate with an inclination of his head. "That I remember, Mrs. Devereux," he said. "You gave us, I recall, an alibi in tea rooms at Tavistock. I think we can tell you right away that we checked that alibi, as it was our duty to do, and you were remembered in the tea-rooms on the luncheon and tea-time occasions to which you referred."

"You also said, I think, that you had not known Colonel Donoughmore before you met him in the Tremarden Arms, when you arrived here?" The Chief Constable paused and awaited her reply.

"That is so."

"That seems to us very strange, Mrs. Devereux." The Chief Constable spoke very quietly and very slowly. "Surely Colonel Donoughmore was a staff officer in the Command in India to which your late husband, Lieutenant Devereux, was attached. Were you not there at the time?"

There was a silence. Superintendent Burns, who sat directly facing Mrs. Devereux saw the look which flashed into her eyes. It was there only momentarily, and vanished almost as soon as it appeared. When she looked at the Chief Constable her eyes showed only a cool reassurance. "That is quite correct," she answered. "I knew OF Colonel Donoughmore, of course. I did not know him personally. There is no reason why I should have done. My husband was not at Command Headquarters. And I did not go out much, anyway."

"Is it not a curious thing that, knowing who he was, and he knowing that you were the widow of one of his officers who died so tragically while under his orders, neither of you recalled each to the other's notice?"

"Why should I do so? I was not interested in the colonel. I doubt whether he remembered my husband at all. And I am not the only Devereux in the world."

"You think that he had no knowledge of who you were?"

"Quite likely, I should say."

"Supposing we told you, Mrs. Devereux, that Colonel Donoughmore had asked a London press-cutting agency to send him all the details printed in the Indian Press about yourself, would you not think that a very strange circumstance, taken in conjunction with the fact that you had met and fraternised at the hotel as perfect strangers, meeting for the first time?"

"I am not conversant, Sir William, with what Colonel Donoughmore may have had in his mind. I can conceive no reason why he should want to know anything about me."

A little of the repose had left the woman now. A tenseness displayed itself in the straightened back which had, so far, nestled to the shape of the armchair. A tinge of colour suffused her face.

"Well, we'll leave it at that," said the Chief Constable. "Now, about the day of the colonel's death. You lunched at the Devonshire Tea-rooms in Tavistock, going in about mid-day and leaving at 12.45. You returned to the rooms for tea at 4.45, picking up the scarf which you had inadvertently left behind at lunch-time, and you returned to Tremarden on the 6.30 train. Is that correct?"

"Quite correct, Sir William."

"That, then, leaves all your movements accounted for except for the short period between your lunch and tea. Would you tell us where you were between 12.45 p.m. and 4.45 p.m.?"

"Certainly. I spent the time in the town of Tavistock. It was my first visit to the place. I looked round the church, I did some shopping, and generally inspected the shops and places as strangers usually do."

"Could you, if we asked, produce anybody who could vouch for your presence anywhere at a given time—such as you did for lunch and tea? The assistant at the shop, or shops, into which you went might remember you. You are an elegant woman, Mrs. Devereux, and one easily to be remembered. Whose were the shops?"

"That I cannot say. They were in the main street and a side street. That is all I can say. I did not notice the names. But what does it matter, anyway?"

The Chief Constable polished his monocle with elaborate care and replaced it in an eye before answering. The arrival of the crucial moment in the interview found him in a somewhat abashed state of mind. He was a gentleman and was, he apostrophised himself, about to call a lady a liar. He did not relish the task, yet it had, he realised, to be done. "Well, you see, Mrs. Devereux," he explained, somewhat apologetically, "Doctor Manson here has a somewhat different version of your movements during the times I have mentioned."

"And pray, what would that version be?" she asked. Transferring her gaze from the Chief Constable she rested it on the scientist.

Manson spoke decisively, without qualms—in fact, sternly.

"I suggest, Mrs. Devereux," he said, "that when you left the tea rooms after lunch you hurried to a bus terminal stop. I suggest that from there you took the 12.55 bus to Tremarden. You left the bus by the lane just past a wayside carters' café, walked up the lane to the river near the Pylons—on the beat which you were supposed to be fishing—and there met Colonel Donoughmore. I should say you met the colonel there by appointment. Something occurred between you and the colonel there—I am not at the moment sure what it was, though I could, I think, guess. However, you were at, or around, that spot until 2 o'clock, when you were seen with a rod in the vicinity of the Pylons, by Major Smithers, who was leaning near the bank, below eye-level on his beat.

"I suggest that you then returned down the lane and walked along the main road towards Tavistock. It had been your intention to board the 2.35 bus, but the vehicle had its full complement of passengers, and passed on. You continued walking for about half-an-hour until you reached a stile on the left-hand side of the road, and lying slightly back from the road. There you waited, wiling away the time with a cigarette, until the next bus came along, on which you rode into Tavistock.

"I suggest, further, that, arrived at the terminus, you walked to a women's cloakroom just off the main street, where you cleaned your shoes, which had been muddied from contact with the sides of the cattle pool near the Pylons, had a wash and brush-up, and then walked to the tea rooms to collect the scarf, which you had purposely left there at lunch in order that you should be remembered, and noted as having visited the rooms for tea. Thus you completed a carefully prepared alibi."

The scientist paused, and the four men regarded the woman with professional interest. Burns, who was nearest to her, was the only one to see the vein throbbing in her neck—that danger signal of a woman's emotions.

The Chief Constable spoke. "What do you say to that, Mrs. Devereux?" he asked.

"I say that it is a great pity that Doctor Manson has nothing better to do with his time than to utilise it in telling fairy stories," was the reply. "May I ask what evidence he has to support this preposterous invention?"

"Plenty of evidence, madam," replied Manson. "The conductor of the bus from Tremarden to Tavistock recognised you by this photograph." He produced and handed over a copy of the photograph taken by the street cameraman. "The driver of the second bus has also recognised the photograph and description as that of a woman who stepped from that stile and stopped, and boarded, his bus. The attendant at the cloakroom has recognised it as that of a woman who came into her cloakroom and had her shoes cleaned of mud. She described your dress and your appearance before she had seen the photograph.

"Finally, from beside the stile of which I spoke, I picked up this." From his wallet Manson took a cigarette stub. Bending forward, he picked up from the ash-tray almost at his elbow, the stub which Mrs. Devereux had deposited there a few minutes before, and at which, at the time, the scientist had peered intently. He placed the two stubs side by side. "They correspond, you see, perfectly, even to the colour of the lipstick," he pointed out. "That is the main evidence, Mrs. Devereux. Will you agree that it is pretty convincing?"

She sat very still. The colour had gone from her cheeks, leaving a pallidness that gave the waiting quartette their answer without the necessity for words. For two minutes they waited; two minutes, which must have seemed like an hour to the woman, before she looked at the Chief Constable and spoke.

"I see I have been very stupid," she said. "I did not think for a moment, that it would have been possible for my movements to have been traced like you have done—minute by minute." She turned swiftly to the scientist. "I congratulate you, Doctor Manson, and apologise for my deprecating remarks just now." A wan smile crossed her face, but did not appear in her eyes. "I thought you were trying to jump me," she explained.

Manson inclined his head in acknowledgment, and Mrs. Devereux continued: "Now I will tell you the truth."

She paused, as if thinking over the words she was about to speak. Then:

"I *DID* go down to the river, and I did see Colonel . . ."

Before she could continue, Superintendent Burns, at a whispered word from Manson, broke in. "Mrs. Devereux," he said, "we do not, of course, know what you are going to say. It may be harmless to you, or it may not be. But I should warn you that the consequences may be of some seriousness. It is, therefore, my duty to warn you that anything you now say may be used in evidence. I do not say that it will be, but it *may* be. Do you understand quite clearly?"

"I quite understand, Superintendent. There is nothing in what I am going to say that can have any bearing on the death of Colonel Donoughmore."

"Very well. I shall take such notes as seem to us fitting, and you may be asked to sign them after they have been read over to you."

The woman composed herself and began her story.

"Well, I *DID* take the bus to Fisherman's Lane and I did go across the fields and I did meet the colonel at the spot where I had, indeed, arranged to meet him," she said. "I am now going to tell you the truth, about that meeting and the reason for it, so far as it concerns—"

She paused, and then in a voice filled with bitterness said: "Colonel Donoughmore was blackmailing me. Something he knew of in my past life, something which does not concern this case at all, gave him the weapon."

Again she paused, as though inviting comment. The four men, however, remained silent.

"You know that I am engaged to be married to Sir John Shepstone," she continued. "The something which Colonel Donoughmore had found out about me would, I fear, have had the effect of making that marriage impossible. It was highly probable that Sir John would not marry me if he was aware of it. Within a day or two of my arrival here Colonel Donoughmore revealed what he knew to me. He suggested that I should buy his silence. The alternative, he made perfectly clear, would be that he would send to Sir John, anonymously, proof of the things he knew. The amount he asked from me was impossible."

"What was it?" asked the Chief Constable.

"He wanted £5,000. I haven't that much in the world. He had become more insistent during the last two or three days, and told me he must have the answer, yes or no, on the next day. I arranged to meet him near the Pylons on my fishing beat. I was prepared to pay something, but not £5,000, and went to argue with him that it was better to have what I could pay than for him to tell Sir John and receive nothing at all.

"I met him on the beat, quite close to the Pylons, and we argued for half-an-hour. He was quite adamant on the sum for which he asked. He said it was nothing to the wife of Sir John Shepstone. I answered that I could not possibly ask for the loan of such a sum from Sir John before I was married, and that all I had of my own was £1,000. He then made an alternative suggestion of a vile character. I lost my temper and did what any woman would have done placed in such circumstances. I struck him."

"With what?" The query came from Doctor Manson.

"With his priest."

"What happened then? Be very exact, Mrs. Devereux; as exact as you possibly can," said Manson.

"I snatched the priest from his hand and hit him on the fore-head. He moaned and fell on his back. Then he moaned again, and after that he was silent. I was terrified. After a moment or two, I recovered myself. I leaned down and called him by name, but he did not speak. He was quite still. I unbuttoned his water-proof jacket and felt his heart inside. I could not feel it beating. I thought he was dead. And then I saw that I was in a terrible po-sition. I thought first of going for help. Then I remembered that I had seen nobody on my way there, and I could not see anybody now. I knew that there could not be anyone on that part of the river, because it was the beat which I was supposed to be fishing. So I ran back across the field to the road, where I waited for a bus which I knew should be along presently. You know what happened after that. It was just as Doctor Manson said just now.

"I still thought that I had killed him; but when I heard that he had been found drowned down by the gulley I knew that I had not done so, and that he must have recovered after I had left him and gone back into his own water. Because, you see, we were nowhere on the river-bank when I hit him, and he could not possibly have fallen in. So, knowing that I had not killed him, I kept silent. That is the story. I am sorry that I did not tell it to you the first time. I did not do so because I saw no reason why it should come out." She finished and leaned back in her chair, glancing anxiously from one to other of the men.

The Chief Constable looked across at Doctor Manson, his eyes lifted in inquiry. The scientist nodded.

"There are one or two points I would like to take up with you, Mrs. Devereux," he said. "Did you say that you unbuttoned the waterproof coat of the colonel?"

"Yes. When he didn't move I did that to feel if the heart was beating."

"Did you fasten it up again?"

"No, Doctor Manson. I left it just as I had unfastened it." Manson pressed the point. "It is a matter of very great importance, Mrs. Devereux," he insisted. "You are perfectly sure that you did not rebutton the coat?"

"I am absolutely sure, Doctor. I was terrified, thinking that he was dead, and did not dare go near him again."

Doctor Manson turned to the Chief Constable. "The point is important, Sir William," he said, "because when the colonel was taken out of the water the coat was tightly buttoned. It was, in fact, this which rendered the wading outfit waterproof, and kept the body floating in the Round Pool." He turned again to Mrs. Devereux.

"There is one circumstance in your story which seems to me peculiar. You say that you arranged to meet the colonel on your beat that morning. Firstly, why meet him there? Why could you not have seen the colonel in the hotel and talked it over. Each of you had rooms."

"I was too terrified. There was always the chance of someone coming into the room—a chambermaid, or Mrs. Baker. The colonel had some knowledge about me. I had hopes of being able to silence him. In my state of mind I saw danger everywhere, and did not dare run the risk of anything being overheard by someone who might themselves use the information."

"Well, conceding you that point, why this journeying to Tavistock arranging an alibi? Why could you not have gone direct to the river from the hotel and had your private interview?"

"There was no idea in my mind of an alibi at that time. I was, as I have said, agitated and thought that it would calm my nerves to get right away and have lunch in Tavistock. I knew that there would be time to get back to the river, since I had fixed two o'clock as the time I was to see Colonel Donoughmore."

"So you had no intention of going back to Tavistock afterwards?"

"None at all—not till afterwards. Then I realised that I had left my scarf in the tea-rooms where I had had lunch. I saw that, if I went there for tea and asked if the scarf had been found, it would look as though I had been in Tavistock all the time."

"That is all I have to ask you, Mrs. Devereux. Is there anything you can think of, Sir William?"

The Chief Constable nodded. "There is just this, Mrs. Devereux," he said. "You say that when you heard that Colonel Donoughmore had been drowned you realised that you had not killed him. Why then, did you not tell us this at the time we questioned you previously? We told you that we were seeking information of anyone who might have seen the colonel on the river-bank. You not only withheld this knowledge, but actually denied that you had even seen the man that day. Now, when you are found out to have been speaking an untruth, and are placed in a very serious position, you come forward with this very circumstantial story. It is, on the face of it, pretty suspicious, do you not think?"

"I know that it must seem that way to you," was the answer. "But I have told you that the one thing above all others which I wanted was to keep all knowledge connecting myself with the colonel quiet. Then where the colonel fell in the river was nowhere near where we talked. So what did it matter?"

Doctor Manson broke into the questioning. "Where do you think the colonel went into the river, Mrs. Devereux?" he asked.

She looked up in surprise. "Where? Why, surely we have all seen the marks, Doctor Manson," she said.

Manson bent his gaze upon her. "I have no doubt you have seen certain marks, like most of us, Mrs. Devereux," he said, and his voice was grimly clear. "But you see, Colonel Donoughmore did *not* fall into the river at that point. He went into the water by the Pylons, in fact, within a few yards of where you were talking with him. And a woman with a rod was seen on the river-bank somewhere about that time."

"Oh!" The woman's ejaculation was almost a scream. "Oh!" Her hands flew to her mouth and she bit a finger until the blood came. Manson waited until she had composed herself. Then: "There are just two more questions, Mrs. Devereux. Did you go alone to the river?"

"Yes . . . yes. Quite alone."

"And did you see anyone at all while you were going, while you were there, or while you were returning? I mean anybody—even at a distance."

"I did not see a soul, Doctor."

"That is all, Sir William, unless . . . ?"

"Burns?" The Chief Constable looked at his Superintendent. Burns shook his head.

"Well, Mrs. Devereux, that seems as far as we can get at present," he said. "You will understand that we cannot make any promise that what you have told us can be kept confidential. And, in the meantime, we shall have to ask you not to leave the hotel without permission."

He rose, walked to the door, and held it open for her to pass out. Closing the door after her, he returned to his chair.

"Now . . . what?" he asked.

"Before we go any further, tell me, Sir William, have you any plain-clothes policewomen here?"

"We have a couple," Burns broke in.

"Then I want them in the Tremarden Arms as chamber-maids," said Manson. "They can take turn and turn apiece. They must be on duty in the corridor into which Mrs. Devereux's room opens. There is a vacant room at the end of the corridor; put them in there. Their job is to watch, report what she does and where she goes in the hotel when she leaves her room, and to whom she talks. It is vitally important. Impress this upon them, but impress, also, that it must be done without Mrs. Devereux seeing that she is being watched. Is that clear?"

"Quite clear, Doctor. You want that done at once, of course." The superintendent turned to Penryn. "Will you see to that, Inspector?"

"And now, Doctor, what are we to make of her story?" asked the Chief Constable.

"I think we should have arrested her." Superintendent Burns put in the suggestion hastily.

"On what grounds?" asked Manson.

Burns looked nonplussed. "Well, surely, Doctor, it has worked out just as you seemed to know. She did exactly what you said she had done. She was the only person there—she admitted so to us, didn't she? She is the only person who could have killed the colonel at that spot . . ."

"Except one other."

The words came in a slow drawl from the scientist. "Except one other, I think."

"One other?" Burns echoed. "What other? We have no evidence of any other person there."

"No identifying evidence, Burns, no. But we certainly have evidence."

"What evidence, and what person?"

There was a pause while the scientist considered his answer. Then he gave it like a judgment. The effect on the other two present was much as would have been the effect if a Judge had given judgment acquitting a prisoner who had entered a plea of guilty.

"I believe what Mrs. Devereux has told us—to a certain extent," he began. "It corresponds to my own theory of what happened. Mind you, I am perfectly sure she has not, even now, told us everything. I think she may tell us some more yet, unwittingly—and to your policewomen, Burns. But what she has said happened on the bank I believe to be true, except for one thing."

"And that?" The demand came simultaneously from the Chief Constable and Burns.

"When she said that there was nobody else near, she is wrong. She may not know she is wrong, or she may—I have not decided about that as yet. But you can take it from me that there was someone else there."

"There . . . was . . . someone . . . else . . . there?" Burns repeated the scientist's words parrot-wise. "Who?" he demanded.

"The person who stood in the copse watching the pair through the brambles. The person who made that footstep. How comes it that you have forgotten that very interesting and informative footprint?"

CHAPTER XXII
"MR. X"

DOCTOR MANSON had one axiom which he never ceased to drill into such men at Scotland Yard as came into contact with him during the course of investigations. "There is no secret conceived in the mind of man," he insisted, "which cannot be laid bare by the mind of man." And time and again he had proved the truth of the axiom to doubters. All that was required, he maintained, was an ordered mind and a logically trained method of thinking, plus knowledge of the line of country through which the secret ran.

His own logical thinking consisted, mainly, in accepting no theory, in starting with no theory; but only with proved facts and then, commencing with the lowest common denominator, gradually cancelling out until the remainder would cancel no more. That remainder, however improbable it appeared, was, he insisted, the only possible answer. In plain language, it was the process of elimination. But not elimination by theory, supposition, or guesswork; but elimination by fact.

That had been the principle upon which he had worked in the investigation into the death of Colonel Donoughmore, and he had now, he felt, reduced the case to its lowest common denominator.

All that was left was for the remainder to be identified. He viewed it as something of an algebraical problem. He wrote it down on a pad on his table as such:

$X = ?$

Who was "X"? That was the problem to which he now had to devote his reasoning. He began by writing underneath his symbol x—? the various quantities. The completed form read thusly:

a = the colonel's body.
b = bootprint cast.
c = the artificial fly.
y = the colonel's fishing-rod.
z = maker of marks on bank.

Pondering over this he wrote the equation:

a + (b + c + y) = z.

Next, he wrote the further quantities:

m = photographed newspaper cuttings.
n = Mrs. Devereux.
q = the date July 15.
r = the motive.

From this he set out his second and third equations:

m + n + q = r. Then:
z + r = z.

Satisfying himself that he had correctly set out the problem, the Doctor, with Sergeant Merry, settled down to its solution. "A" and "B" he decided, were easily disposed of. It was obvious, from the position of the footprint, that the owner had pressed forward on his left foot to peer through the brambles at something ahead. It was reasonable to suppose that the only thing that could have interested him was the scene between the colonel and Mrs. Devereux since, after Mrs. Devereux had left, the colonel—if her story was true, and he (Manson) believed it was—was lying on the ground, unconscious. The time which elapsed between the wound on the head and entry into the water had been shown, by pathological examination, to be at least half-an-hour. Therefore, Mrs. Devereux had left the colonel alive, which put "b" on the spot when the colonel became, pathologically, a body.

Thus, Manson argued, "c" and "y" became at once associated with "b". Because, as he pointed out to Merry, before the colonel became a body, he had had his rod and his priest with him. The priest had vanished. But the rod was placed on the river bank near the scene of the supposed accident. Nobody but "b" would have taken the rod to the bank so far down the river. If "b" took the rod down, then he also attached the fly to the line. Therefore, it could reasonably be assumed that he also made the scratches on the bank. "Now," he reflected, "is there any more to be got out of that?"

Merry regarded the equation with a critical eye. "Have you, Harry, sought any possible connection between 'b' and 'z'?" he asked.

"No. I don't see how we can. . . ." He stopped. "Of course," he said, "the bootprint cast. How utterly careless of me."

"We worked out that the marks on the bank were made by a right boot," Merry hazarded. "You would hardly be likely to find a similar nail protruding from the heel of the left boot which made the footprint."

"No. But if the measurements are the same it will be a strengthening of the equation quantity." Manson produced from the cupboard the casts taken of the bank indentures and of the copse footprint.

He measured the heel breadths and lengths with a micro-gauge, checking over the measurements three times before he was finally satisfied. The two presented identical figures. "That then, seems to prove the equation," he announced.

"Now we arrive at the second equation. And that is not going to be so easy, 'm' and 'n' we can add pretty easily and certainly. The newspaper cuttings and Mrs. Devereux are definitely connected. But where does 'q' come in? What led Colonel Donoughmore to write in haste on July 15 to the press-cutting agency for those cuttings, and go himself to London to collect them, when they could have been sent to the hotel by post?"

"Mrs. Devereux said that he knew something in her past, Harry."

"Exactly! He *knew* something in her past. Then why did he want the cuttings? And why *send* for them? He knew Janice Devereux. He must have known who she was, because he described her to the agency and referred to the Indian newspapers. Her engagement to Sir John Shepstone had been announced six months previously. *Why wait to send for the cuttings until she had been several days in the hotel? Why not have begun the blackmail weeks before, or even on the first day she appeared— or the second?* He knew something in her past. Then the cuttings were not going to help him. The only credible explanation that I can think of is something in the hotel. But what?"

"I suppose you mean something between July 12 when Mrs. Devereux appeared and July 15 when he sent for the cuttings?"

Manson nodded. "It could only be something connected with those dates," he said. "An idea did strike me on that." The scientist sorted among his dossier and produced the copy he had taken of the hotel register. The two men bent over it. "Now, this is what I mean," Manson explained. Taking a pencil he indicated the entries in the register. He spoke rapidly for a few minutes, emphasising his remarks with jabs of the pencil on the table-top.

Merry sat back and whistled softly. "That, Harry, would be a hell of a mess," he said.

"It is the only satisfactory explanation I can see at the moment, and if we prove it, that is the end of the case," Manson retorted.

For half an hour the two men discussed a plan of campaign to meet the new development. At the end, Merry suggested the first move. "I think, Harry, we ought to know more about the fly which Franky says is his," he said.

The two proceeded downstairs. The hotelier was in his office when they entered. Manson explained the visit. "Sorry to keep harping on that fly, Franky," he said. "But are you still certain that you didn't lend it to anybody?"

"Certain sure, Doctor," was the reply.

"Where do you keep these flies of yours?"

Baker pointed to the writing-desk in the lounge. "In there, Doctor," he said. "I keep all my fishing bits and pieces in there. In case anybody wants anything, you know."

"Locked?"

"Noa, Doctor. We don't lock up things like that in Cornwall."

"So that anybody coming in for a drink, or anybody staying in the hotel, could go off with a cast, or a fly, if they liked?"

"I suppose they could, yes. That is, if they knew such things were kept there. But who would want to go stealing a fly, Doctor, when they know that they have only to ask for one?"

"That is what we want to know, Franky."

"That certainly lends colour to the idea, Harry," said Merry, as they walked back towards the staircase and up to their room.

"And may explain the phenomenon of the wet fly and the rod in the grass," added Manson. The words, spoken aloud, awakened a thought in the mind of the scientist. He glanced at the rod on the wall, with, below it, the landing-net. Both were covered over with mutton cloth. "That reminds me, Merry," he said suddenly, "we have not yet tried the rod for finger-prints."

The scientist lifted it down from the hook and unwrapped the two lengths, laid them on the table. It was a split-cane, seven feet long, and the cane closely bound. The handle, to the extent of some 12 inches, was of the usual cork, which affords a better hold on the rod, and also prevents slipping of the hand when casting. Merry eyed the cork doubtfully. "Not likely to help us much, I'm afraid, Harry," he suggested.

"I wonder," was Manson's retort. "We can try the cane sections first, and then there is a possibility that Aubert may help us."

It was early apparent, however, that the cane was not going to produce any desired results. Though the sergeant covered the polished surface with a layer of Hydrang. c. Creta—the grey powder used for outlining unseen finger-prints on darkened surfaces—no trace of prints made an appearance. It was evident that the rod had been carefully wiped clean of any possible marks. If not, there should have been, at least, the marks of some fingers on it. The joints had had to be pieced together.

"That leaves us only the cork as a possible medium for traces," commented Manson. "We had better have Burns in on this. We will have to have access to a photographic dark-room."

The superintendent, the possibilities explained to him, was sceptical. "We could use a dark-room in Dawson's, the chemist, here," he agreed. "He does most of the developing roundabouts."

"And he will understand, to some extent, the process, then," said Manson. "I would like someone familiar with photographic reactions as an independent witness."

Mr. Dawson expressed his eagerness to place himself at the service of the scientist. He was considerably intrigued by the suggestions put forward. "So I understand, sir, that you think you can photograph unseen prints on a cork handle?" he asked. "I had always understood that only smooth surfaces would take impressions of the skin."

"That is the generally accepted idea," Manson replied. "I have, however, been experimenting on the lines of Aubert and Forgeot."

"Aubert?" Superintendent Burns looked inquiry.

"A French surgeon in 1878. He made investigations into the products of the sweat glands. His experiments demonstrated that perspiration products reacted to silver nitrate. That, mark you, was some years before finger-prints became recognised as a means of identification. Three years later, Forgeot, another Frenchman, demonstrated that finger-prints could be developed with silver nitrate. Curiously enough, it was not until quite recently that the works seem to have been remembered by medical jurisprudists, and now the silver nitrate process is hailed as a recently devised method of finger-print development!"

The chemist was displaying considerable interest in the discussion. He now ventured an opinion. "I take it," he said, "that the principle is that the nitrate, reacting on the sodium chloride present in the perspiration, throws it up black. That would be the natural reaction of the two substances."

"Exactly," said Manson. "You are familiar with the subject?" he asked.

"Moderately," was the reply. "I took a science degree at London."

"Excellent. Then you will, I think, be able to follow the experiment I am about to attempt. You said, just now, that you doubted the possibility of developing such prints on a rough surface, such as cork?"

"That is so, Doctor Manson. On a smooth, level surface, I can understand. It would take impressions in the way that a surfaced paper would."

"That is true. But my suggestion is that the sweat ducts must, perforce, deposit the same sodium chloride on uneven surfaces. Now I see no reason why they should not be developed up to a degree that should give a reasonable chance of identification."

"In that case, they could be developed on cloth, or fabric, or inside a pair of gloves," the chemist suggested.

"I think they could be," was the reply. "Shall we go into the dark-room?" he suggested.

"Now, if you, Mr. Dawson, will prepare me a 5 p.c. aqueous solution of silver nitrate, I will fix an orange light over the window. And I shall want a camel hair brush."

"Brush?" asked the chemist.

"Unless you have a three feet long developing tank, which would be better, Mr. Dawson," the scientist replied. "It would be impossible to submerge the rod handle in an ordinary dish, of course. We shall have to paint on the silver nitrate."

The requirements placed handy on the developing board, Doctor Manson began his test. Dipping the brush into the silver nitrate solution, he applied the liquid delicately to the rounded surface of the cork, turning it slowly round and making certain that every minute portion of the area received a coating. Not until both the chemist and himself were satisfied on this point did the scientist cease handling the brush, and lay the rod gently across the edges of the sink.

"How long do you suggest the rod should be left, Mr. Dawson," he asked.

"I should say with the amount given, that five minutes should be sufficient to coat any sodium chloride there may be with silver chloride," was the reply.

"That corresponds with my own opinion," Manson agreed. "I think that the most difficult part of the operation will be the washing. It has to be very thorough, and yet without force enough to sweep away the chloride."

"I suggest, sir, that the handle be held upright in the sink filled with water, and the tap left running slowly enough to keep the water moving," said the chemist.

"Excellent." Manson nodded delightedly.

Superintendent Burns bent forward eagerly as the rod was lifted from the sink some minutes later. It revealed to his eyes "no difference in appearance from before. Nothing," he said.

Manson smiled. "You're in too big a hurry, Burns," he chided. "We haven't finished yet. You cannot hurry science or chemistry, you know. If there are any prints on the handle, they are still invisible to us, but they will be coated with silver chloride. It remains now, to reduce the silver chloride, when the pattern will appear black."

"That, sir, is where my knowledge ends," the chemist said, with a smile. "How do you propose to achieve that?"

Manson considered the question. "There are two methods. I could expose the handle to the daylight, and when any prints have obtained sufficient intensity, treat them with sodium thiosulphate. That is, however, a little rough-and-ready to my mind. I think a better way would be to develop them with ordinary H.Q. photographic developer. It will be slower, and we can obtain a more level intensity and development. We shall have to paint on the developer in a way similar to that in which we applied the silver nitrate."

The first application of the brush produced results which heightened the hopes of the four watching men. A number of black smudges sprang up on the light-coloured cork. With each touch of liquid, as the rod was slowly turned, the smudges increased in number and density. Manson and the chemist watched the intensity of the markings.

"I don't want them too far advanced," the scientist explained. "There is a jumble of prints, as might be expected. Over intensified, they will be difficult to separate."

He waited a few seconds longer. Then, with a "That should do it" he plunged the rod once again into the running water in the sink.

"Now, I think we may let daylight in, and view the results," he said.

There was, however, to be a further delay. So thickly was the cork handle spread with the prints of fingers that, though the scientist searched it thoroughly with the aid of a powerful magnifying glass, he could reach no decision as to whether the experiment had produced any identifiable pattern. Patterns there were in plenty, superimposed one upon another. Manson turned to Mr. Dawson. "I'm afraid I shall have to encroach further upon your goodness," he said. "Would it be possible for you to enlarge for me, in that excellent apparatus I see there, a photograph which Sergeant Merry here will take of the handle. If you could enlarge any part he may show you, up to say six or seven magnifications, we could then judge whether any print is sufficient for coding and classification?"

"I shall be delighted," was the reply. "I have seldom spent a more entertaining half-hour than that I have just experienced."

"That is very kind of you, Mr. Dawson. Then I will leave Merry with you. We have our miniature copying camera in the hotel."

The two men shook hands and parted.

Superintendent Burns and Manson, on their return to the hotel, were greeted with Inspector Penryn. "Been looking for you, Doctor. One of the policewomen has reported. There does not seem much in it to interest you, but you'll probably like to see her."

He left the room to return a minute later with a neatly attired chambermaid. "Policewoman Mary Trewilliams, Doctor," he introduced. "She has been told to report to you."

"Report away, Mary," invited the scientist.

The woman produced a note-book. "On receipt of certain instructions," she began—Manson groaned inwardly—"I kept watch on room number 3, and its occupant. I was on duty when she came upstairs from lunch. She entered her room, where she remained for some minutes. She then left and, walking down the corridor in the direction of the bedroom in which I was secreted, knocked at the door of number 15. There was no reply. She attempted to open the door, but it was locked. She then returned to her room—at 1.16 p.m. At 1.24 she emerged again and descended the stairs. She returned at 1.31, and again entered her room. At 1.45 she once more left her room carrying an envelope in her hand. She walked to the room number 15, and slipped the envelope underneath the door. She then returned to her own room. We have not seen Mrs. Devereux since.

"At 2.30 the occupant of room 15 returned, and entered the room. Five minutes later, the occupant of number 15 left and walked to the room of Mrs. Devereux, opening the door and entering. Left again at 3 o'clock and returned to number 15. Five minutes later, room 15 occupant left again, locking the door of the room and going downstairs. There has since been no sign of room 15. That is all, sir."

"Right. Thank you very much. Keep a close watch and if anything else happens let me know at once."

As the woman left the room, Merry and Mr. Dawson entered. The latter advanced to the table, laid upon it a 16 x 12 inches developing porcelain dish. It held a photographic enlarged bromide print still wet. "Sergeant Merry thinks the chance has come off," he said, and stood back.

"Then the experiment is successful?" The chemist waited the reply with obvious eagerness.

"It is, Mr. Dawson, thanks to your help, for which I am infinitely obliged."

(It may be of interest to remark that Doctor Manson's method of revealing finger-prints on rough or unpolished surfaces was successfully used in America some ten months later, when it produced prints on to a step-ladder. These proved the principle evidence convicting Hauptmann of the kidnapping of the Lindbergh baby.)

With the chemist gone, Manson turned sharply to his Sergeant. Rapidly, he acquainted him with the contents of the policewoman's report. "Now, we must get busy," he said, the recital concluded. "I am going into room 15 and I shall want about ten minutes there. You had better station yourself at the bottom of the staircase, and should number 15 appear, engage that individual in conversation. It is imperative, as you will realise, that

15 shall be kept away from that room until I appear at the top of the staircase. Is that clear?"

"Quite, Doctor."

"Right. Off we go. And pick up a master key from Franky."

As the sergeant took his stand at the bannisters' foot, Doctor Manson proceeded up the stairs and along the corridor to number 15. A knock at the door produced no reply, and the scientist, inserting the master-key, opened the door and entered, locking it carefully behind him. With his back to the door he surveyed the room. It looked more like an unoccupied chamber than a guest's sleeping apartment. No toilet articles were on the dressing-table and no articles of clothing lay in the disarray customary in hotel bedrooms. The eyes of Manson, as they roved round the room, closed almost to slits in the deep-set sockets, and his dynamic personality vibrated into action.

A half-filled paper basket was his first objective. Quickly he tipped the contents out on the floor, and then, taking them up one by one, examined each piece before depositing it back into the basket. Only four pieces seemed to call for further attention. Pieced together, they made the form of an envelope, and bore a name written in a woman's handwriting. "The envelope pushed under the door by Mrs. Devereux, undoubtedly," Manson said to himself, and slipped it into a pocket. But, though he searched thoroughly, no trace was to be found of the message which had been contained in it.

Next, the scientist crossed to the wardrobe. It was when he opened the door that the state of the room was explained. The cupboard was as bare as that of Old Mother Hubbard. "Getting out, eh?" Manson spoke softly to himself. "It seems that I was only just in time."

Two trunks stood on the luggage trestle-stool in a corner of the room. Manson moved one and tried the lid. "Unlocked! That's lucky!" He opened the lid and ran his hands among the folded contents. "No papers, no . . ." The sentence broke off as he exposed a tweed suiting. With a jerk he pulled out half a dozen or so strands, and taking an envelope from a pocket, tucked them safely inside.

The second and smaller trunk gave him further confirmation of that for which he was seeking. His searching hand brought out a boot—a left boot. Quickly he turned it over. The sole had been patched neatly. Through the patch was driven a hobnail. Diving once more into the trunk he produced the right foot counterpart. In the heel, standing out from a set of three, was one protruding hobnail. The Doctor searched no further. Closing the trunk, he surveyed the room again. Then, satisfied that he had left no trace of his intrusion, he emerged, locked the door again behind him, and hurried to his own room round the corner. Leaving the boots he returned to the staircase and slowly descended.

Merry's questioning glance received a confirming nod.

"The police station," Manson said, as the sergeant joined him.

CHAPTER XXIII
ARREST

THE GOLD-RIMMED monocle fell from the eye of Sir William Polglaze; the Chief Constable for once let it remain dangling at the end of its cord.

"Who . . . WHOM did you say, Doctor?" he asked.

Manson repeated the name.

There was a stunned silence. Then Superintendent Burns found his voice. "I suppose there isn't any chance of a mistake, Doctor?" he questioned. "I mean to say, there has never been the slightest suspicion directed against . . ."

"You mean you have had no suspicion, Burns," the scientist interrupted. "But it has been in my mind for a day or two. You can take it from me that there is no mistake. I never speak until I am perfectly sure. I have the boots, the right foot with the hobnails in, and the left boot with the patch on. They are the evidence for the arrest. Here they are."

Burns and the Chief Constable examined the upturned soles.

"Yes, Doctor," the Chief Constable said. "We'll accept that. But what about the other—the identity?"

"I'll prove that after you have made the arrest and returned with the prisoner. After all, it is a secondary consideration you know. Besides which, I hope before long to have final evidence." He took from his pocket the envelope pieces reclaimed from the wastepaper-basket in No. 15.

"We'll go right away." Burns took up his hat.

"Oh no, you don't. Not that way." Manson was emphatic. "Watch number 15 on the train, and board it. Better have two men with you. Make the arrest at Exeter. I've a good reason for wanting this. But you had better come back in an Exeter Squad car."

The Chief Constable agreed. "How about the arrest, Doctor? Do you want a warrant?"

"Just as you like, Sir William. A warrant is not necessary. You can arrest for murder without it. But I will swear an information if you like."

The most complete news of the arrest was given in the columns of that popular newspaper, the *Daily Examiner*, the following morning. It read:

COLONEL IN RIVER: SENSATIONS LIKELY.

From our own Correspondent.

TREMARDEN. Tuesday.

Following the investigation by Chief Detective Inspector Manson, Scotland Yard's scientific expert, and Superintendent Burns, of the Cornish County Police, into the Tremarden river tragedy, a man was arrested late last night at Exeter, and will appear before the Bench to-day.

He is described as William Braddock, a Canadian, of Calgary, and he has been charged with the murder of Colonel John Donoughmore, retired, late of the Indian Army.

Braddock had been staying at the Tremarden Arms, where the colonel was also a guest. The colonel had failed to return from a day's fishing in the River Tamar, and though search was made for him during the night, he was not found.

Next morning his body was seen by a farmer in a deep salmon pool. It was at first thought that the colonel had fallen into the water while fishing; but subsequent investigations by Doctor Manson, who was in the hotel, also on a fishing holiday, resulted in the distinguished scientist coming to the conclusion that the case was one of murder.

I am able exclusively to state that when the case comes before the court, evidence of a sensational nature will be given.

At the police court the following day, Braddock was remanded. "The accused made a certain statement after his arrest," Superintendent Burns stated. "I do not propose to put the statement before the court at this stage. I ask for a remand for seven days in order that the Director of Public Prosecutions can be communicated with."

Two months later Braddock, standing in the dock at the Assize Court at Bodmin, heard the Judge, a square of black velvet perched precariously on his head, pronounce sentence of death.

CHAPTER XXIV
THE JIGSAW COMPLETE

EVENING IN SEPTEMBER. Across the fertile Tamar valley the declining sun played hide and seek amid the shadows of the trees. Leaves, whispering in the zephyr breezes, rustled the prying beams away from the secrets behind their branches; and spoke softly of the peace of darkness so soon to fall, and of the nectar to revive their jaded sap that the night would bring. Over all, Nature, that supreme artist, had painted the yellow and bronze tints from her Autumn palette on to the canvas of landscape, splashing it in masses, and then deftly touching in the magic of sere and yellow, so that the shadows behind seemed to speak of dark days, and the darker deeds of man.

Autumn in Cornwall—where the castle of Tremarden looks across at the weather-worn, granite hills, hard as man's fight for livelihood on the wind-swept, rugged moors below their peaks; and then down in the deeps beneath, where the Tamar flows swift to the sea, as it has done for a thousand years or more, carrying on its turbulent bosom the fallen leaves whose sands of time have run out for ever.

The sun sank lower, until only one thin shaft could peer through a window of a room in the grey, square building across the moors at Bodmin. Three men sat enclosed within its white-washed walls. Two were in uniform—the uniform of the Law. The third wore a tweed suit that spoke of the open fields, and rising birds from the stubble, or the smell of hay in the newly built ricks, or the plops of trout as they come up for the fly. For three weeks two men had never left the side of the other. Night and day they sat near him; hour in and hour out; and now their task was nearly done. To-night, they watched for the last time. To-morrow, at eight o'clock, the sands of time would run out for the man they guarded. He, himself, stood watching that last thin shaft of sunlight grow smaller and smaller, and then, in a flicker, withdraw from the window of his cell, and vanish from his sight—for ever.

* * * * *

In the smoking-room of the Tremarden Arms eight men sat in a semi-circle round the fireplace. They had eaten an early dinner, and as the other hotel guests wandered into the dining-room at the sound of the gong, the eight had filed out and made for the room prepared for them. Within the inside curve of the semi-circle, Franky had loaded a coffee-table with bottles of liqueur, a box of cigars and another of cigarettes. A waiter added to its burden a coffee-pot and cups, and as he made his exit, Franky crossed to the door and turned the key in the lock.

That makes certain that we shall be able to spend the evening by ourselves, he promised and, turning waiter, he poured out the coffee, placing by the side of each cup a glass of Benedictine. "Very special this is, Doctor," he said. "It's some of the real stuff and there isn't another hotel in Cornwall that has any, I can tell you that."

"In honour of the occasion, eh, Franky?" Sir Edward Maurice suggested.

"That be it, Sir Edward," was the reply in the drawling tones of the Cornishman.

Licking tongues of fire from the log in the great open fireplace, threw up shafts of yellow, to light up the ancient glory of the room. From floor to ceiling it was, and still is, panelled in blackened, carved oak. In the ceiling the huge rough hewn beams, themselves dark with the smoke of ages, stared down as they had stared at gatherings of men for 900 years. The great table was nearly as old, as was the chest which stood beneath the window. Strange and diverse were the men who had sat round that table in its many days. Cavaliers had dined there; the Roundheads had followed them. Once, the Norman had put his legs beneath it and ate and drank, while his Captains stood, silent, alongside its length. That was when William had come to inspect the Castle that his chief captain had built high above the Inn—the castle that to-day stands in ruins above the same room.

The eight men sampled, with the appreciation of connoisseurs, the liqueur. Lighting cigars, they lay back in their chairs. Sir William Polglaze demonstrated his satisfaction by allowing his monocle to dangle at the end of its cord on to his waistcoat. Sir Edward Maurice sniffed the aroma of cigar smoke and Benedictine with the air of having been seduced. Major Smithers turned his cigar round and round in his fingers before he decided that it was perfectly seasoned and blended. Franky, Superintendent Burns and Inspector Penryn eyed each other, and Penryn whispered: "These blokes at the top do themselves well, don't they, Super?" to which Burns made answer in the affirmative. Sergeant Merry, used to such meetings with Manson, took what the Gods sent without giving undue thanks. Doctor Manson himself, eyed his fellows in contemplative satisfaction.

It was the Chief Constable who spoke at last the words for which the company were waiting.

"Did you see him, Doctor?" he asked.

"I saw him—in the condemned cell this afternoon." Manson twisted his cigar. A sternness seldom seen in that scholarly face accompanied the words. He flicked off a length of ash before he continued.

"You know, Sir William," he said, "it was the first time that I have come away from such an interview without a feeling of, shall I say regretful sympathy for the unfortunate fellow inside, without the nasty thought that there, but for the grace of God, go I—I failed completely to register or experience the least compunction in having been instrumental in putting this man there. He was the worst man I have ever hanged.

"Here was a man who murdered, not because he had been done a great wrong, or for revenge for some fancied wrong. Nor did he murder in a fit of anger, or on the spur of the moment. He murdered deliberately, with careful planning—and devilish careful planning, it was too—and for what? Because he wanted money for himself which Colonel Donoughmore was about to receive in blackmail. Honour among thieves?" The scientist laughed. "It's a fallacy. I have never yet met it. The thief, and the criminal of any kind, would sell anybody, even his own mother, to safeguard himself. The criminal has only one rule, and it is the rule of most people, from whatever society they come—the rule of self-preservation. You see it in this case as regards the thieves—one blackmailer blackmailing another!

"Nor was Braddock's crime a sudden lapse. He was bad all through. Here he was, first a wife deserter, clearing off and leaving a woman to fight her way alone in the world. Then he becomes a blackmailer of a woman, until he graduates to murder. Who could feel sorry for a man like that?"

"Did he tell you all the missing bits, Doctor?" The inquiry came from Superintendent Burns.

Manson nodded. "At least, he asked me what I conjectured to have happened, and I told him. He listened carefully and at the end said: 'You might have been there, laddie. If I had known I'd have rid myself of you, too.'"

"What *did* he do, Doctor?" Major Smithers asked the question hopefully. "The fact that he pleaded guilty at the trial robbed us of the story. I hoped to have heard from your evidence how you worked the thing out. Would it be too much to ask if it can be told, or is there any official secret about it?"

"No, Major," Manson answered. "I think you can all hear it. It may be a warning to you. Also I think you are justified in hearing it in the circumstances—all of you. Do you not think so, Sir William?"

The Chief Constable smiled broadly. "I think so, Doctor—shall we say as a little apology and recompense."

"Recompense?" came from Sir Edward Maurice.

A chuckle escaped Doctor Manson. "That is the word, Sir Edward," he said. "Because you and the major, and Emmett here, were all under suspicion at one time, and we combed you all pretty thoroughly."

"Me?" Sir Edward asked, murdering the English grammar!

"Certainly you," Manson retorted. "It looked a toss up once between you and Emmett. Look at the position in which we were. Emmett, after threatening to pitch the colonel into the river, said the scoundrel walked back into his own beat. Within a few minutes you appear on that very beat. You told us that you did not see either Emmett or the colonel. You walked all along the colonel's beat and even stopped to search for a cigarette case. Yet you saw nothing of them, so you said. Looked as though someone was not speaking the truth, did it not?"

"By gad, sir—yes," the startled Baronet agreed.

"I think you would have been in a nasty spot, Sir Edward, if Doctor Manson hadn't got you clear," said Superintendent Burns.

"How did he do that?"

"By proving to us that the colonel did not go into the river at the spot we thought," was the reply.

"Very nice of him," commented Major Smithers, humorously.

"Yes?" The query came from Penryn. "Well, it made things look pretty black for you, then, Major."

"For me? How was that?"

"You were then on the next beat to where the colonel was *really* killed, you know, and *you* said you did not see him. You were in a tighter place than Sir Edward, because whereas Sir Edward had only the slightest of motives, you had a very powerful one. We talked it over very seriously." The inspector paused before, very diffidently, he continued: "You see, Major, we knew all about the share-pushing frauds and the words which you had used about the colonel. They had been overheard. 'One day I'll send him the same way.'"

"I . . . I . . . see," Major Smithers answered, and his voice shook a little. "You found that out, did you. You're very thorough, Doctor. How did you get me out of that spot?"

"I didn't, Major. The colonel's fishing-rod did that. It also saved Mrs. Devereux from being arrested on suspicion of being the actual murderess. There was a time when I was almost convinced that she, alone, was concerned. Then Merry went down to the river, and his story when he returned, made me quite sure that there was someone else in the affair with her. The colonel's rod again."

"The colonel's rod?" echoed Penryn. "This is the first I've heard of this. What the deuce has the colonel's rod to do with it?"

The scientist lit a cigarette and watched the smoke rise in a spiral to the ceiling before he answered. "When we examined the spot at which the colonel was supposed to have fallen in," he said, "you will remember that the rod was lying in the grass on the bank. That was one of the first things to excite my suspicion, because no fisherman would lay his rod down like that; a fact upon which I remarked to the Chief Constable here, at a later stage, and to Burns.

"When we had broken Mrs. Devereux's alibi, and there was a strong suspicion in my mind that she had, in fact, committed the murder, I sent Merry down to the water where she was fishing, with instructions to ask her any sort of questions, so long as he got her up from the water and away from fishing. I asked him to watch carefully, every thing she did, and to report all her actions to me. I did not tell him *what* to watch. When he returned he described how Mrs. Devereux had come up from the water at his request and had *carefully rested her rod against a bush and that her second rod, a wet-fly one, was also standing upright by an adjacent bush.* Then I knew that she was a fisherman, and could not have so far departed from the training of a fisherman as to lay a rod down in the grass. That meant, in conjunction with other evidence I had, that someone else—and to my mind a non-fishing someone else—was in the business. So that cut out both Sir Edward and the major, and also Emmett, all of whom would instinctively have propped their rods clear of the ground.

"Curiously enough, however," the Doctor went on, "it didn't let out Franky, despite the fact that he is a better fisherman than any of us. Franky did all he could to prove that he was the fellow we were after."

Baker looked up, startled; and Manson grinned humorously at his expression. "Oh, yes you did, Franky," he insisted. "Attached to the colonel's dry-fly fishing-line was a wet fly. The colonel did not put it there. He hadn't a wet fly, and he did not fish wet fly. The murderer put it there. Now I couldn't find a wet fly in anybody's fly-case except that of Mrs. Devereux, and we had a good look through them all. Mrs. Devereux had none of the pattern of that on the line. I showed the fly to Franky, hoping he might be able to recognise it for me, and tell me who used such a bait. He *did* tell me. He said it was his! He *insisted* that he had tied it, and that nobody but he used such a fly. He had never lent a fly to anybody, nor had he sold one. When, rather disturbed, I asked him if he was absolutely certain, he replied: 'Sartin sure, Doctor.'

"Then I remembered that Franky had gone down to the bank the previous night to search for the colonel, and might easily have done him in, so to speak. I was in a devil of a quandary until, later, I found out that his flies were kept in unlocked drawers of the writing-desk in the lounge of the hotel, for anyone to borrow or purloin."

"So one by one you eliminated all the suspects, Doctor," Emmett said. He was following the recital with eager attention.

"All except one, Emmett. I had no idea whom he was, and wrote him down as 'Mr. X.' Although I could not put a name to him, I could follow him from the moment that he turned up on the river bank near the Pylons. I knew exactly what he did, and how he did it."

"What DID he do?" The question came from all three fishermen. The police officers, of course, were already aware of the story.

"Well," responded the scientist, "it was pretty obvious from a footprint in the copse nearby that he stood, hidden behind the bushes, and watched the quarrel between the colonel and Mrs. Devereux, who had invited Donoughmore to meet her on her beat. Mrs. Devereux herself confessed to us that she had struck the colonel unconscious with his own priest and, believing him to be dead with a fractured skull, became terrified and fled. That was her story and I believe it to be true. When she had disappeared, Mr. X, or as we now call him, Braddock, came out of his hiding place. The colonel was still unconscious; in fact he never regained consciousness. Now, although the major here did not see Braddock, Braddock caught a sight of *him*, and that settled the colonel's fate. Braddock could not be sure that the major had not recognised him. He did not dare, therefore, to have the colonel found dead at that spot. So he tipped him into the cattle drinking pool.

"That was the mistake that will hang him to-morrow morning. Except for that, I should never have known the spot where the colonel was drowned. If Braddock had only carried or dragged him into the river, detection would have been pretty well impossible.

"Fortunately for us, he did not do so. Fortunately, every murderer makes a mistake, and thereby leaves a clue for those of us who trail after him."

Emmett broke into the Doctor's soliloquy with a question. "How was pushing the colonel into the pool instead of into the river a mistake, Doctor?" he asked.

"And why should that have led you particularly to the Pylons," added Sir Edward.

Doctor Manson bent forward eagerly. He loved these questions, not because they revealed his abilities, but because they justified science in the eyes of the man in the street as a means of detection of wrong-doers. And he liked to describe the process. It was his one weakness, or vanity, if you like that word better. So he proposed to impress the company with the recital.

"Well, it was like this," he began. "At the post-mortem on the colonel we found in the throat a few fragments of weed. There were a few more fragments in the liquid taken from the lungs. As a precaution, I took samples of the liquid and collected a piece or two of the throat fragments. That was purely careful routine on my part. I had no reason to suspect that they would be of any use, but it is a precaution I always take. You cannot have too much detail when investigating crime. I identified the weed later as *Elodea Cunardensis*. The jars containing them I placed on the mantelpiece of my room.

"The following day—I think that was the date—the superintendent, Merry and I, made a thorough inspection of the banks of the Tamar. That, by the way, was the day I definitely proved that the colonel had not fallen in the river at the fancied spot. As we walked along the bank, we spoke of the water, of its crystal clearness, by reason of which we could see the shale and gravel-lined bed of the stream. And we spoke of the smallness of the trout compared with those in the Devon or Berkshire waters. The superintendent gave us the reason. There was no feed in the water, he said. The swiftness of the stream would not allow green stuff to grow. It was swept away as soon as it got to any length. Now, no green stuff, no food, and therefore small fish," he explained. "I really ought to have seen the anomaly then, but I didn't," the scientist digressed.

"However, back in the hotel the superintendent, in putting a glass of beer on my mantelpiece clinked it against one of my jars of exhibits. I looked across at the sound, and my eyes caught sight of the jar in which was the liquid taken from the colonel's lungs. *At the bottom was a thin layer of sediment, the result of the jars standing there for a considerable time undisturbed.*

"It staggered me. Merry and I at once tested it by filtering the liquid out and drying the sediment. It was mud."

He eyed the three fishermen. "No?" he queried. "Well, well, I'll have to go into more detail. When a man has been underwater while breathing, he draws water into his mouth, lungs and stomach. Whatever is in that water goes inside him with it.

"How did the colonel come to have water with a mud deposit in it from the crystal clear waters of the Tamar and its shale and gravel bottom. And how did he come to have specimens of Elodea Cunardensis *in his throat and lungs, when there isn't any* Elodea Cunardensis *in the Tamar river?"*

NOTE: The reader is referred back to the problem set him in Chapter IX.

"Well, I'll be dashed!" The major slapped a thigh. "So then you were sure that . . ."

"That the colonel had not been drowned in the Tamar at all," broke in Sir Edward.

Manson nodded. "That is so," he agreed. "And I began to look for somewhere he *could* have been drowned—somewhere where there was mud and *Elodea Cunardensis.* Now *Elodea* usually grows in ditches and small, still streams. Merry and I spent an entire day trudging over the fields round the Tamar without finding any. Then, we dropped on the cattle drinking pool, practically by accident. And it was there, also, that we found the footprint in the copse which gave us the complete story. It was more or less conjecture still—until Braddock confirmed it to me this afternoon. That's all there is to tell"—and Doctor Manson sat back in his chair.

There was a protest from the Chief Constable. "Oh, no, Doctor, we aren't having that!" He shook a disapproving head. "We know the fellow was the killer. We know why he killed. But how did he come to kill. That's what we aren't sure of. Only he and you know, because you said just now that you told him what you conjectured to have happened and that he confirmed it.

What *DID* you conjecture, and what *DID* he confirm? Out with it! Give him another drink, Franky. It will make his tongue wag a bit more."

There was a ripple of laughter, in which the scientist himself joined. The silence which followed was an appreciation of Franky's Benedictine, that amber nectar of the Gods, growing less and less plentiful as the great monastery on Monte Cassino, overlooking the plains in Rome, find its distillation harder and harder. It was some minutes before Manson replaced his empty glass on the coffee table and resumed his story.

"Well, if you want the full story I suppose you will have to have it," he said. "Right! Mrs. Devereux told us at the interview, when we confronted her with the fact that, despite her alibi, we knew that she had been on the river bank and had seen the colonel, that the colonel was blackmailing her. What she did not tell us was that Braddock was also blackmailing her. She did not dare do that for reasons which you will soon appreciate. The facts are that Braddock was first in the field. He had made himself known to Mrs. Devereux and her visit to the Tremarden Arms was expressly for the purpose of seeing him and arranging the terms of his silence.

"The Arms was an unfortunate choice for him. He met the colonel there—and the colonel knew who he was. At least he thought he knew, though, as it happened, he could not be sure about it. But when Mrs. Devereux appeared in the hotel, too, he no longer had any doubts about it, and he at once put out his 'demand with menaces.'

"Knowing what we now do, we can realise that there was no escape for the woman. Braddock, knowing Mrs. Devereux's resources in the way of finance, also had no delusions as to the outcome. His vision of a tidy income for the remainder of his life was going to be halved with the colonel, unless the colonel could be silenced. And it was pretty plain that there was only one way to silence him, and that was the way he planned—murder.

"Now he must have been very exercised in his mind as to how he was to get rid of the man. Then, the colonel's impatience spelt his own undoing. He insisted on Mrs. Devereux finding the £5,000 he wanted within twenty-four hours. Mrs. Devereux arranged to meet him on her beat the following afternoon in a last endeavour to reduce his terms. But before doing so, she sought the advice of her other blackmailer, Braddock. She told him of the appointment, the place of it and the time. Braddock told me that he arranged to be hidden there, and in the event of Donoughmore proving adamant, he was to emerge from the copse, at her signal, and the united threat of them both was to be used against the colonel.

"What went wrong we shall never know. Whether the colonel smelled a rat or not, only he knows. But he moved away from the river bank. As we know, Mrs. Devereux hit him with his own priest. Braddock, watching from the copse, said nothing and did nothing. Mrs. Devereux, seeing no sign of Braddock in answer to her signal, concluded that he had not arrived and she fled. Braddock saw a way to turn the events to his own advantage. Here was murder put into his hands with no risk to himself. It took him half an hour to realise it, but when he did so he heaved the still breathing Colonel into the cattle pool.

"If he had had any medical knowledge at all, he could have made himself safe. The colonel was almost dead; his skull had been badly fractured. He lived only about half a minute after he went into the water.

"I think that had he, even then, left Donoughmore where he was, in the cattle pool, he might still have cleared himself of a charge of murder. But he dare not do it. The colonel was on Mrs. Devereux's beat. You must bear in mind that Braddock, at this time, knew nothing of Mrs. Devereux's morning visit to Tavistock, and could have no knowledge of the alibi which she was, even while the colonel lay in the pool, preparing. He realised that if the colonel was found dead there, suspicion would be directed against the woman—and he couldn't trust her not to betray him to save her own skin. He wasn't a good reasoner.

"He told me that since he had been toying with the idea of removing the colonel, the river had been in his mind. It seemed the most likely kind of 'accident' to happen to the man who was on and in the water all day. He had, accordingly, spied out the land and had decided on the spot where the colonel might, some day 'fall in.' Carrying the colonel's fishing-rod, he walked down the riverside and placed the rod on the grass, and made the false marks of a supposed fall down the bank. He says he was walking across the field to the road, when he suddenly remembered that he had left the colonel's fishing-net at the side of the cattle pool. He had to go back for it; it would never do to have it found there. He unscrewed the net from the shaft, concealed it under his coat and walked into the drying-room of the hotel, swinging the stave. There, he screwed the net back on it and placed the complete landing-net with a collection of rods in the room. It was taken into the lounge with the rods when the owner picked up his belongings. That is the story."

"But where does my artificial fly come into it, Doctor?"

"You *would* ask that, Franky!" Manson smiled, but the smile had a touch of sheepishness about it. "It didn't come in at all. *The thing that gave me almost the first inkling that the case was one of murder had nothing really to do with it.* Braddock's version of it was exceedingly simple. In carrying the rod down the bank he either snapped off the fly or the colonel had done so before he went across to Mrs. Devereux. Anyhow, Braddock thought that a trout-rod would look more natural if it had a fly on it. He had one with him, and he just tied the thing on! He had picked up Franky's raincoat in mistake for his own, and half a dozen flies were stuck in the lapel, where, I gather, Franky usually keeps them. That's what gave Braddock the idea of tying a fly on the line. It just shows you how one can be misled by guessing at things. Though it did serve a useful purpose in exciting my suspicions."

"Any more questions?" Manson concluded, after the laughter had died down.

"How did he get the colonel's body down to the Round Pool?" asked the major.

"Braddock dragged it through the neck of the cattle pool into the river, and then let it drift down the stream. I worked out the run of the water with the weight of the body, and it came somewhere about right," answered the scientist. "Braddock worked out that the colonel's waterproofs, all in one piece, would keep him watertight, and keep him afloat."

"There is just one more thing, Doctor." The speaker was Sir Edward Maurice. *"How did you tumble to whom Braddock was?"*

"Ah! Now that was the one piece of the investigation for which I do pat myself on the back," Manson replied. "In the colonel's flat we found some reproductions of some newspaper cuttings referring to Mrs. Devereux and her dead husband. A press-cutting agency in Fleet Street had been asked by the colonel to supply them in a letter which he had written from the hotel, here, on July 15th, I asked myself what could have happened in the Tremarden Arms, on, or immediately before, July 15th to cause the colonel to write post-haste for those cuttings.

"Franky, here, knew of nothing. There had been no quarrel, so far as I could find out, and no scenes of any sort. I came to a dead end. It was not until I thought of the hotel register that I got an inkling of the truth.

"If you look at the hotel register for July, you will find that of the people who entered the hotel as guests between July 1st and the 14th, *only two of them were still remaining there on the 15th*, namely, Mrs. Devereux and Mr. Braddock. I asked myself was there anything in this. Braddock had arrived on the 8th, so there was not much in that, for a week had elapsed without any haste on the part of the colonel to dash about for Mrs. Devereux's life story. Mrs. Devereux arrived on the 12th—and within about thirty-six hours the colonel sent for those cuttings—and wanted them urgently, so he told the agency. I began to consider whether Braddock might be mixed up with Mrs. Devereux.

"Now, Mrs. Devereux had said that the reason for the blackmail was that the colonel knew something about her past life which, if it was revealed, would make her marriage with Sir John Shepstone *impossible*. She used that word; not, say, the word unlikely or doubtful, but sheer impossible. Now we knew that she had met Sir John in Monte Carlo. We also know that she was known in Monte Carlo as a woman of very loose principles as far as men were concerned. Sir John had lived in Monte Carlo. He must have known her reputation. It was hardly likely, as I saw it, that an affair with a man or with men, would make him break his promise of marriage; if he had qualms of that kind he would never have proposed to marry her.

"I reviewed in my mind all the circumstances which it seemed to me might result in marriage being made not just un-likely or improbable between a man of the world and a woman of the world such as these two were, but *absolutely impossible*. For the life of me I could conceive only one such circumstance— *that the wife, or husband, of one of them was still alive.* There is no other *insurmountable* impediment to marriage. Now, it was not Braddock who was being blackmailed. Therefore, if I was thinking along the right lines, *the 'circumstances' had to be connected with Mrs. Devereux. Yet her husband was dead. He had died in India. Then I remembered that the body of Devere-ux had never been recovered and his death had to be presumed.*

"*Taking all things into consideration I became certain that Braddock was Ronald Devereux.* As you all know I was correct.

"The final evidence is provided by a thumb print we were able to develop on the cork handle of the colonel's fishing-rod. It corresponded exactly with a thumb print left by Braddock, or Devereux, on a glass which Franky placed for us on his table at the last meal he had in the hotel here."

There was a span of silence. Sir Edward broke it with a question.

"What happened in India, Doctor?" he asked. "Why did Devereux allow himself to be regarded as dead. What was his reason?"

Doctor Manson hesitated. "I don't know whether I can tell you that," he replied. "Devereux left behind a written confession and the full story of that episode. It was, however, written in the condemned cell, and is therefore, an official secret. The Chief Constable has the document. Whether he can tell you anything without infringing police rules I do not know." He looked across at Sir William Polglaze.

The Chief Constable nodded. "It is not altogether in accord-ance with the rules," he said. "But I think, perhaps, that I might stretch a point, since you were all, more or less concerned in the matter." He extracted a document from a pocket and opened it. "I will read you one or two salient paragraphs," he continued. "It is understood, of course, that it is not mentioned outside this room."

There were murmurs of assent.

"Well, here is what he said, in his own words:

"My wife I had known when we were boy and girl in England. I'd always wanted to marry her, but her family was in County class and mine was—well—middle class tradesmen. Then one day I met her in India, again. She was a companion to a rich old woman. We resumed our boy and girl acquaintance and within a few months we had married. I thought she was in love with me, but I hadn't been married more than a few weeks when I realised that all she had married me for was to get back into the kind of life she had known as a girl and young woman. She wanted to get back into a social standing with its advantages. I had very little private means; what I had I had saved, and we had to depend chiefly on my pay as a Lieutenant. My savings soon went. Then she pressed for more and more money. We had continual rows and when I could not provide the money she wanted she took it from other men. I knew this, but I couldn't prove it, otherwise I would have divorced her.

"In the end I decided to get out of the position, even though it meant giving up the Army. I wasn't too fond of the Army, anyway. I spied out the land and made arrangements for disappearing. On the day of the hunting trip, a couple of half castes had a horse and a change of civilian clothing waiting for me at a spot we had fixed upon. Within easy reach of the rendezvous I ordered my boys to stay behind, while I went forward. I crossed the river in a native boat which was tied up to the bank. I landed on the other side, higher up, and overturning the boat, sent it into mid-stream. I knew it would go down with the current, which was pretty swift, and that my boys would see it and presume that I had gone in the river. I made my way on horseback to a station some miles down in the plains, and there took train for the coast. It was an easy matter to work my way on a ship, and eventually I reached Canada."

The Chief Constable ceased reading the manuscript. "The next few pages," he said, "explain that Devereux tried mining, factory work, fur trapping, and was no great shakes at any of them. Then, one day, in a hotel in Calgary, he said, he saw in the *Graphic* a photograph of his wife and learned that she was about to marry the wealthy Sir John Shepstone." The Chief Constable turned again to the manuscript.

"I saw that I could make good use of Sir John's fortune," he read. "I borrowed the money for my passage and came to London and wrote to my wife, suggesting that we should meet and discuss the position. She arranged to see me at the Tremarden Arms, where she would go for the fishing. We were not to make any acquaintance or seem to know each other, but were to meet in her room at night, after the rest of the hotel had retired."

The Chief Constable ceased and replaced the document in his pocket. "That's all I think I should read you," he decided.

"I can carry on from there," said Doctor Manson. "Braddock, or Devereux as we may now call him, told me to-day that soon after he arrived in the hotel the colonel eyed him curiously, and even suggested that they had met somewhere before. Devereux, though he denied it, and spoke humorously of everybody having a double, said that he saw the colonel was puzzling over him. He said that he would have left the hotel except for the fact that Mrs. Devereux was coming down, and he did not know where she was, in order to stop her. He felt pretty safe, he said, in his 'death.'

"The arrival of Mrs. Devereux, however, despite the fact that the two did not speak or greet each other in any way, revived all the colonel's suspicions, and then an unfortunate occurrence—for Devereux—happened. He was washing in the lavatory when the colonel entered. Through the mirror over the basins he caught sight of Devereux's bare arms. Now, during a hunting trip Devereux had been mauled on the right arm by a tiger. Marks scored thus deeply by a jungle beast never disappear; the scar remains always. The colonel saw, in the mirror, *the scar left by the Indian adventure with the tiger*. Then, of course, he remembered—and was certain. He taxed Mrs. Devereux with her husband and her forthcoming marriage the next day."

There was a brief silence as the scientist finished the narrative. Then the Chief Constable voiced the feelings of the company. "Well, all I can say, Doctor, is that it's the finest bit of reasoning I've ever heard," he commented. "When I think how nearly we buried the colonel as an accident . . ." His voice trailed off.

"But you nearly missed him, Doctor!" Franky Baker put in a sly dig at Doctor Manson. "He was well away before you arrested him."

Manson looked at the hotelier; and the friendship of years was in the look, and in his voice when he spoke.

"Franky," he said. "I've known you many years, and I knew your father before you. I know and love this hotel. I've spent many happy days and nights here, and I hope to spend many more.

"I told the superintendent, here, that I had a very good reason why he should follow Braddock as far as Exeter before he took him into custody. I had! I did not want it to be reported in the newspapers that a murderer had been arrested in the Tremarden Arms Hotel."

He rose, and placed a hand on the hotelier's shoulders; and thus the two walked out.

THE END

CPSIA information can be obtained
at www.ICGtesting.com
Printed in the USA
LVHW020216080222
710478LV00015B/2040